Mr Smi
Miss Patel

By Ray Burston

© 2019

Ambitious and successful, Wes Smith is in the prime of life – even if the pursuit of a lucrative, globe-trotting career has come at the expense of a failed marriage and a string of relationships that have gone nowhere. Therefore, the promise of a new start in another new country proves a challenge too tempting to pass up.

It's a new start that abruptly goes awry. Finding himself the sole survivor from an airliner that is mysteriously lost at sea, he is suddenly confronted with a very different and unexpected challenge: how to survive on a small, uninhabited island in the middle of nowhere and with little hope of rescue in sight.

It's a challenge that will take on a whole new dimension upon the discovery that Wes Smith was not the sole survivor of the flight's disappearance after all.

To Glory...

... whose bright smile and childlike faith inspired this story.

"If I rise on the wings of the dawn,
And dwell in the uttermost part of the sea,
Even there shall Thy hand lead me,
And Thy right hand lay hold of me."

Psalm 139, verses 9 & 10

1

"My father, after shewing a great concern at my plans, said to my mother with a sigh, 'That boy might be happy if he would stay at home, but if he goes abroad he will be the miserablest wretch that was ever born'... But I that was born to be my own destroyer could no more resist the offer than I could restrain my first rambling designs."

Robinson Crusoe

"Ladies and gentleman, this is your captain speaking. If you will kindly return to your seats and fasten your seat belts, we will shortly be commencing our descent into Perth – where the time is just coming up to ten o'clock and the temperature on the ground is a pleasant twenty-five degrees. I hope you've had a pleasant flight; and whether this is your final destination or whether you'll be connecting with an onward flight, on behalf of my crew can I thank you for flying with Qantas Airlines and wish you good day and a safe journey to wherever you're heading."

The pilot's words caught me staring out of the window at the city's familiar skyline, as well as contemplating again the new job I was on my way to take up. What's more, it was a relief to learn that the temperature where I was about to land was a good ten degrees cooler than where I'd taken off from two hours earlier.

As I recall that morning, I was still in two minds whether my lucrative spell in Port Hedland on the remote north-west tip of Australia had been a boon or a voluntary prison sentence. Sure, this mining town of fourteen thousand souls had possessed enough diversions for a Pommie ex-pat worker looking to part with a few dollars: a gaudy shopping emporium; a smattering of bars, night clubs and restaurants; a yachting marina; a racecourse; and – if you didn't mind sharing your surf with venomous box jellyfish and the odd shark or two – a pleasant if unexceptional beach.

When I'd first found out the summer temperature in the Pilbara region can hit forty degrees I confess to being unfazed. Having just passed another tepid and overcast summer in my native England I rather missed the more idyllic climes I'd enjoyed during previous job postings in southern Africa. Yet even I was at my wit's end when, that first summer in Port Hedland, the mercury in the glass topped *fifty* degrees centigrade, the air-conditioning in my apartment broke down, and it was two weeks before the engineer eventually fixed it (awaiting a spare part from China, he'd pleaded). Sleeping had proved all but impossible, while even at seven o'clock in the morning it was possible to fry an egg on the pavement! Thereafter, I resolved to never complain about indifferent English summers again.

Though Oz was good to me, it had not been long before, possessed of incorrigible itchy feet, I was pondering another well-remunerated career move – this time, I promised myself, to somewhere with a more benign climate. Until it presented itself I'd sought consolation in the company of whichever sexually-frustrated Sheila I happened to get chatting to in the bars where I found myself increasingly frittering away the handsome pay cheques I was pocketing. I was reminded of the Billy Joel song that talks of people *'sharing a drink they call loneliness'* because *'it's better than drinking alone'*?

In due course, my plane touched down in Perth. With several hours to pass before I boarded my long, connecting flight to London, I dumped my case in the left luggage facility so that, unencumbered, I might savour Australia for one last time – for it was not without sadness that I was leaving her behind.

* * * * *

Truth to tell, Melbourne might enjoy a more agreeable climate; Adelaide is more 'English'; Brisbane boasts the best surfing; while Sydney remains indisputably a fabulous (if expensive) place to live and work. However, Perth will always be my favourite Australian city. It was where I'd first touched down in the 'Wide Brown Land' upon my arrival from England, prior to heading up the coast to that job in the Pilbara. Like Australia's other coastal cities, it too boasts superb beaches, great eating out, fabulous night life, and matey people to chat to over a beer at a barbie. Yet somehow Perth feels different. Maybe it's the sheer isolation of the place – situated, as it is, closer to Jakarta in Indonesia (3,013 kilometres away across an empty blue ocean) than it is to Canberra, Australia's capital city (3,718 kilometres away across an empty red desert). Indeed, travelling to Perth from anywhere is a jaunt – even if one flies: three hours flight time from Adelaide (the nearest large city) and five hours from Sydney. Meanwhile, driving the 1,646 kilometres from Port Hedland involves a mind-numbing eighteen solid hours on the road – much of it spent trundling along dusty, desert trails.

On the bus ride into the city I was tempted to look up an old friend before I jetted out of the country for good – for it would be good to meet up with her one last time and hear her seductive voice again. However, I thought better of it. My unannounced intrusion into her life would not be right. After all, whatever we'd once had going, it had been six long months since we'd parted. We'd both moved on since.

Instead, I made my way to Perth Underground station and to more innocent memories: of the day I'd strolled into this place for the first time, there to fall head over heels in love with another seductive voice – namely its female platform announcer. On lonely, wakeful nights during that first summer in Port Hedland, when I was being slow-roasted by the torturous summer heat, I contemplated seeking out that anonymous lady – if only to tell her how weak at the knees she'd rendered me announcing the arrival of the trains to Joondalup and Currambine! Her jaunty, yet silky-smooth voice seemed an apt analogy for a city that just oozes fun and enjoyment. Perhaps it was these qualities that had always drawn me back to Perth whenever the opportunity of a long weekend break had presented itself. It would be on one of those weekends that I would first meet that 'old friend' whose charms had almost tempted me to stay and make a life in Oz (alas, not the platform announcer at Perth Underground station, where the arrival and departure announcements have since been automated).

Today – on my last day in the city – it was just such a bland, disembodied broadcast that heralded the arrival of the train to Mosman Park in the city's suburbs, from where it was a hop, skip and a jump to Cottesloe Beach. Alone with my thoughts – and beneath one of those balmy blue skies with which Australia seems uniquely blessed – I continued to reflect upon my time in this exhilarating country: the places I'd seen and the people I'd met; the money I'd made and the money I'd spent; the love I'd found and the love I'd lost.

Halting on the dunes and gazing out to sea, I was captivated by the same curious thought that had intrigued me on the first occasion I'd lingered at this spot three-and-a half years earlier: how the next landfall from here was South Africa – almost eight thousand kilometres away across the vast ocean I was staring out across. Now, as then, it set me thinking: how tiny and insignificant is one human being in the great scheme of things. Lingering to savour those billowing breakers, I pondered anew that by this time tomorrow I would be on my way to somewhere else – to another new country where there would be more places to see and people to meet; more money to be made and to be spent; and more love to find and to perhaps lose again.

* * * * *

"I'm sorry, Madame, but that seat has already been taken by another family. I can only apologise for the booking error."

"But my elderly mother: she must sit by me, you understand. She is not accustomed to flying and gets very nervous."

"I'm checking the system for you, Madame. But I'm afraid there appears to be nowhere left in Economy Class where I can seat you both together. And all I have unallocated in Business Class is just one seat on its own."

From my place in the queue a few heads back I could see that the check-in clerk was as embarrassed as the oriental lady was aggrieved whose elderly mother looked like being separated from her. Meanwhile, seemingly possessed of only a tenuous command of the English language, the hapless and diminutive octogenarian could only look on in trepidation until her daughter turned to explain to her what had happened.

"Look, it states clearly on our tickets: seats D55 and E55. I told the travel agent when I booked that I must sit together with my mother," she remonstrated with the clerk again.

"Once again, Madame, I can only apologise. But it is too late now for me to rectify the error. Those seats are already taken. Otherwise, I can only suggest you let me see if I can find you two seats together on a later flight."

His proposition was met with an irate huff and the plunging of ornery fists into slender feminine hips. Upon which, I flipped open my passport and stared down at the seat number printed on my own ticket. Stepping out of line, I wandered forward to the check-in desk.

"Excuse me, mate, but I might be able to resolve this lady's problem," I announced. "Look, I'm booked to sit in seat C55," I held up my ticket for the clerk to study, "which – correct me if I'm wrong," I said, glancing at it myself, "must be across the aisle from seat D55. I'm happy to take your unallocated seat in Business Class if surrendering my seat ensures this lady remains close by her mother."

I can't deny there wasn't an element of cunning as well as charity in my generous offer. After all, who wouldn't pass up the opportunity to upgrade to a superior standard of travel under the guise of helping an airline rectify its inglorious mistake!

For a moment the clerk's anxious eyes flitted between the two sets of tickets that had been presented to him.

"Er… Yes. I can do that. If that's okay with you, Madame," he put it to the lady still scowling at him. The creases in her forehead were eventually ironed out by a hasty exchange in Mandarin with her elderly mother.

"Yes, that will be acceptable," she grudgingly nodded. "Thank you very much, sir. It is most kind of you," she then turned to address me. Her mother too doffed gratefully and offered me a toothless smile.

* * * * *

Having cleared security, the first reward for my good deed was learning that my upgrade entitled me to access the airline's exclusive Business Class lounge. No need to aimlessly wander the duty-free shops to kill time when I could instead pass the hour or two before my flight boarded browsing the free newspapers in its opulent seating area. First though, feeling peckish after bidding my fond farewell to Perth, I decided to stroll over to the buffet to fill a plate or two from the free selection of salads, oriental delicacies, and desserts.

Balancing the tray, I spotted a free table and sat down, taking the opportunity between mouthfuls to survey the better class of passengers with whom I would be sharing my journey – well, at least until we landed in Singapore for our only stop-over (the check-in guy having qualified my glee by pointing out that thereafter I would be consigned to my original seat in Economy Class). Not that the giant Airbus A380 we would be boarding wasn't capable of completing the nine-thousand-mile flight to London Heathrow non-stop. However, selecting a stop-over flight option had shaved a few hundred dollars off the ticket price. Even so, the agreeable ambience in the lounge – the soft lighting, the discreetly-piped music, and the *sotto voce* phone calls of crisply-attired business leaders catching up with their CEOs – chided me to not be so hard on myself when purchasing air travel in future. For goodness sake, on my salary I was hardly a backpacking pauper! In the meantime – and though I might only be a Business Class passenger for the first leg of the long, twenty-one-hour flight home – I resolved to make the most of it.

Meal consumed, I diverted to the coffee machine to round it off with a mocha – only to discover that the instructions on the device baffled me. Perhaps it was an auspice that I was meant to divert to the bar instead. I was on the cusp of throwing up my hands and doing just that when, from the corner of my eye, I spotted a slender hand reach around to assist me. I turned to behold a gorgeous South Asian lady trailing a slim, painted finger across the requisite symbols.

"I think you'll find you need to press this button first," she instructed me in well-spoken English, tossing her head to expel a strand of her long, auburn-tinted hair that had intruded across the eye she fleetingly fixed upon me.

Together we waited while the machine whirred away, both of us unable to resist the urge to glance at the other while the jet of steaming brown slurry filled the cup. A nervous smile played at the corner of her mouth.

"There. Simple when you know how," she announced, this time letting slip a jovial grin.

"Thank you. The feminine touch saves the day!" I marvelled, lifting the cup from the tray and slotting it onto a saucer. "And to think: I was about to go order a beer instead."

Unable or unwilling to summon a further witty riposte that might have kept this tantalising encounter going, she smiled again – this time slightly awkwardly – masking her coyness by inserting the cup in her own hand onto the drip tray. A few more deft instructions with that dainty feminine digit and the machine was whirring again, dribbling a cappuccino into her cup.

I offered her an unconscionably dreamy parting smile before drifting back to my table. My rescuer too wandered evocatively back to her own table on clicking stiletto heels, there to tuck her gorgeous legs beneath it. Resting her elbows on the table, she sipped from her coffee and recommenced perusing the laptop she'd left open. Templing her fingers, she rested her chin upon them. After a moment or two during which she feigned to scan the screen, she took her phone from her handbag. Glancing over at me again, she then called someone on speed dial before settling into a *sotto voce* conversation of her own.

* * * * *

Dusk was already advancing by the time the departure gate opened. At last the mighty plane could commence boarding its three-hundred-and-eighty passengers. It was while queuing on the jet bridge that I heard a soft clunk on the floor and glanced down at my feet to discover that a gaily-coloured object had come to rest between them. I stooped to pick it up and search out its owner – a sheepish little girl with spectacles and black, shoulder-length hair who emerged from between her parents' hips.

"Thank you, sir," she smiled up at me as I handed it back – a cheesy grin that prompted me to beam back at her with avuncular enchantment.

"Oh, Preema. Your father told you to put it away until we are on the plane," her mother turned to berate the child indulgently. "I do apologise, sir," she then looked up to beseech me in her pronounced Indian lilt.

I beamed a second time.

"No worries. A Rubik's Cube: I haven't played with one of those since I was a kid. Not that I could ever figure the thing out!"

"I can, sir," Preema held it up to me and crowed.

Chancing her mother's rebuke again, the youngster then challenged me to jumble up the cube. After polite hesitation, this I did, only to hand it back and watch her deftly twist it this way, then that, then this way again, then that way a final time until – hey presto – the colours on the sides matched.

"Wooh! I'm impressed. You've certainly got that thing sussed," I commended her.

"Yes, sir, our daughter is very intelligent for her age," her father explained proudly.

"Preema, you say? That's a pretty name," I noted. "A pretty name for a pretty little lady."

"Thank you most kindly, sir. Every day we give thanks to God that He has blessed us with such a special child," he chortled, draping a protective paternal arm across his prepubescent seed. Nestling up to his side while staring up at me, another cheesy grin had spread across Preema's smooth russet chops.

Stepping aboard the plane, I presented my boarding pass to the flight attendant, who courteously bade me make my way to the spiral staircase that led to the upper deck.

Although this was not the first occasion I'd been privileged to fly Business Class, the wicked thrill one derives upon being able to shear away from passengers heading for the cheaper seats – Preema and her parents included – was no less animating. More so, because things had moved on since I'd last flown 'up top' several years earlier. Emerging at the summit of those stairs, a pretty attendant ushered me to a centre seat cubicle that was brimming with all manner of thoughtful little luxuries – the kind one might expect for the eight thousand Australian dollars I'd otherwise have had to shell out to sit here. There were blankets and pillows in the stowage area (all sealed in polythene for freshness); illustrated menus in the side pocket, along with glossy in-flight magazines that showcased the exotic destinations the airline served; a video screen in the seat back booted up ready to select an in-flight movie (together with a set of headphones so as not to disturb one's neighbours); a fixed side table with a built-in, touch-screen handset to adjust the recline of the seat; a pull-out tray that unfolded to form a larger table; reading lights; laptop sockets; a USB charging point; even a pop-open vanity mirror. However, some items were familiar to a gate-crasher from Economy Class: in the stowage pocket I located a pair of vomit bags – provided just in case!

"Oh. Hi. It looks like we meet again," my rummaging was interrupted by a refined and pleasantly familiar voice, its owner having halted at the adjacent cubicle to claim her seat.

This was uncanny. Of all the flights taking off that evening; and of all the seats in the Business Class of this one! I bit my lip to suppress the urge to thank aloud my lucky stars.

"Just as well," I playfully suggested. "I might need your expert hand to log me onto the free internet."

"What? A system-savvy guy like you?" she replied. "I take it you *are* a software engineer? Or something to do with computers?" she added, by now having sat down, her gorgeous brown eyes just visible above the partition that divided the cubicles. Once again, she swept her hair from one of them with a discreet brush of her fingers across her brow.

"I'm a mining engineer, actually."

"Forgive me then. From the way you're dressed I imagined you managing the kind of breezy, laid-back set-up where young men with beards, tattoos and piercings programme computers. And are those Timberlands I noticed you're wearing?" she craned over the partition to spy my footwear.

I too glanced into the well of my seat at my denims and my boots. Might she perchance be suggesting that I was underdressed for this class of air travel? My retro-slogan T-shirt and SuperDry hoodie certainly contrasted unfavourably with the chequered bodycon dress and black three-quarter sleeve tunic my new next-door neighbour was wearing.

"Needs must, I'm afraid. I've done a fair bit of walking today."

"Ah, but not good for flying. Your feet expand. You'd best remove them if you want a comfortable flight. Ask the attendant for a pair of flight slippers once we're airborne."

"I will. You sound like you're a regular Business Class flyer," I probed.

"I clock up a fair few air miles each year. I own my own high-class fashion business. We sell all over the world. Our Australian outlets are especially profitable. Maybe Aussie women are so accustomed to trotting about in shorts and vest tops that when they do dress up they want to look fabulous."

"You can say that again," I said, buckling myself up and nestling into my seat.

"I'm sorry?"

"I said: you're right. I can think of at least one Australian lady I know who, well… Yeah, she too always looked fabulous," I called over, conscious that my sojourn in Perth today had not exactly helped expel from my head the memory of the said lady.

"Mind you, you look fabulous too," I added, chancing my luck with my new flight companion. "In that outfit, I mean. It's beautiful. One of your own creations?"

From the coy manner with which she arched her eyebrows, I could deduce the answer to my question. And that my luck might be holding.

"Mint?" she offered in this spirit of newfound repartee, retrieving a packet from her bag. She offered me one over the partition before taking one herself and popping it into her mouth. "It's good for your ears: for when we take off," she insisted.

I grinned mischievously.

"I'm afraid it won't fit!" I insisted, rather clownishly attempting to insert mine into one of my lugholes.

I thought I detected laughter dancing in the depths of her eyes as she stared at me and sucked on her mint. Upon which, I popped mine into my mouth too.

"Crew: arm doors and cross check."

Just then our blossoming acquaintance was interrupted by the video screen flashing into life, upon which the image of a delightful oriental attendant was pointing out the safety features of the plane, as well as explaining the routine for take-offs, landings, and – God forbid – forced landings. Meanwhile, the generators had powered up and I felt the plane being nudged away from the terminal gate. Taxiing under its own power, while we were halted in the queue at the head of the runway I nestled into my seat and returned to my previous introspection.

Australia could have turned out so different; and yet in one crucial matter it had turned out to be depressingly the same. *'For what profits a man if he gains the whole world but loses his own soul?'* I vaguely recalled my old RE teacher once preaching – not that I went near churches, except for the obligatory weddings, christenings and funerals. It was one of the very few passages from the Bible that I'd memorised. As time had passed, I'd done the weddings (including one of my own) and the christenings (ditto). I guess I was now fast approaching the time of life when it would increasingly be the funerals that would summon my infrequent church attendances. Yet what had I got to show for having 'gained the whole world'? A failed marriage and an eight-year-old daughter who I seldom got to see; a few flings on the rebound; out of one of them a tenuous love affair that might just have healed the trauma of that failed marriage; and then back again to more flings on the rebound. I posed the question again: had it all been worth it? The career? The money? The exhilaration of living and working on one of the most awesome continents on the planet? And now the opportunity ahead of me to live and work on yet another?

The engines opened full throttle and the huge airliner raced down the runway with these questions still assailing me. The plane then lifted into the evening sky, climbed, banked, and headed out to sea, where the illuminated skyline of Perth that I craned to catch a last glimpse of could beguile me – and reproach me – no more.

2

"I must go and leave the happy view I had of being a rich and thriving man in my new plantation, only to pursue a rash and immoderate desire of rising faster than the nature of the thing admitted."

Robinson Crusoe

"Good evening, ladies and gentleman, this is Adam Lim, your captain, speaking. Firstly, can I apologise once more that we were a little late taking off from Perth. However, we are now flying at our cruising altitude of forty-thousand feet. With the wind in our favour, we should therefore make good progress to touch down in Singapore at or around our scheduled arrival time of 2355 hours. Otherwise, please relax, enjoy the in-flight facilities, and allow my cabin crew to be at your service."

With a five-hour evening flight across the Indian Ocean ahead of me, I'd already plugged my phone into the charging jack and was availing myself of the complimentary wi-fi to catch up with e-mails and social media posts. I was happy to avail myself too of the complimentary food and drinks the attendants were bringing round. Boy, I could get used to this lifestyle!

I have to say that, for such a colossal jet, the engine roar was remarkably subdued – testament to advances in air travel since I'd first flown long-haul over twenty years earlier. However, smooth as the A380 was, even it was no match for the spot of in-flight turbulence we briefly encountered.

As we bumped and jolted, I caught wind of a sudden clinking of glass, along with a cuss word being spat out. It sounded like my next-door neighbour's pricey little outfit had just been doused in Veuve Cliquot. The turbulence having passed, I heard her unclip her seat belt and, above the partition, observed her rise to her feet, her expensive solitaire diamond necklace glinting in the glow of the cabin lights.

"I do hope it doesn't stain, madame," an attendant had meanwhile rushed up to her in full-on apology mode.

"No, it'll be fine. Fortunately, champagne washes out quite easily. Just fetch me a damp cloth, if you'd be so kind."

"Of course, madame."

"It could have been worse then. It's cheap red wine they're probably spilling in Economy!" I attempted humour while she was loitering in the aisle waiting for the attendant to return. I unclipped my belt too and rose to survey the damage.

"My fault really, I suppose. I should have clung onto my glass," my acquaintance explained, putting on a brave face.

"Thank you," she bade the attendant, running the cloth over the wet patch in her lap. Her distraction afforded me another opportunity to lustfully eye that incredible figure. Too late I spotted her observing my interest in her.

"I apologise. I haven't introduced myself, have I," I sought to mask those ulterior motives, reaching over the partition to offer her a hand. Having dispensed with the cloth she leaned over to tentatively slip her own inside it.

"I'm Wes. Wes Smith," I said, shooting her a boyish grin.

"Anila. Anila Patel," she replied, motioning to slip back into her seat. Then she halted herself, as if intrigued.

"Wes, you say?"

"It's short for Wesley. But no one ever calls me that. Except for my mother. And then only when she's dismayed about something I've said or done," I joked.

My amateurish attempt at humour goaded one corner of her mouth to tuck in and her alluring smile to return. Otherwise, she sat down and buckled herself up – a hint perhaps that I should return to my own seat and leave her in peace to watch the in-flight movie. Maybe my equally amateurish stab at chatting her up had bombed after all.

"Anila – that's a pretty name," I noted even so as I sat back down behind that partition, following it up with my other well-worn chat-up line: "A pretty name for a pretty lady."

There followed a dispiriting silence from the other cubicle, leavened only by the hypnotic hum of the plane's engines.

Ah well, some you win, some you lose! I nestled back into my seat and resumed surfing my phone. However, just at the point when I was resigned that I would not be joining that celebrated 'Mile High Club' tonight, I spotted two sets of dainty fingers reaching up to fiddle with some clips. Lo and behold, that confounded partition was suddenly no more.

"Thank you," Anila stared across at me with a tantalising smile. "For the compliment, that is. So if the intention is that you would like to conduct a proper conversation with me I guess we might as well lower this thing!"

Perhaps all was not lost after all. I scrabbled about for something to say with which to restart our dialogue.

"See – I heeded your advice about the slippers," I announced, holding one of my feet aloft. "I found a pair in the amenity kit."

She proffered another one of those indulgent smiles.

"I must remember to sneak them downstairs with me when we touch down at Singapore," I explained, adding with a conspiratorial hand pressed to my mouth that "at which point I'm afraid I shall be obliged to return to Economy."

"Oh, so you…?"

"Yes, I bagged an upgrade," I confessed. "Well, at least for the first leg of the flight. I guess that makes me a bit of an imposter."

"Not at all," she smiled. "In fact, I might just be glad of the company. I think I've seen most of the in-flight movies on offer," she then feigned to have me believe. What – all two-hundred-and-fifty of them?

Switching off the screen, she retracted the fold-away flight table and adjusted her seat to make herself more comfortable.

"So, did I hear you say you're a mining engineer?" she glanced across at me from her new, more horizontal repose, training those rich brown eyes on me as she awaited my reply.

"That's right. I was the safety manager at a huge iron ore mine about seventy kilometres south of Port Hedland," I enlightened her in between likewise playing with the controls of my own seat until it too was set to the same relaxed recline. "It extracts close to ninety million tonnes of the stuff; and sits on proven reserve of over a billion tonnes more, making it one of the most important mines in Western Australia."

"Was, you say? Do I take it you no longer work there?"

"That's right. I'm heading off to Canada to take up a new role as operations manager at one of the largest copper mines in British Columbia. That's after I've spent a few weeks in England catching up on what's happened since I've been away."

"And how long was that – if you don't mind me being nosy?"

Having run a hand through her long, silky hair, and with those probing eyes still trained on me, she could see I didn't mind at all. Far from it. I was positively revelling in this classy bird's company.

"Three-and-a-half years, to be precise."

"That is a long time. I hope the reward was worth it."

"Mining's not exactly a badly-paid occupation. But then I guess it depends on how you define 'reward'."

She must have noticed my self-assurance falter. *'For what profits a man if he gains the whole world but loses his own soul?'*

"So you have regrets about leaving Australia?"

"A few," I admitted after some hesitation.

"Or is it also the case that you have regrets about your decision to work there in the first place?"

Wow! How quickly my prospective chat-up bid had turned into dissection at the hands of my attractive new flight companion. Strangely though, I was unfazed. Perhaps an earthly confessor in whom I could confide was what had been missing from my life during my final, lonely months in Oz. Therefore, I psyched myself up to be candid.

"If I told you that my decision to take up that job in Australia was what broke up my marriage, would that make me sound foolish? Or callous even?" I put it to her.

She glanced away and pondered that question for a moment.

"Yes and no. The higher the climb to the top, the harder the journey can be on those we love. However, one has to be true to oneself. If managing a massive mine in Australia, and now in Canada, is what you were cut out to do, then I doubt you'd have found your fulfilment in life stacking shelves in a supermarket.

Besides, someone has to run the place. Were you married long?" she continued her soft-spoken interrogation.

"Ten years."

"Children?"

"One daughter – eight-years-old. I've tried to keep in touch with her. I flew home once a year. She also came out to see me last year – accompanying my parents on an extended holiday."

"That time must have been very precious to you," she surmised.

"It was."

She permitted me a caesura in the conversation while I recalled that amazing vacation – the places Emily and I visited; the laughter we'd shared; and the sadness when the time came for her to board the flight home with her grandparents – treasured memories that had earlier been stirred by my touching encounter with that cute little Indian girl on the jet bridge (who I guessed was the same age as Emily; possessed of the same happy smile too). I imagined her at that moment, probably fumbling with her Rubik's Cube on the deck beneath me – showing off her expertise to her proud, adoring father. Meanwhile, this proud, adoring (but absent) father had been reduced to wiring a portion of his pay cheques to a bank account ten thousand miles away – maintenance and pocket money stumped up in lieu of being a vital presence in his child's life and of watching her grow up.

"Did your wife not want to follow you to Australia?" the dissection resumed.

"Sadly not. Leaving aside that much of its wildlife either bites you, stings you, or eats you, I suspect the Australian heat would not have been for the likes of Leanne – that's my ex-wife – even had she elected to join me. I'd pleaded with her; but, well… she found Africa bad enough. Mind you, Port Hedland got a bit too hot for me at times!" I snickered ironically.

"Africa? So this was not your first job overseas?"

"No. In 1997, before I met Leanne, I worked at the huge Konkola mine in Zambia. Back then I was young, carefree, and single. And it was good money – far more than I could make in England. Hence in 2005, when I was offered the opportunity of working in South Africa on a similar healthy remuneration, I jumped at it.

"However, the difference this time was that I was a married man. Reluctantly, Leanne fell in with my plans. However, it proved to be a desperately lonely time for her; stuck in a strange country where she had few friends; and with me focussed too much on the responsibilities that went with my well-paid job. What's more, it was while we were in South Africa that Emily was born. I guess the strain of caring for a new baby without the support of her family proved too much. She was desperately homesick. She spent most of her time in South Africa counting down the days until she could return to England."

"I can imagine."

"Then you can probably imagine her dismay too when, no sooner we were back home, I announced my next big challenge – in the shape of a plum job in Oz. It was the final straw. Though I begged her, Leanne was adamant. 'Choose', she put it to me bluntly: 'the job and the money in Australia; or Emily and me in England'. Perhaps it was the stubborn streak in me that didn't take kindly to ultimatums. We had many rows about it. In the end though, I made my choice. The rest, as they say, is history."

"That's sad."

From the dolefulness of her sigh, I sensed that maybe Anila now regretted her crass statement about being 'true to oneself'. Even so, she shuffled on her seat and turned onto her side to face me, brushing her hair from her face again as if to bid me unburden myself of the sequel to that fateful decision.

"Looking back though, I now realise that, in truth, we were just two different people who wanted different things out of life. You see, we'd been drifting apart over a long period of time. Perhaps what happened was inevitable – although they do say that hindsight is only true after the event!" I smirked forlornly.

"Anyway, after I'd split from Leanne, left behind my child, and cried it all out of my system, I threw myself into my new job, while in my personal life I was soon behaving like a kid let loose in a candy store," I continued. "I promptly drifted in and out of a succession of relationships. Well, hurried encounters, really – as divorced and frustrated thirty-something males often do," I noted, offering her a one-sided smile. "Never anything serious. That was until one night, while weekending in Perth, I ran into Willow."

"Willow?" I watched my listener's eyebrows arch.

"Yes, I know – as in the tree," I chortled. "It was at the beginning of last year. Like me, she too was hanging around the club on her own that night. Like me, she too was acting cool and untroubled – even as her eyes told a different story."

"So is she the Australian lady you alluded to earlier – the one you claimed always looked fabulous'?"

I drew breath and, in my mind, was transported back to that humid January night in Perth when I'd outwitted the not inconsiderable competition for Willow's favours and won the right to strut alongside her on a strobe-bathed dance floor.

"Yes. She was blonde, beautiful, and leggy. She captivated me the moment I set eyes on her – as she probably did the other men who'd had their eyes on her that night. Afterwards, I invited her to join me for a beer on the verandah overlooking the street, where we could chat and chill. She immediately warmed to my English reserve and understatement. Likewise, I warmed to her brassy and irreverent Aussie humour. It was then that I discovered she was married. However, one thing led to another and we ended up back at my hotel. Boy, what a night to remember that was!

"Looking back, our moment of passion should have ended there – every man's dream of a one-night-stand! However, I was utterly mesmerised by her. So, at my insistence, we continued to meet up. As I learned more about her situation, it became apparent that her husband was something of a psycho: controlling, pathologically jealous, and given to terrifying fits of rage; and, if that failed, by threatening to kill himself – and her with it! By all accounts, he was one disturbing character. No wonder Willow was desperately unhappy and was looking for something more from her miserable life."

"So how come this 'controlling' husband of hers let his 'beautiful, blonde, leggy' wife out to play, knowing she might well be 'playing' with other men at that?" she proffered the next logical question. To which I smirked sardonically.

"He was an airline pilot, so fortunately he was out of town a lot – off to Europe, America, or wherever. So long as we were careful there was no reason why he should ever find out."

"It still sounds to me like this 'Willow' woman was playing a very dangerous game. And so were you too, Wes."

"Undoubtedly. I reckon he must have had his suspicions that his dutiful, but otherwise resentful wife was finding her emotional fulfilment in someone else's arms. What woman in that situation wouldn't? Sure enough, a few months into the affair, she informed me he'd been trawling her phone and had come across one of my text messages to her – despite Willow insisting she'd been religiously deleting them once she'd read them. Nothing too incriminating, she assured me. But enough for him to maybe work out that some out-of-town ex-pat called 'Wes Smith' was sniffing round his missus.

"There and then, she insisted that our affair had to end – for both our sakes. Of course, I begged her to remove herself from her unhappy marriage; to leave with me for Port Hedland; or at the very least to go stay with her sister in Cairns – at the other end of the country. However, she would have none of it. Dutiful wife to the end!" I hissed angrily.

"What's more, she had it in her head that, given the kind of man he was, wherever she ran to he would find her and, well… Who could say what a bastard like that was capable of doing!

"It would be the last time I would ever see Willow – even though I was tempted to look her up whenever I was in Perth. Neither did she ever phone or text me; nor return my calls. It was as if she'd just disappeared off the face of the Earth. Perhaps I was a fool to have expected a different outcome from a heady and insane infatuation with another man's wife," I sighed languidly.

"And her husband? Did you ever think he might have been enraged enough to want to follow up on the little clue Willow had inadvertently left on her phone? Isn't the fear of constantly having to look out for 'a bastard like that' the real reason why you've reluctantly decided to leave Australia?"

I chewed on the inside of my cheek and shook my head at the absurdity of such a suggestion.

"I can take care of myself. No, it's Willow I feel for. I still wonder whether I should have been more insistent that she leave him. But then maybe I was the coward – walking away like I did. It felt like I was abandoning her to whatever retribution she would likely face. And though you might conclude that what we'd had going was just one more hopeless fling among many, even now I find myself unable to forget about her. Maybe I was in love with her. I often wonder whether she felt the same."

Anila drew an elbow out, propped her head in the platform her hand thus formed, and stared at me empathetically.

"Or did it not occur to you, Wes, that, ridiculous though it might sound, all along this woman was feeding you a total pack of lies; that there never was any violent, psychopathic husband; that – just as you'd had your one-night-stands – so you too were just one more fling among many to her; a diversion of which she'd now tired and was looking to wash her hands of."

It was a brutally honest assertion of a possibility that I had myself entertained. After all, I'd never met the guy, nor seen any photographs of him – either ones on her phone that she could have showed me, or ones she might have posted on her otherwise heavily-redacted Facebook page. When all was said and done, this man was a mystery; a phantasm that I needed to put to rest, along with the memory of the mixed-up woman who'd maybe dreamed him up as a way of eliciting sympathy from her lovers (as well as a means of subtly menacing them too).

"Who knows?" I conceded, despondently.

"Then again, assuming what Willow told you is true, it was *her* decision to stay, Wes," Anila consoled me. "You can't keep beating yourself up over that. Neither would you have been able to successfully build a life with someone who was always looking over her shoulder; someone who'd maybe yet to sort out her own head; or confront her own demons. Not every love story can have a fairy tale ending. So just be grateful instead that you're now turning the page and moving on – beginning a new chapter in your life; and in a new country too."

I genuinely appreciated Anila's sincerity and her willingness to listen. Therefore, after time spent in quiet reflection, we chatted instead about more light-hearted matters, periodically giggling and flirting while the digital maps on the screens of the neighbouring seat cubicles plotted our progress northwards.

"Anyway," I eventually pointed out, "you haven't told me much about yourself – apart from the fact that your name is Anila Patel and that you own your own fashion business."

"Well," she shuffled again and shot me a coy grin, "I'm thirty-two years old; I live and was born in London, the youngest of three sisters; and, yes, I run my own fashion business. For what it's worth too, a few years back my face made it onto the cover of *'Cosmopolitan'* magazine when I was voted 'Asian Businesswoman of the Year'. Following that, I was invited to head up a government task force set up to encourage more girls from ethnic backgrounds to consider careers in business."

"Wow! I'm impressed. And are *you* married?" it was *me* now delving into *her* personal life, though not consciously seeking to skate over her entrepreneurial achievements.

"No, I'm not – though it's a source of mounting despair to my mother!" she flared her nostrils in dismay. "However – and in anticipation of your next question – I am in a relationship with someone at present."

Drat! I tried not to permit my disappointment to show.

"And do you have any…"

"No, I have no children," she intercepted my next question too. "I hope to one day though… before it's too late."

"Hope?" I quizzed.

She glanced away as if to choose her words with care, those pretty eyes roaming everywhere except at me.

"I'm up for it. But I can't say Mike's keen on the idea."

"Mike? He's your partner, I assume?"

"Don't sound so surprised. We Asian women do find you white guys attractive, you know!" her gaze returned – and with it a coyly reproachful smile upon lips that glistened. "But maybe Mike and I are two different people too – like you and Leanne. We certainly seem to be spending more and more time apart lately. But then he has his interests and I have mine. Sure, he's been good to me," she conceded, "and we've had some good times together. Maybe it's because he's quite a bit older than me that he's not keen on having more children. You see, he's been married before; and he has three by his first wife."

"Do I take it then that you've immersed yourself in your fashion business as a means of seeking revenge on him for frustrating those maternal yearnings?" I ventured to be so bold. "And that, like Willow, sooner or later you might also be tempted to find emotional fulfilment elsewhere?"

Even as I said it, I feared my supposition was a chat-up line too far. Or at least it crassly pointed to emotional turmoil that – unlike me – Anila was unwilling to be quite so candid about.

"I haven't always been faithful to Mike – if that's what you're driving at," she huffed. "However, like you, I've had my fingers burned; bad choices I made and corners I regret turning."

She sullenly rolled onto her back, reaching across to power her seat to a more upright setting. Maybe, like her strange and sudden reticence, it was an acknowledgement that by indulging in this *tête-a-tête* with me she risked playing with fire again. Perhaps my penchant for flippancy was grating on her. Perhaps I'd flattered myself unduly and that she didn't have the hots for me after all. Perhaps, like her harsh assessment of my own adulterous *paramour*, all along she'd being toying with my patent interest in her but had now tired of stringing me along. Or perhaps instead she *was* up for being wooed, but (unlike me) could also summon the mettle to halt this seduction before it risked her turning another regretful corner. Perhaps Willow Mackenzie wasn't the only woman who was wrestling with demons.

Soon it was time for the other passengers to return their seats to the upright position. The plane had commenced its descent into Singapore – the glittering city state where we would be passing all of one hour and twenty minutes before setting off again on the long, overnight leg to Heathrow.

Once the plane touched down and docked, those passengers who were leaving the flight at this point shuffled from their seats and began gathering their belongings. I meanwhile jiggled my feet back into my Timberlands before rising from mine, grabbing my shoulder bag, and stretching exaggeratedly in the aisle.

"Alas, I'm afraid at this point I must leave you," I called over, hoping Anila wasn't angry with me.

If it was a play for sympathy it appeared to work.

"Listen, Wes. I'm sorry – for clamming up on you back then," she looked up at me with fluttering, remorseful eyes.

"And here was me thinking it was something I'd said," I replied as a smile ran away from my face.

"Don't be silly. You've been great company. Fascinating too," she reciprocated, rising to offer me a hand across the redundant partition. "It's a pity our brief time together is at an end."

"And you've been a wonderful listener. Perhaps a session on the couch with you was just what I was looking for," I thanked her, savouring her soft, slender hand in mine. "...The psychotherapist's couch!" I qualified my remark when she curled an eyebrow at my bumbling *double-entendre.*

"Look, I do understand why you're wary of things that might get complicated," I apologised again. "But then maybe I too have had way too much complication in my life of late."

"As you've just spent the last four hours telling me," she puckered her lips in jest.

It was my turn to permit a plaintive snigger to escape.

"You up for maybe stretching your legs?" I half-asked-half-suggested, hinting in the direction of that spiral staircase.

"Thanks for the offer. But I've hung around enough deserted airport terminals in my time. If it's all the same, I think I'll change into the pair of flight pyjamas they provide so that I'm ready to bed down when we get airborne again."

I permitted myself a last fond glimpse of those seats, which – absent the partition between them – reclined to form an expansive double bed. I pondered the 'Mile High Club' once more.

"In which case, I'll bid you sweet dreams, Miss Patel,"

"You too, Mr Smith. And all the best with the new job."

Then, totally unexpected, the contemplative demeanour I'd been sporting throughout must have tugged a heartstring. She reached into where she'd stowed her handbag, drawing it out. She then proceeded to delve inside and pull out a small business card.

"Here," she simpered. "My number and e-mail address. Perhaps if you have some free time on your hands once you're back in England – in between spending it with your parents and your little girl, that is – you'll give your 'psychotherapist' a call. Maybe we can meet up again for another session on the couch."

At first staring down at it while battling to suppress my excitement, I filed it away in my passport wallet.

"Oh, and Wes," she called out as I was shuffling down the aisle to tag onto the line of exiting passengers.

I turned about.

"Your flight slippers!" she grinned, waving them aloft and shaking her head in the manner of an indulgent mother.

I ambled back to collect them and stuff them inside my travel bag. Then I sneaked her one more grin – this time a knowing one, like a kid with a teenage crush. After the 'dangerous game' I'd carelessly played in Perth would I ever learn!

3

"'You see what a taste Heaven has given you of what to expect if you persist. Perhaps this is all befallen us on your account, like Jonah in the ship of Tarshish. Pray,' continues he, 'what are you? And on what account did you go to sea?'."

Robinson Crusoe

Anila was right about one thing: international airports are not the most thrilling places to hang around at midnight. With its tall, verdant palm trees shielded beneath towering glass atriums, Changi International Airport might rank as an exception if for no other reason than the sheer scale and magnificence of this air-conditioned temple to modern air travel – even if it was largely deserted. Wandering it at least afforded me an opportunity to loosen my joints, watching the ground crews refuelling the plane and loading additional baggage into its cavernous holds. As we were scheduled to touch down in London at 0625 hours GMT I intended to spend most of the flight catching up on my sleep.

It was as I was ambling back to the departure gate that I felt a buzzing in my groin. Trawling my phone from my pocket, I unlocked the screen to tap open the text message that had arrived. To my surprise, it had been sent from Willow's phone.

"Enjoy your flight home, Wes. And please don't worry about me. Very shortly I will be in a better place too. Goodnight, sweetie. And sleep tight."

Having had no contact with her for several months, I was stunned. How on Earth had she found out I was leaving Oz – and, more to the point, that today was the day I was heading home? Even so, it felt good to hear from her again – even if doing so rekindled memories I was still endeavouring to put behind me.

Not unnoticed however was the allusion that she'd finally summoned up the courage to walk out on that brute of a husband and make a new life for herself.

Whatever my churned-up emotions at that moment, I felt I simply had to call her – if only to wish her well and to confirm from her own lips that she had indeed finally broken free of him. Somehow replying by text didn't seem right – even though I knew hearing her voice again risked churning those emotions still further. Swallowing hard, I took the plunge and dialled. The text had only been sent a few minutes ago, so I reasoned she was still awake.

However, her number merely rang out before diverting to answerphone. Meanwhile, another disembodied voice echoing around the departure lounge was announcing the last call for my flight. Knowing I would be unable to call her from the plane (and that once we were over open sea there would be little hope of connecting an illicit call from the toilet), I dialled again. Hovering at the gate, I flashed the boarding clerk pained smiles in between the frowns occasioned by Willow's refusal to answer me.

If I'm truthful, right then I was in such a funk that I was tempted to board the next flight back to Perth – even if it meant letting my luggage carry on to London without me. However, with the clerk leering at me impatiently while readying the gate for closure, I knew that – while such impulsiveness plays well in romantic movies – it would prove expensive and most probably futile. I could only assume Willow had deliberately sent the message this late precisely to ensure I'd passed the point of no return for changing my mind and staying in Australia. Reluctantly, I flashed my boarding card and hurried down the jet bridge. My phone was still pressed to my ear as I boarded the plane – the very last passenger to step inside before the attendant sealed the door.

"I know. No phones!" I rolled my eyes at her apologetically.

This time she gestured for me to make my way down the gangway towards the back of the plane. Bodging at my phone to switch it to 'airplane' mode, I counted off the row numbers. Locating Seat C55, I slung my bag into the overhead locker, sat down, and sullenly buckled myself in.

Though nowhere near as spacious and palatial as where the wealthy Anila was at that moment readying herself for take-off, there were still plenty of thoughtful little flourishes provided to make the overnight flight comfortable for the two-hundred-and-fifty passengers below her (for whom money was rather tighter). Included among that number were that cute little Indian girl and her parents. Having spotted the bonny little lass across the aisle from me, still spinning that Rubik's Cube, it clicked that hers was the 'family' that had cuckooed the elderly mother of that Chinese lady in Perth – and Preema the culprit who was sitting in what should have been her seat! While I was glancing across and exchanging grins with the youngster, her mother niftily confiscated the cube lest her daughter annoy the willowy, middle-aged woman sat next to her in Seat D55 (and who was fidgeting nervously as the plane taxied).

Reminded too that it was long past her bedtime, Preema removed and folded her spectacles and stuffed them into the pocket of the hoodie she'd meantime donned – having shooed away an offer by her mother to place them in her handbag. The little girl then twisted over and buried her head of jet-black locks into a puffy white pillow. Demonstrably pretending to be asleep, she was unable to resist the temptation to pop an eye open and observe me fidgeting too. However, her pretend slumber was interrupted by a patrolling flight attendant softly chivvying her to sit upright in the seat – at least until we were airborne.

With the lights dimmed, the engines roared into life, sending the jet hurtling down the runway. We were skywards again, the whirring of the undercarriage being retracted preceding a bank to port that briefly afforded the passengers next to me a magnificent, panoramic view of Singapore by night.

Ordinarily, I too am an avid window-seat flyer, eager to imbibe high-flying vistas of mountains, deserts, forests, glaciers – and, yes, sprawling cities too. However, given that most of my return flight to the United Kingdom would be undertaken in darkness I contented myself with an aisle seat. Indeed, twenty minutes out of Changi and everything was pitch-black outside – save for the flashes of a distant electrical storm somewhere on the far shore of the Straits of Malacca.

It might be approaching two in the morning; however, nothing was going to interfere with the cabin crew serving final in-flight refreshments before the lights were dimmed again and everyone could make themselves comfortable for the night. Having eaten my fill, both on the ground in Perth and on the first leg of the journey, I settled for an orange juice and a bowl of nibbles.

It was while munching them that I decided to take my phone from my pocket and study Willow's message again. My earlier excitement at hearing from her out of the blue had given way to a gnawing sixth-sense about that text. For example, why send it well after midnight when she could have sent it much earlier – by which time I would have long since departed Australian airspace. Perhaps she couldn't sleep. Maybe instead she was celebrating her newfound freedom in Queensland, watching the sun come up at her sister's beachside house in Cairns. Or maybe she'd idly tapped it out while making eyes at some other lustful sucker who'd spotted her across a bar in Perth! A 'better place' indeed!

And why 'sweetie'? She'd never addressed me using that term before. The more I thought about it, the more that sixth-sense told me things didn't add up. Far from being in a better place, had something more disturbing happened to Willow instead?

However, my second-guessing was cut short when a sudden violent jolting of the plane snatched both phone and tumbler of orange juice from my hands. All around me, passengers were screaming, their food, their drink, and their paperback novels also flung from their grasps. Meanwhile, in the aisles, the 'trolley dollies' were being pummelled against seat backs, the items they'd been serving crashing hither and thither. Elsewhere along the plane, oxygen masks were dropping down to further alarm hysterical passengers, while overhead lockers had also burst open to deluge their contents upon them.

Even more heart-stopping, the plane then tipped into a steep dive, the attendants clinging on for dear life as their trolleys hurtled down the aisles. Glancing across again, I spotted Preema wailing in her mother's embrace – the eyes of both her parents shut tight as they clung onto each other, her father mouthing prayers with a fervour that suggested they would be the last ones he might ever offer. Eyes closed too – and gripping the arms of the seat for all she was worth – the woman next to them had also discovered an urgent need to commune with her Maker!

For several more seconds that felt like an eternity, the screaming jet yawed and pitched until finally it levelled out – by which time even its most stoical passengers were palpitating.

"Bloody hell, love. They didn't see that one coming!" some guy in front of me exclaimed as an attendant hurried along the aisle, comforting her charges – a blooded handkerchief pressed to her forehead.

It was the most shocking episode of turbulence I'd experienced in all my years of flying, made worse (as the man in front had pointed out) by the fact that Captain Lim had plainly not spotted it in time to flick the seat belt sign on and hurry his passengers back to their seats. Neither was that pretty flight attendant the only person nursing an injury. What's more, several more minutes would pass before finally, at the behest of the senior flight attendant in the galley behind us haranguing the flight deck on the intercom phone, someone up front elected to offer an explanation – someone, to my surprise, sporting a broad Australian accent...

"Ladies and gentleman, this is Rick Mackenzie, your First Officer, here. Can I apologise for the spot of turbulence we encountered back there. Hopefully it hasn't caused you too much discomfort..."

"Discomfort? My wife's a bloody nervous wreck, mate!" the man in front yelled in disbelief, glancing up from consoling her.

I shared his anger. While the attendants desperately sought to placate their passengers or collect up the wreckage of the meal trolleys, that anger was magnified not just by the manifest understatement of First Officer Mackenzie's remark, but by the glibness of his manner too. 'Spot of turbulence'? Whatever happened to the good old Aussie penchant for calling a spade a bloody shovel!

"Yours, mate?" I meanwhile felt a tap on my shoulder, the guy behind inserting a stubby hand around the seat back to hand me back my phone.

"Thanks," I turned around, panting.

Otherwise, I tried to be philosophical. I'd read about this kind of extreme turbulence, which – though rare – could toss even the largest airliner around like a child's toy. I thought of Anila upstairs and wondered if her delightful little dress had once more been drenched in expensive house champagne.

* * * * *

A further twenty minutes would pass before we would hear from the cockpit again, the cabin crew having meantime done a sterling job of patching up cuts and grazes and tidying up the chaos occasioned by our freak encounter with nature.

> *"This is First Officer Mackenzie again, just informing you that we might need to make a few sharp manoeuvres in the next few minutes…"*

The compliment of travellers directed voluble sighs of anger and trepidation at this unseemly, laid-back voice breaking further bad news to them. However, at least this time he'd illuminated the 'fasten seat belts' signs in good time; and offered an explanation.

> *"… This is because of a large military exercise we've just been informed is taking place in the Andaman Sea. There's no need to worry though, and we should be able to return to our normal flight path once we've steered around the exclusion zone…"*

As the huge jet executed a sharp (if more controlled) bank to starboard, my innate sixth-sense was troubling me again. 'Large military exercises' don't just 'take place' on a whim. They take weeks, months even, to plan. Surely air traffic control in Singapore would have advised Captain Lim beforehand that he needed to file a new flight plan to avoid it. Besides, where was Captain Lim? Even though long-haul A380s carried two flight crews – one flying while the other rested – surely our abrupt and unprecedented encounters, first with extreme turbulence and now with a flotilla of missile-firing warships, demanded that he return to the cockpit and take charge – if only to reassure his fretting passengers. So why had the first officer been delegated the task of piloting this mighty airliner in the manner of an evading fighter jet – a bizarre thing to be doing if we were supposed to be steering clear of a large naval exercise. Meanwhile, the digitised maps that had been plotting our course on those seat-back screens suddenly all went blank.

Alas, my frayed nerves – as well as those of the passengers around me – were shored up when the jet finally returned to a steady flight pattern. Having been buffeted (literally!) by enough excitement for one night, I slumped down into my seat and tried to snatch the shut-eye I'd promised myself – though not before our Aussie pilot had one more anodyne announcement to make.

> *"Ladies and gentleman, just a quick call to say we've now resumed our normal flight path. I do hope those last few manoeuvres we had to make weren't too alarming. However, we're still on course to arrive in London at or around six-thirty local time. Therefore, I will request that the cabin crew dim the lights so that you can get some rest before we do. In the meantime, this is your first officer, Rick Mackenzie, wishing you goodnight... and sleep tight."*

* * * * *

Unsurprisingly, 'sleeping tight' proved impossible the more I began to figure out answers to my own questions. My brow furrowed and my blood ran cold as I lay there mulling over what I'd pieced together so far – including that name: Rick Mackenzie. Willow's surname was Mackenzie; her husband's name was Rick; he was Australian; and he was... an airline pilot!

Yet surely not! Of all the flights I could have travelled back to England on had I really booked myself aboard one being piloted by a man I'd cuckolded? If so, it was uncanny.

While my anxious persona was struggling to recall which airline Willow had told me her husband flew with, my rational persona insisted that it was absurd to imagine that someone up above had pre-determined that I should fly with him. And anyhow, how could this man possibly know who I was; or that I would be travelling aboard his plane? Even assuming he'd got to browse the passenger list, there must be dozens of Smiths aboard this flight (though rather fewer with UK passports, I surmised; and fewer still called 'Wesley'!). Was it really credible to believe that it was for my benefit that he'd taken his passengers on that joyride across the Bay of Bengal? And that *goodnight and sleep tight'* that he'd bade them: might it just be a chilling, coded message for one passenger in particular? As with the term *'sweetie'* that I dwelt upon when rereading Willow's text message: had she really typed that? Or had her husband gotten hold of her phone again, typed it, and then purposely sent it to me instead? And if so, what fate had become of her now that her phone was in the hands of her pathologically jealous husband?

Unable to rid my mind of this awful scenario, I rose from my seat and wandered down the aisle to the rear of the plane, nervously noting where the exit doors were as I went. On my way I passed the galley, where I spotted the cabin staff huddled together in some kind of confab (and who abruptly halted their anxious deliberations upon spotting me). It further deepened my foreboding that all was not well with the flight that First Officer Mackenzie was at the controls of.

Meanwhile, the dramas so far had occasioned a run on the wines and spirits aboard among those passengers who also couldn't sleep. Consequently, though it was four in the morning, the plane's bathroom facilities were much in demand. Queuing outside the toilet was a middle-aged man who, bored with the wait, had taken to staring out the window of the adjacent exit door. He too was clearly perturbed by something.

"*Coalsack Nebula*," he mumbled, observing me hovering.

"I'm sorry?"

"Or the Southern Coalsack, as it's sometimes called," he tilted his head as if to bid me join him there. Intrigued, I nudged myself away from the bulkhead I'd been leaning against to peer out at the night sky.

"It's that dark patch in the heavens there," he pointed out. "A nebula is a cloud of dust or gas, often thrown up by a dying star.

Although that one is over six-hundred-million light years from Earth, it's large enough to be visible to the naked eye."

"Do I take it you're an astronomer then," I replied, straining to make out the object he was directing my gaze at.

"Only an amateur one," he grinned uneasily. "However, enough of one to know that it's only visible in the southern hemisphere. As is Alpha Crucis, its nearest large star," he likewise pointed out the bright white dot adjacent to it.

"The thing is we shouldn't be able to see it this far north – assuming, that is, that we're following our normal flight path, which by now should be taking us across the Himalayas."

"So what are you saying?" I said, perturbed.

"Given its position in the night sky at this time of year, it means we're certainly not heading on a north-easterly course, as we should be."

"Maybe the plane sustained damage during that turbulence we encountered," I frowned. "Maybe the pilot's taking us back to Singapore... or even to Perth," I joked more fancifully, though I was no longer sure the latter place was where I wanted to be heading in any eventuality! "And anyway, surely we would have been informed of such a drastic change of plan."

"If it's Singapore, we'd have landed by now," my astronomer friend insisted, studying his watch. "And Perth?" he paused before shaking his head. "We're heading in the wrong direction. Make no mistake," he fired me a look of foreboding, "we're flying due south."

"South? What? Out into the Indian Ocean?" I gasped, muffling my surprise when, at that precise moment, a woman passenger joined us at what she assumed to be the end of the queue. At that moment too, the occupant of the toilet emerged.

"No, be our guest," I said, insistently urging the new arrival forward to the vacated cubicle. My fellow male passenger also bade her take up the offer.

"Oh... thank you," she twittered, pleasantly surprised by our collective act of supposed chivalry.

It got a pair of wagging ears out of shot. Once the door was closed, and the lock clicked, we huddled together again by the window, this time our voices purposely lowered.

"We've been flying due south for well over an hour now. Based on our last position before those map monitors went blank, I reckon we're well out over it now. Quite where the pilot is taking us I can't imagine. But assuming he holds this course, there is no other landfall between here and Antarctica – just millions of square miles of ocean!"

I was stunned. A second opinion was confirming that something untoward had indeed happened to our flight.

"You don't suppose we've been hijacked, do you?" the guy was meanwhile endeavouring to answer his own questions.

My brow furrowed again. I agonised whether to reveal to him my own suspicions about the pilot (and, more pertinently, a possible motive for this seemingly inexplicable act).

"I don't know. But I do know this 'Rick Mackenzie' guy has got the cabin crew spooked," I glanced back up the aisle.

"You don't suppose he's taken over the cockpit, do you?" he put it to me. "I mean, killed the rest of the crew, like. Perhaps that accounts for that chaotic dive we plunged into. Rather than hitting an unexpected air pocket, perhaps some kind of struggle took place to seize control of the plane. But, if that is the case, why on Earth would he be flying us out to nowhere?

"Look, we took on fuel at Singapore," I recalled. "The A380 has a range of over eight thousand miles," I further remembered reading something in one of the in-flight magazines. "If he's working on behalf of some terrorist group or other then it's possible he might yet change course and land somewhere – in the Middle East maybe. Perhaps that's why he's heading out to sea first: to throw air traffic controllers off the scent."

Though it sounded intuitive, my theory was but a foil for a no less worrying probability: that Rick Mackenzie – the jealous, unbalanced husband whose wife I'd bedded, and who might have finally plucked up the courage to leave him – was on some kind of suicide mission. And that it was a one-way jaunt he intended I should accompany him on – as well as every other passenger aboard this flight.

"In which case, it must be why he's switched the navigation lights off," my knowledgeable friend observed, staring out of the window again. And as if that dire prognosis wasn't bad enough, the only other passenger aboard who'd twigged that something was amiss had noticed something else while staring out of it.

"See there," he pointed to what appeared to be a vapour trail billowing from the plane's wing. Except that it wasn't. "That's aviation fuel – and the pilot is jettisoning it. Look, thousands of gallons of the stuff!" he exclaimed, dragging me over to observe the same spray billowing from the starboard wing.

"But why?" he shook his head, baffled and fearful.

I couldn't bring myself to tell him what I strongly suspected. For the first time in my life, I became overwhelmingly conscious of my own mortality.

"Look, I'd forget your 'eight thousand miles', mate," he gripped my shoulders and put it to me bluntly. "If whoever's flying this plane carries on dumping fuel he won't be making landfall anywhere – and neither will we!"

* * * * *

"Are you absolutely sure, sir?" the senior attendant likewise quizzed the flight's sojourning amateur astronomer.

He repeated his calculations. He also urged her to peer through the windows herself, where it was possible by the light of those stars to make out aviation spirit still gushing from the wings.

Even so, she appeared to need little convincing that something was awry in the cockpit, where First Officer Mackenzie was refusing to take calls on the intercom phone. Neither was the armoured cockpit door responding to the access code her colleagues up front had entered. Rick Mackenzie had sealed himself inside and there was no way the door could be forced.

"Oh – my – God!" she muttered under her breath as the realisation sank in that all three-hundred-and-eighty of her passengers – as well as the remaining crew members aboard – were now entirely at the mercy of their deranged first officer. Quickly regaining her composure, she urged us back to our seats while ordering her colleagues to calmly, but firmly urge those passengers to stir from their slumber, don the life jackets under their seats, and listen out for further announcements.

Returning to my seat, I spotted Preema anxiously petitioning her parents in her native language as they, like other startled passengers around them, looped life jackets over their heads, tying them securely. Placing one over their daughter's head too, her mother anxiously stroked her cheeks. Nestling her head against the child's, they then closed their eyes and began to pray.

For the first time in more years than I cared to remember, I considered it a sound move – for I could foresee no way that this was going to end well. At the very least we would be ditching in mid-ocean. And I'd watched enough documentaries on the *'Quest'* channel to know that when airliners crash-land at sea it seldom, if ever, ends well. I too now found myself desperately trying to remember prayers I'd been taught at school. Assuming that was that there was someone up above who was listening.

* * * * *

No sooner had the lights dimmed again to accustom our eyes to the darkness outside than the tannoy crackled into life again, this time with the oriental accent of the senior flight attendant.

> *"Ladies and gentleman, it may shortly be necessary for this plane to make an emergency landing at sea. In that eventuality, the pilot will ask you to assume the brace position as shown on your safety notices. Once the plane has landed, calmly and quickly make for your nearest exit, using the floor lighting to find your way. Do not – repeat do NOT – attempt to inflate your life jackets until you are clear of the plane."*

A thousand tremulous thoughts flashed through my mind – not the least being what if I'd indeed let my luggage travel on to London without me and never set foot again aboard this accursed plane! Meanwhile, around me similar trepidation was assailing even the flight's most stolid passengers. Women and children – and even grown men – were openly weeping, while others were petitioning whatever deity they thought might spare them. Once more I observed that Preema's father had his arm extended around his family protectively, mouthing another fervent prayer that their particular deity would protect his family. Alas, the woman next to them had no such assurance, biting at her knuckles in palpable, impotent dread as if, by so doing, she might expunge the reality of our peril.

Given what I suspected, I very much doubted whether any kind of warning would be given by our vengeful (and now ominously taciturn) first officer. However, amidst my own dread and impotence, a far more fearful realisation dawned: that it might just be too late for my own increasingly desperate and ineloquent prayers to save me now. After all, I'd expended my entire adult life affecting disinterest in religion or spiritual matters. Therefore, I imagined a supposedly all-knowing, all-seeing God gleefully reminding me that I'd felt no such propensity to call upon Him when, in the pride of life, I'd been raking in the money and lapping up the good times. Likewise, had I turned to Him when I'd absent-mindedly ship-wrecked my marriage? Or when I'd consigned to emotional turmoil the daughter I'd left behind in England? Had I bothered to seek His counsel while lapping up the hedonistic, playboy lifestyle in Australia – where I'd seduced a succession of women (as well as lustfully pursued another man's wife)? Would I have cared to heed his voice a few hours earlier when contemplating something similar with the wealthy South Asian beauty who was now on the cusp of perishing with me?

No, why should this God listen to me now – much less forgive me – when it was *my* headstrong adultery that had so enraged Willow's husband that it had caused him to hurl himself into this cruel and senseless act? It was an act of premeditated evil for which all these innocent people around me – the godly and the ungodly alike – were about to forfeit their lives to a remote watery grave.

One by one, the jet engines flamed out and there descended upon us an eerie stillness disturbed only by the faltering flow of air across the plane's wings, as well as by the petrified whimpers emanating from its doomed passengers. The huge airliner was silently gliding to its demise – and ours with it.

In the dimness, I turned one final time to behold Preema sobbing in her parents' prayerful embrace. I thought of Emily back in England, the daughter who I would never see again; and whom I'd let down so badly. Unsure whether to curse or cry, I wrapped my arms around my head and pressed them into the seat back in front of me. Sobbing pitifully myself, there was nothing more I could do except cast myself upon the mercy of whoever this deity was that I could hear the little child and her parents behind me calling upon. If such a deity existed, then maybe – just maybe – He was a loving and forgiving one after all.

4

"Nothing can describe the confusion of thought which I felt when I sunk into the water... I was ready to burst with holding my breath, when, as I felt myself rising up, so to my immediate relief, I found my head and hands shoot out above the surface of the water. And tho' it was not two seconds of time that I could keep myself so, yet it reliev'd me greatly, gave me breath and new courage."

Robinson Crusoe

Though it lasted only seconds, it felt like an age. The thunderous jolting of the huge jet careering and cartwheeling across the waves became strangely inaudible to me. Instead, like an insanely speeded-up movie, before it came to rest every individual who'd crossed my path during the forty years I'd walked the Earth – Leanne, Emily, Willow and Anila included – flashed before my eyes. Finally, I found myself gazing in awe at a radiant figure dressed from head to toe in blinding white garments – more radiant than I'd ever seen. So this was it: the end!

And then – miracle of miracles – I was lucid again; back in the land of the living, my ears filled by the roar of the rushing water that was flooding into the cabin. I'd survived!

Neither was I alone. In the darkness and the commotion other passengers were gasping in disbelief too. Some of these survivors were already clambering for the exits; others were detaining themselves by trying to revive those crumpled members of their families who'd not been so lucky.

Hastening to make my own escape, among their horrified screams I suddenly picked out Preema's too, the little girl shaking her parents in a desperate bid to rouse them. Making out their blank stares and blooded faces in the dimness, I surmised they were both dead. Therefore, in the fleeting moment available to me to think, I fumbled for the child's seat belt buckle and hauled her kicking and screaming over the equally mangled and lifeless frame of the woman she was sat next to. However, having lost valuable seconds doing so, our escape risked being imperilled by the water that was engulfing the cabin. Amidst the fearful cries of those behind us who were already being overwhelmed, it was every man for himself!

Alas – fatally, and in their panic – other passengers had forfeited their chances of escape by prematurely inflating their life jackets; desperate acts that pinned them impotently to the roof of the cabin – its last, rapidly-vanishing pocket of air.

Having been sat just a few seats ahead of an exit door – and with Preema still wailing in my arms – I battled to force it open, elbowing aside two guys who were clawing at my shoulders to get past me. However, like a waking nightmare, in the murk and the melee my shameful triumph came at the price of losing my grip on Preema. I looked but she was gone.

Thereupon, the surging flood impelled me out of the exit door. In the instant it did I was sucked underwater and the speeded-up movie was replaying for a second time. Desperately, I fumbled with the toggle of my own life jacket. Finally, it too inflated.

Breaking the surface, I was afforded respite from my struggle. However, I was soon animated instead by the groaning and hissing of what was left of the jet slipping beneath the waves. Instinctively, I turned and swam to avoid being pulled under – desperate thrashing made more gruelling by those Timberlands laced uselessly around my ankles (and which I'd been too preoccupied during the flight to remove).

Exhausted, I eventually halted far enough away to turn about and marvel at the sheared-off rear end of the huge airliner sinking fast, its twenty-four-metre-high tail silhouetted against the starlit sky like the pectoral fin of some gigantic, submerging whale. Then, to my horror, the mighty airliner was gone – all five hundred tons of it, entombing those passengers who'd failed to escape. In the darkness and the haunting silence, all that I could make out were the small, scattered items of wreckage that I was now paddling amongst. Furthermore, the only traces of humanity to be found were odd corpses here and there that floated past among this harrowing jumble of flotsam. Alas, they would not be floating about for long: already in the distance that silence was being disturbed by frenzied thrashing in the water. The scent of blood had attracted the attention of gleeful sharks.

Though I called out in the night there was no response to my cries. It left me numb: of all the four hundred people aboard, had I really been the only one who'd gotten out alive? Surely someone else must have escaped? Yet absent too in the gloom were any of the escape chutes that were supposed to activate to form rafts when the exit doors had been opened (and which might spare me the attention of the sharks if only I could locate and clamber aboard one). I could only assume they'd been shredded by the impact; or had failed to detach and been sucked down still strapped uselessly to what was left of the aircraft.

I was alone. Surely no vengeful deity could have dreamed up so cruel and lingering a means by which a man should perish. Otherwise, if there was any succour to be had as I bobbed about in the darkness – with only a flimsy yellow life jacket to keep my head above water – it was that the sea temperature was curiously bearable. And though it might only serve to postpone my appointment with divine wrath, it did hint that, wherever I was, the stricken plane that I alone had been spewed from had perhaps not travelled as far south as I'd feared.

* * * * *

I reckoned I'd been in the water for at least an hour by the time dawn broke and I could better survey my utter desolation. The assortment of wreckage I'd swum through earlier was now nowhere to be seen. Meanwhile, with the advent of daylight the wind had picked up and the waves were rising.

During my years in Australia I'd heard surf instructors say that remaining largely motionless in the water not only helped conserve body heat but was also the posture less likely to attract sharks. That I'd avoided their attention so far I could only ascribe to the fact that, as far as I could determine, I'd sustained no cuts or injuries during my ordeal aboard the plane.

However, a few hours into that first day and the need to conserve body heat became less pressing. Instead, the sun was bearing down on me without mercy from a clear cobalt sky – an intense, blistering heat from which my only protection was to haul up the hood on my sweatshirt. No less disconcerting, cupping my hand to my eyes and searching that sky revealed nothing that might hint at impending rescue; just the pencil thin contrails streaming from a silent, high-flying jet which soon dissipated and vanished. Plainly, it wasn't looking for me.

Indeed, that solitary, high-flying passenger jet would be the only sign of human activity I would spot that day. I reasoned that it was unlikely that First Officer Mackenzie had fired off a mayday call; or given any indication of where or how the plane he'd been piloting had come to grief. Therefore, there was a distinct possibility that no one on the ground would have the faintest idea where it had been heading. To all intents and purposes, our flight had disappeared.

As I pondered all this I spotted a fleeting glimpse of a more sinister trail: the wake carved by a black triangular shape slicing briskly through the waves a short distance from me.

Then it was gone. Though I fretfully jerked my head about to survey all angles of possible attack, it too had vanished (though I had no doubt that this inquisitive observer would be back).

* * * * *

If nothing else, a day spent bobbing in the ocean afforded me the opportunity to put my life in perspective. To think, just twenty-four hours earlier I'd been strolling around a busy metropolis, looking forward to seeing my folks in England *and* taking up another exciting new job overseas. Yet here I was, countless miles from anywhere and barely clinging to life.

My dire predicament was surely a rebuke to the ambitious and acquisitive streak in my nature that had first tempted me to chase after ever more well-rewarded jobs in far-off corners of the world. After all, who needs a fancy house, or a flash car, or money in the bank, or even the favours of willing women when you can lose the lot tomorrow – along with life itself?

* * * * *

In an attempt to while away the bleak, endless hours of that first day, I endeavoured to fix my thoughts on all those seemingly banal blessings I'd once known. For example, I recalled sunny childhood afternoons playing cricket over the park with my friends, and how afterwards we would congregate on the swings to debate what we would do with our lives when we were older. I dreamt wistfully about the first time I'd kissed a girl – on those same swings, aged fourteen, when Susan Parker from across the estate had offered me a brisk peck on the lips (in the manner of a bird snatching an ear of corn) before treating me to a more leisurely one. I remembered too the first time I'd made love to a girl – aged eighteen, on my first clubbing holiday in Ibiza – some bint whose name I'd been too drunk to remember.

More ruefully, I recalled the first time I'd set eyes on Leanne – across a crowded marquee at a friend's wedding reception; as well as the day two years later when we'd exchanged marriage vows of our own – an occasion brimming with good intentions that I'd failed to live up to. It went without saying that I recalled too the idyllic moments I'd been privileged to spend with our daughter, Emily; strolling through forests or collecting shells on the beach while she shared with me the trivia of her own childhood. I looked back with fondness upon those times when I would excitedly debate the trivia of adulthood – politics, football, and fast cars – with my father over a beer or two down the local pub. Finally, I looked back with crushing yearning at the times when my mother would comfort me in her embrace as a child whenever I'd been overcome with fear – as I was now.

Forcing that fear from my mind, I fast-forwarded to the present and imagined my rescuers arriving by helicopter and discovering – to their amazement – that I was alive. More fancifully, I tried to visualise how, a few months down the line, the crash and my extraordinary escape from it – the horror of witnessing passengers being drowned or their corpses being devoured by sharks; and now the hunger and the thirst assailing me while I awaited my own imminent devouring – all this would be just a memory (albeit a harrowing and most probably indelible one). I imagined

returning home to the welcome arms of my disbelieving family –
a survivor from the loss at sea of a huge airliner from which,
incredibly, I alone had escaped.

It reminded me that if I ever did survive to tell this tale, then,
henceforth, I would conduct my life with the greater sobriety that
became such a miracle. Maybe I'd settle for more modest career
aspirations in England, where I could be a better father to Emily.
After all, what is material success or acclaim in one's career when
life itself is so tenuous and transient!

* * * * *

This hankering remembrance of happier times, allied to the
soporific effect of bobbing on the waves beneath an unrelenting
tropical sun, meant it was with quite a start that I was suddenly
roused by an abrupt nudge beneath me. Instinctively, I tore away
the hood of my sweatshirt and swung my head about in a frantic
search for the culprit.

Then I spotted it. The tell-tale swept-back fin had surfaced
some distance away. Once more it swept past within a few feet of
me. As it did so, I swivelled in the water to retain it in sight.

What a way to die! I was about to become someone's
afternoon snack! Or was this passing visitor just playing with this
strange, defenceless human he'd come across floating in the
ocean. For a second time that day, I prayed aloud with all the
earnestness of one whose time on Earth was up.

*"... Our Father, hallowed be Your Name. Your kingdom come,
Your will be done, on Earth as it is in Heaven... Give us this day
our daily bread, and forgive us our trespasses, as we forgive
those who trespass against us...."* I mouthed as best as I could
remember, all the time my eyes fixed in terror upon that chunky
black fin. *"... And deliver us from evil!"*

Suddenly, the great fish set a course directly at me. Sweeping
in at speed, a huge, gaping jaw full of razor-sharp teeth rose out
of the water. Acting upon another nugget of my surf instructor's
advice, with all my might I raised my legs and thrust one of my
Timberland boots into the creature's eye as it lunged past,
followed by a similar hefty thud from the other that struck it

square on the gills – the two spots on a shark's body where I'd been assured it was most vulnerable.

The animal thrashed before plunging beneath the waves and resurfacing some distance away. There it circled again, albeit warily. I readied myself once more, convinced I'd so pissed the thing off that this time it was in no mood for games.

Then, to my surprise, it turned and swam away, perchance to alight upon less feisty prey. Heart still thumping, I gave thanks that once again I'd been 'delivered from evil'. Even so, I wondered how much longer whoever was smiling down would indulge me – for to be awake again was to be reminded anew of the hunger and thirst gnawing at me. How much longer could I survive alone on the open ocean?

* * * * *

For a second time that day I awoke from a fitful daydream to discover that I was surrounded by circling black fins. However, unlike that earlier encounter, these jolly fellahs were more benign. It was a pod of dolphins, also curious about a human they'd come across floating alone so far out in the ocean. They too gingerly swam in closer to investigate.

Perhaps it was the maddening effects of that hot sun upon me, but I had this outlandish idea of grabbing hold of one of them to see if it might tow me nearer to land. After all, I'd heard tales about dolphins rescuing stricken sailors. However, this pod was content to circle at a distance instead, standing sentinel over me as the wind and the ocean currents took me where they willed. It was a heartening service they performed nonetheless, playfully breaking the surface to snort spray from their blowholes. So long as they were present, the sharks weren't – for again, I recalled my surf instructor sharing tales of dolphins protecting injured surfers from the depredations of sharks.

For what must have been several hours they swam alongside me – the most surreal sight imaginable on an already utterly surreal day. Then suddenly they were gone. I was alone once more as the afternoon sun began to dip

* * * * *

Dusk was at hand – the time, I'd been told, when sharks are at their most active. It looked like I would be spending a second night at sea – assuming the shark I'd affronted didn't return to wreak his revenge! What's more, in the distance dark clouds were massing. Beneath their sombrous canopy I spied the almost perpendicular threads that indicated rain. A storm was brewing. I found myself praying in earnest again.

However, at first vaguely, and then with gathering certainty, I strained to study a commotion in the distance. My ears too could discern the continuous roar of breaking waves.

I could only assume there must be some kind of reef up ahead, which accounted for both the noise and the milky white froth that disturbed the water. Then, behind the crests of those waves, I glimpsed the tops of trees swaying to-and-fro in the breeze. It was an island. And I was drifting towards it!

However, it was still some distance away. With the settings sun silhouetting it ahead of me (and that storm advancing behind me, it would be touch and go whether I would make it before darkness fell and veiled this glimmer of hope from my disbelieving eyes. Therefore, despite my enervated state, I made haste to swim for it, though knowing full well that doing so would further attract the attention of sharks. However, it was a glimmer of hope to which I simply had to cling.

Yet upon pressing closer to that frothing surf I feared that island sanctuary might yet prove beyond my grasp. As I edged closer to it, the waves began to mount with ominous violence, troughing to reveal the formidable jagged obstacle that was the offshore reef (and upon which I was about to be dashed).

However, as if to impel me ever forward, my desperate paddling was indeed attracting unwanted attention – more sharks this time. Paddling faster, at last I felt my feet brush against the first coral outcrops. With the creatures too numerous to fight in my weakened state, I knew I had to chance it.

For a second time, the bizarre fate of being flung into the sea wearing a pair of stout walking boots was to prove fortuitous, enabling my feet step onto the reef with impunity. Even so, flailing about with my hands to gain balance resulted in me nicking my fingers on it as I did. The trace of blood in the water now drew those sharks into the shallows to chance their luck too.

However, aided by the boots, I was able to clamber up on to the coral. Buffeted by the surf, I spent anxious moments balancing to prevent myself being swept back out into their waiting jaws. Then, advancing a step at a time, the sea became sufficiently shallow (and the surf sufficiently weak) to enable me to progress more assuredly towards safety. Soon I was wading on shingle. Then, at last, I was clear of the water altogether.

Trudging up the beach to rumbles of thunder and flashes of lightning over my shoulder, I tore the cumbersome and now superfluous life jacket from over my head and flopped down onto my back exhausted. Lying there in the twilight, panting heavily and gazing up at the clouds massing overhead, I gave thanks that I'd made it ashore. Even though I had not a clue where I was, the opening chapter in my epic struggle for survival – and certainly the most arduous and terrifying one – had drawn to a close.

5

*"I walk'd about on the shore, lifting up my hands,
and my whole being, wrapt up in the contemplation
of my deliverance, making a thousand gestures and
motions which I cannot describe, reflecting upon all
my comrades that were drown'd, and that there
should be not one soul sav'd but myself."*

Robinson Crusoe

I had no idea how long I'd been slumbering in the hollow in the shingle that I'd stumbled into. Too dark to go exploring when I'd landed, it had afforded little shelter from the storm, leaving me cold and wet. Who would have thought one could be at risk of hypothermia on a tropical island! However, with the advent of daybreak the sun was climbing in the sky and my clothes were drying on my body – or at least on the side that was exposed to it. Discarding my trousers to assist the process, I removed my wallet and my phone from the pockets. I switched it on, amazed to discover that the device was still working – despite its immersion in the ocean! Unsurprisingly, there was no signal to be had, so I switched it off again to conserve power. However, the battery was fully-charged. Who knew: my phone's flashlight would come in handy in emergencies.

Mercifully too, last night's torrential rain had enabled me to slake my thirst. Otherwise, my skin was coarse and reddened from the ravages of sun and saltwater. Having removed those boots that had so incongruously proved their worth, I hauled off my socks to reveal feet that were similarly shrivelled and sore. And I was hungry too – boy, was I hungry! Yet the priceless knowledge that I was alive, uninjured, and sitting up on *terra firma* tempered my eagerness to explore my new home. Instead I passed the next few minutes in contemplation of those remarkable blessings, and that – because of them – my chances of seeing my family again had improved immeasurably.

Encouragingly too, rising to my feet and gazing around me, it was as if I'd woken up in Paradise. Spread out before me was a turquoise sea that was becalmed, white surf lapping indolently over the reef in the foreground. Along with the cawing of seabirds massing above me, its hypnotic roar was the only sound to be heard. Meanwhile, aback from the shingle, a stretch of bleached white sand curved into the distance, fringed by verdant palm trees that swayed lazily in the warm breeze. However, there was no sign of fellow humanity to be seen. Once again, I found myself alone with nature – albeit in a much better place.

Strolling up the beach and into the shade of those swaying palm fronds it didn't take me long to alight upon something edible – for the floor of the forest was littered with coconuts in varying hues of ripeness. Picking one up and placing it to my ear, I shook it. It was full of juice – so I wouldn't have to rely wholly on passing rain squalls for liquid sustenance. Also present on that forest floor were land crabs – so a source of meat was to hand too. Indeed, some of those crabs were quite sizeable, though wary of this human crouching down and studying them. One or two could even be observed climbing the trees!

Neither had I ventured far before I reached a clearing in which a large, tranquil body of water spread out, tightly fringed by dense green bushes. It appeared to be some kind of shallow lagoon. However, any hopes I'd entertained that *it* might prove a source of fresh water were soon dashed: squelching through the purple-green sludge at its edge, I bent down and scooped a mouthful of water in my hand, only to discover it was brackish.

Unsure what else might be lurking in the forest, I'd taken the precaution of strapping my boots back on. This was a tropical island after all, and I had no idea what snakes – venomous or otherwise – might also inhabit it. Neither could I be entirely certain what that lagoon was home to. For example, the saltwater crocodile that lurked in the swamps of south-east Asia and northern Australia was known to cross open sea when seeking out pastures new – having thereby colonised many offshore islands. I stepped back into the forest and continued my exploration.

Returning to the beach with an armful of coconuts, an even more promising discovery was that the island was not totally unknown to human visitation. Aside from the washed-up detritus of plastic waste that had presumably drifted here by ocean current, I discovered other manufactured items that I could find a use for: a piece of rusted corrugated sheet that could form the basis of a shelter, both from the rain and that demon sun; ropes and sea-bleached wooden stakes that would enable me to fashion that sheet into a roof; discarded netting too that might enable me to snare fish inshore of that coral reef.

More importantly, they hinted that, at diverse times, other human beings had landed (and possibly domiciled) on this island. This too gave me hope that the time I would be compelled to spend here would thankfully be brief.

* * * * *

The first problem I encountered on my new island home was how to open a coconut when in possession of neither a knife nor a hammer? Unfortunately, the stones I found on the beach were neither sharp enough nor large enough to do the job. Indeed, bashing at it with the largest stone I could find barely put a dent in it. I imagined Bear Grylls never had this problem!

After several minutes of hungry human versus unyielding coconut, I decided to put the contest in abeyance and stroll along the beach in search of sharper or more sizeable rocks. It was while doing so that I would come across further, fascinating evidence of human activity on the island.

Alas, it had been a long time since this particular manmade object had partaken of the purpose for which it had been unleashed. Yet, though badly corroded by the elements, part-buried in sand, and missing its tail section, it was still recognisable as a World War Two fighter plane – a Japanese Mitsubishi Zero if my juvenile days spent gluing together *Airfix* models served me correct. Nosing around inside the cockpit revealed that smaller, more portable items like its controls and instruments had long since been pilfered. Even so, I was unable to resist the urge to clamber inside, squat down on what was left of the pilot's seat and grip the rusty stump that was the joystick.

"Banzai!" I hollered as I pushed it forward to place the Zero into an imaginary steep dive. For a one surreal and carefree moment I was that eleven-year-old model-maker again.

"Nya-a-a-a-a-r-r-r-r-r!" I screamed at the top of my voice in an impersonation of it swooping out of the sun upon some unsuspecting enemy patrol. Having selected my victim, I thumbed the imaginary trigger, juddering the stick in my hands.

"Dagga-dagga-dagga-dagga-dagga-dagga-dagga-dagga…!"

"Nya-a-a-a-a-r-r-r-r-r!" I screamed again, this time pulling back hard to climb steeply, glancing back over my shoulder at my imaginary foe spiralling to Earth in flames.

This uninhibited act of childlike regression must surely have been a sight to behold. However, for all I knew there was no one else within a hundred miles of me, so why should I care! Indeed, worryingly, I'd been uninhibitedly talking aloud to myself on my peregrinations through the forest and along the beach − posing questions and furnishing answers to them; punching the air upon solving a problem, while cursing to high heaven if I couldn't. They do say it's the first sign of madness.

Otherwise, this rusty old Zero provided salutary evidence that I probably wasn't the first person to have wound up marooned on this remote speck of sand and palm trees. Climbing back out, I spent a moment surmising the likely fate of its pilot had he survived that forced landing. How long had it been before he'd been rescued? Or rounded up and captured? Or maybe he'd succumbed to the desolation of this place and gone doolally? Like I was in the first stages of doing?

Such rumination reminded me of a weekend I'd spent on an adventure tour of the Outback not long after I'd arrived in Australia; and of sage advice the guide had imparted to us campers should we ever find ourselves lost and alone in such a wilderness. He'd told us that one of the most important factors determining who would and who wouldn't make it out alive was a positive mental attitude. Therefore, if I was to survive my time as a castaway I knew that maintaining a sense of hope would be essential. In my mind I fixed a picture of my daughter and resolved that *she* would be my hope: the reason for maintaining a positive mental attitude in the face of whatever my lonely island incarceration had yet to confront me with.

* * * * *

Armed with a couple of hefty rocks, I wandered back up the beach to where I'd gathered together the items I'd found so far. After narrowly escaping being struck on the shin by one (which ricocheted my way when I launched it at a particularly implacable coconut), I managed to crack a nut open, down the refreshing water inside, and scrape out enough white flesh to comprise my first modest meal. Even so, the experience reminded me of further sage advice the tour guide had imparted: that to survive in a remote and hostile environment it's essential to avoid injury at all costs. In a tropical climate – and with no recourse to modern medical care – even the smallest wound can quickly turn septic. And God forbid you should break a limb! Swishing my sticky fingers in the sea, I surveyed the cuts and grazes I'd acquired while clambering over the reef, hoping that the salinity of the ocean might provide some kind of anti-bacterial prophylactic. After all, seawater is good for healing wounds. Isn't it?

Once I'd eaten, I set myself to the task of fashioning that corrugated sheet into a primitive beach shelter, employing the same stone-age tools I'd used to break open and gouge out the coconuts to hammer in the wooden stakes and slice through the rope. Feeling chuffed with my first amateurish attempt at desert island D-I-Y, I duly crawled into the shade beneath it.

Once the initial relief at being out of the midday sun had passed, I mused that the *'Chez Nous'* I'd fabricated would be hard-pressed to withstand a battering by strong winds. What's more, being early March, it was still the cyclone season in the Indian Ocean (assuming that's where I was). I had vivid recollections of some of the destructive cyclones that had struck Port Hedland during my time there. Therefore, it would be wise for me to stake out a more protected location further inland where I could hopefully construct something sturdier.

* * * * *

My empty stomach was nagging me again, this time to round up one of those ubiquitous crabs I'd come across; or even nab one of those seabirds I'd spotted roosting in the bushes that ringed the lagoon. However, to make a meal of either I would first need to get a fire going – something that would be important too for alerting passing ships and planes. It duly reminded me of the second problem: how to start a fire when in possession of neither matches nor a lighter. On the plus side though, there was driftwood aplenty, both for rubbing together as sticks and for kindling. Furthermore, the husks of those discarded coconuts would provide a source of tinder to get one going.

And so I wandered back into the forest to search out my next meal. I didn't need to venture far to come across those crabs scavenging on the forest floor. Some of them were larger than a human hand and would provide a decent-sized meal if only I could catch one. However, as if telepathically aware of my intentions, they promptly scattered into the undergrowth upon spotting me. Besides, those flexing claws looked like they could do some damage.

Chary of inserting my hand inside to grab one, instead I armed myself with a piece of branch, poking and prodding to see if I could force the critters to break cover. Sure enough, I managed to draw back enough foliage to expose one. That said, the little blighter was determined he wasn't going to come quietly, his claws gaping menacing in readiness.

"Ow! You little…!" I yelled in pain and withdrew my hand, nursing the finger he'd nipped. Round One to the crab.

However, offering that branch to him as a decoy I returned to the fray, easing it inside the gape of his claw and goading him to clamp onto it. Drawing him out of his lair with his claw still gripping it, I gently laid him down on a patch of open ground. While his eyes were twitching, as if to weigh up my next move, I grabbed both claws and overpowered him.

Carrying this ten-limbed captive back to my beachside shelter, with my free hand I dug out a hole in the sand and dropped him inside. It would serve as a place of incarceration while I swung into effect the next stage of my plan: lighting the fire. Using a piece of coral scree as a knife, I gouged out a groove in one of the pieces of timber before laying it groove-side up in the sand. Then – recalling how I'd seen it done on TV – I took another stick and began to rub the end of it furiously up and down the groove. And rub. And rub. And rub. And… nothing!

I was sure Bear Grylls never had this problem either. However, after pausing to mop my brow and peer down into that prison pit – where I thought I discerned my prospective supper scoffing at my ineptness – I put my shoulder to the task of trying once more to elicit sparks from those sticks. And though I continued to rub furiously (and that smart-Alec crustacean no doubt rejoiced that he might yet live to re-join his mates in the forest), eventually through the wisps of smoke trailing from the end of the stick I spied the glow of sparks. I'd done it!

Quickly, I trailed a ball of coconut husk over the embers and tentatively blew. It took a few more puffs before that ball flared into fire. Eagerly transferring it to the kindling I'd prepared (and before it consumed the ends of my fingers!), I blew again and watched in amazement as my first attempt at primitive pyromania smoked and flickered and gave off heat. Gleefully, I peered into the pit again.

"Sorry, old chap. But I'm afraid I'm not very good at this."

Well, it was the truth. Absent a few unspeakable lapses involving daddy-longlegs when I was a small boy, I'd never butchered an animal before. And while mammals have jugulars that can be slit and birds have necks that can be wrung, how does one despatch a crab – swiftly and painlessly? I stared down at him and he stared up at me, strangely evoking pity on my part. Amidst such pathos, I pondered whether veganism wasn't a nobler philosophy than I'd credited it.

However, this was no time for squeamishness. He'd been a worthy and formidable foe, but those hunger pangs were still assailing me. Picking up a stick and coaxing him into gripping it once more, I drew him out and grabbed a claw in each hand. Taking a deep breath, I tore his limbs from his body. Then, thrusting the stick into his innards, I skewered him and held his clawless carapace over the crackling fire. I had no idea whether he was dead, nor how long it would take to cook him, but I imagined that at some point during the process of being barbequed his spirit had departed. Assuming crabs had souls, that is. I thought of Emily again – and how I might explain to her this act of savagery on my part.

* * * * *

Though what I served up was hardly *Cordon Bleu* the crab tasted good. After picking him clean of meat I crawled back under my shelter, whereupon I was confronted again with the stark reality of what had happened barely thirty-six hours earlier. As a hot afternoon gave way to my second night on the island – and having fed the fire to keep it glowing – that lowly red crab wasn't the only 'soul' the fate of which I found myself pondering.

I guess they call it survivor's guilt: wondering what on Earth I'd ever done to deserve to live when everyone else aboard that flight had perished. Assuming Rick Mackenzie *had* deliberately crashed that airliner into the sea as an act of revenge upon me, why had I been spared when – alone among my fellow passengers – I bore at least a passing responsibility for his demented rage? For what purpose was I to be incarcerated upon this dot in the middle of nowhere unless, like that crab, it was that I might reflect upon my life in readiness for a grizzlier and more lingering fate that perhaps awaited me?

And yet it was crazy to think like that. I hadn't murdered those people. My only crime was to offer momentary happiness to the desperately unhappy wife of a cruel man. Unless, of course (or so I imagined), it was for other, more grievous sins and omissions that I was being 'punished'. By now it was likely that Emily and my family feared the worst as the search operation to locate the missing flight was intensifying – yet with still no news of its whereabouts. Fearing the worst from a different perspective, I strongly suspected the authorities weren't even searching in the right place. A whole day had passed and I'd spotted neither a ship on the horizon nor a plane in the sky. I mused upon the likelihood that there might not actually be any ships or planes out there looking for me. Like that doomed flight, its sole survivor too had 'disappeared'.

6

"My thoughts were now wholly employ'd about securing my self against either savages, if any should appear, or wild beasts, if any were on the island; and I had many thoughts of the method how to do this, and what kind of dwelling to make...

"I soon found the spot I was in was not for my settlement... so I resolv'd to find a more healthy and convenient spot of ground."

Robinson Crusoe

I slept fitfully that second night, troubled by things that had never previously weighed on my mind. In particular, that little Indian girl and the intensity of her parents' prayers during those final, terrifying moments kept flitting in and out of my consciousness. Was there really a God in Heaven who judged men's 'sins'? And from whom they needed to seek forgiveness? Indeed, was there a Heaven too: somewhere beyond those stars I stared up at that was set aside for the souls of those who – like that Indian family – had placed their trust in Him while on Earth? All my adult life I'd regarded such talk as mumbo-jumbo – tales and myths put about by man-made religions to keep people in submission to man-made rules and regulations (submission which had enriched many a religious charlatan along the way!).

And yet had I too not prayed during those moments of seeming finality aboard that plane and then adrift at sea, when I'd feared the time had come for *me* to discover the truth? If so, who had I prayed to? Was it just a vestigial reflex that had impelled me to implore some divine object that – unlike those billions of stars – had no basis in empirical reality? Besides, despite my godlessness, did I too not ascribe to a set of (admittedly more pliable) moral 'rules and regulations' – do not kill, do not steal, do not bear false witness (if thou can help it!), do not covet thy neighbour's wife (likewise)? If so, then why, when I was just another evolving organism – a link in the food chain whose purpose on this Earth (like that crab) was to feed his face and satisfy his lusts before he too fell victim to another organism higher up the chain? Were those 'rules and regulations' also just an evolutionary response to the imperative of bringing order to otherwise chaotic and selfish human society?

Though there were more practical matters I needed to attend to on that second day – surveying the island to identify things to feed into my face (as well as a spot that would afford better protection from the elements and from creatures in the food chain that might feed me into theirs) – I continued to mull over these things. I was once more talking aloud – though assuring myself that I wasn't really addressing that imaginary divine object.

* * * * *

It hadn't only been that Japanese pilot who fate had drawn to this place. Rounding the island's southernmost tip, I stumbled upon some graves in the shade of a palm grove set back from the beach. From the inscriptions carved on the weathered crosses that marked them they appeared to belong to sailors from a German warship that had foundered here during the opening months of the First World War – a long, long way from the Fatherland.

Venturing a little further along the shingle berms, nearby I came across something even more extraordinary: a railway! Granted, it was only a short section of narrow-gauge track that lay mostly buried beneath sand and shingle (and which had corroded badly in the places where it was exposed). Leading up from the water's edge I followed its course inland to where it terminated in a clearing in those coconut groves. It was here that I found one of the wagon trolleys that had once been hauled along it. Here too – among the detritus of that long since abandoned railhead – I came across a truly useful implement. It was an adze: a small hammer with a rusty pick head on one side that had presumably been used for the maintenance of the track. It would come in very handy for a variety of tasks – not least breaking open coconuts. Locating one, I treated myself to a demonstration of its efficacy. No more pounding at the things with rocks.

I imagined that, at some point, the railway had probably been used to harvest and export those coconuts – of which there was an obvious abundance. Even so, it must have been a fraught enterprise. If there had once been a jetty at the seaward end of the track it had long since been reclaimed by the surf. Meanwhile, the reef that appeared to encircle the island would have made transferring cargo between beach and ship extremely hazardous. Maybe it was for this reason that the operation had many years ago been abandoned; and why – likewise unable to reliably resupply a population ashore – the evidence pointed to only transient human settlement of the island.

Continuing around the foreland I passed through a narrow strip of forest where it was possible to glimpse both the sea and the lagoon at the same time. Brushing against the foliage I noticed the seeds of the trees here adhering to my T-shirt. Unless I was mistaken, they were Pisonias – the legendary catchbird trees I'd seen in the rain forests of Queensland (so named because those seeds adhered to birds' feathers too, the better to aid their dispersal; lethally on occasions, when so many would cling to its feathers that the poor creature would be unable to fly). What's more, there were certainly plenty of birds nesting in the trees – including large, comical-looking seabirds that boasted garish red feet. Catch one of those, I pondered, and I'd be able to feast like a king for the rest of the day.

Otherwise, the density of the forest eventually drove me back onto the beach, which on this side of the island was wide and comprised mostly white, powdery sand (in contrast to the shingle and rough clinker where I'd come ashore). Being the leeward side too, it was here that I came across evidence of further settlement in the shape of two long houses on the fringe of the forest – *ataps* of the kind I'd seen elsewhere on my travels in South-East Asia. They too had long since been abandoned to the elements. There was evidence too that wells had been sunk, though they'd long since silted up. Furthermore, the offshore reef was narrower at this point and the surf shallower – all of which suggested here would probably have been the preferred spot for any attempt at a seaborne landing on the island.

It was here too that I discovered further evidence of its use in wartime. Progressing northwards, I spotted several rusting bombs and artillery shells aback from the beach. Glancing over them, I had no way of knowing why they'd been dumped here, nor whether they'd been safely defused. Suffice to say, my curiosity didn't extend to tinkering with one to find out.

By the time to sun had reached its apogee I'd been walking for what felt like miles. Pressing on further, I rounded the northernmost tip of the island and headed back along the eastern shoreline. In all that time I'd noted that nowhere on the island rose higher than the brow of the beach. There was no mountain fastness here atop which I could light a fire to alert passing ships; nor any caves into which I could retreat to escape passing cyclones.

I returned to my corrugated beach shelter in possession of the collection of items that I'd come across – including plastic pop bottles washed up along the shore in which I could collect rainwater. I'd also found a large 40-litre plastic container that (from what I could discern from its faded label) had been used to transport hydrochloric acid! It set me thinking: last night I'd spotted the more adventurous of those forest-dwelling crabs venturing onto the beach as dusk had closed in (presumably to scavenge for a more varied diet). I reasoned that if I sliced off the neck of this container and buried what remained in the sand, then, by dropping the scraps from my last meal inside, it would make an excellent crab trap. What's more, it would be a less risky way of catching them than probing the undergrowth, where venomous snakes might also lurk. I returned to the forest to nab a crab before rekindling the fire.

Dining on crabmeat and coconuts for a second evening, thereafter I baited my trap with a morsel left over from the one I'd apprehended. Speculate to accumulate, if you like. As I sat there watching darkness draw in, I kept an eye cocked to see if it might lure an unsuspecting crustacean. Otherwise, I decided that tomorrow I would decamp to the leeward side of the island, taking my newfound possessions with me – the crab trap (if it worked); my collection of plastic bottles; and the most amazing find of all – that adze that I couldn't resist playing with. With me too would come the only possessions I'd arrived on the island with – my boots; my hoodie; my wallet containing a superfluous wad of Australian dollar notes (as well as an equally superfluous collection of credit cards that could avail me nothing in this place that modern civilisation had forgotten). Oh, and my mobile phone too. I switched it on for a moment to check that it was still working (which it was, though again there was no signal to be had). More pertinently though, on it was stored an album of photographs I'd taken of Emily during the holiday she'd spent with me Down Under. In that lonely twilight setting of fricative sea and crackling fire – and with pangs of survivor's guilt once more gnawing at me – thumbing through it reminded me anew of why it was imperative that I remain focussed on staying strong and getting off this place.

* * * * *

Day three on the island and my decision to shift location was vindicated. Overnight, the wind had gotten up and a monsoon had deluged the beach, pummelling the corrugated sheet and flooding the trench I'd scraped out. However, with the sun once more drying my clothes, I examined my crab trap to discover that it had worked beyond my wildest imagination. For there, imprisoned at the bottom of that container was the largest crab I'd ever seen. Its body alone was the size of a dinner plate. As my shadow drew over it, like a prize-fighter its guard was up – two humungous claws that looked more than capable of crushing bones.

It was one of those legendary coconut crabs that I'd heard about during my rain forest trek in Queensland – so-called because those claws are more than capable of prising them open. Also known as robber crabs, they are fearless scavengers that will carry off anything they come across (including birds and other crabs). Overpowering this guy was therefore going to be a job for my adze – the claw of which made deft, if unsavoury work of despatching him. Once I'd got the fire going he became breakfast – and a very filling one at that!

Packing up and setting off shortly thereafter, I made my way to the far side of the island by first travelling north along the eastern shoreline. Clambering up the dunes there was evidence that the lagoon had once been open to the sea at this point – one more lesson in how, over time, tropical cyclones possessed the power to shift and shape the low-lying islands that stood in their paths.

It was while approaching the northern shore that I spotted a silver-grey object washing back and forth in the foreshore. Downing my chattel, I waded in to discover that it was all that remained of a floatation raft of some sort. Then it clicked: it was one of those escape chutes from the A380, which must have snagged on the reef. Remarkably, it was the only piece of wreckage from the plane that I'd yet come across (though other items must have spread far and wide on the currents). Was it too fanciful to imagine that someone might have made it onto the shore aboard it? However, though I called out into the forest aback from where it had washed up there was no response.

Meanwhile, the pounding swell along this rugged seaboard reminded me how fortunate I'd been to have gotten ashore at all. And to think: had I heeded Anila and discarded my Timberlands in favour of a pair of flimsy flight slippers I might never have made it, the soles of my feet – like that escape chute – ripped to shreds by the deadly reef that would reveal itself at low tide.

* * * * *

The image of Anila that I'd fixed in my mind had disturbed another night of fitful sleep. Ruminating upon the searching conversation we'd partaken of brought home to me just what mental torture a lack of human company was going to be (notwithstanding that I was a loner by temperament – as Leanne had often chided me resentfully). In this vein, I was talking to myself again – pouring out my soul in the hope that someone, somewhere might be listening. Jean-Paul Sartre had once insisted that 'hell is other people' (or, as he'd most likely meant, 'hell is the wrong sort of other people'). Yet it didn't lessen an awareness that once the challenge of constructing my new abode was complete (and I'd slipped instead into a routine of snaring crabs and harvesting coconuts), I would have time in abundance on my hands with which to ponder the meaning of life – yet without anyone to whom I might pour out my deliberations. For days and weeks to come (and quite possibly months and years!) there would be just me, myself and I. The thought left me cold.

"Couldn't you have washed up on this island just one more survivor from the flight? Just one more!" I pleaded aloud to the ineluctable deity who'd stranded me on this pinprick in the ocean.

If it really was omniscient, then it must be aware too who I had in mind. For though I knew we would have made an unlikely couple – the sophisticated lady and the rough diamond – I knew there were going to be lonely nights when I would find myself fantasising about her fabulous figure, her gorgeous silky hair, her alluring smile, and those avid, probing eyes.

"We could have been so good for each other, Anila – you and me. We could have been Romeo and Juliet; Beauty and the Beast; Bogart and Hepburn; King Kong and Fay Wray!" I called out absurdly, as if she really was staring down at me from a place where her soul might have found repose – and with hankering eyes and a concurring grin.

Then again, no, I gestured Heaven dismissively, as if swatting away a troublesome fly. What's to say that, cooped up on this barren pinnacle of sand, Miss Patel and I wouldn't have sooner or later ended up squabbling and hurling names at each other – like Leanne and I had? Either way, it was not to be. Instead – like Christ's Last Supper – those blissful few hours we'd passed in each other's company, recounting the twists and turns in our lives that had led to us boarding that fateful flight, had transpired to be the calm before the storm. For me, that storm had unfolded as a truly life-changing event; alas, for Anila, a life-extinguishing one.

* * * * *

Rather than attempt to repair the roof and sides of those large *ataps*, instead I cannibalised what remained of them to build a shelter more becoming of a man by himself. By sinking some of the timbers into the sand (digging out the foundations with my adze and hammering them in with rocks), I was able to raise the platform I'd constructed about a metre off the ground to protect me from snakes and other creepy-crawlies. Its canopy I thatched from palm fronds underlaid with a slither I'd cut from that waterproof escape chute. Inside, it was just large enough for me to sit up and to bed down (a few more palm fronds standing in as a mattress). If you like, it was a miniature version of an *atap*.

There was even enough chute and rope left over to string a hammock between two adjacent trees for use during the day. Though it had taken me the best part of the day to knock it all together, I was quite proud of my achievement. Furthermore, I'd come across an old rusting oil drum which (judging by the puncture marks around its base and the scorching inside) had once been used as a brazier. Rolling it into position nearby, it would play host to my camp fire.

I'd sited my new abode in a coconut grove aback from the beach, where it would afford me both shade from the midday sun and yet a reasonably uninterrupted sea view – in case a ship or a plane perchance passed by. However, today – like yesterday and the day before – both the horizon and the sky above had been devoid of either. Yet surely the search teams must have some idea where my flight had gone down. So why was no one looking for it here? In this day-and-age of sophisticated radar tracking and constant satellite communication I refused to believe such a huge modern aircraft could have simply disappeared.

My anxieties flitted from the sublime to the ridiculous: as well as search vessels on the horizon and rescue planes overhead, I made a mental note to keep an eye on the treetops too. I'd read somewhere that dozens of people each year are killed by falling coconuts. Some of the heftier ones I'd gathered up were the size of footballs; and the trees they'd fallen from over fifteen metres tall! I knew Australian beach resorts had taken to pre-emptively de-fruiting their palm trees just to be on the safe side. Perhaps tomorrow I would attempt to shin up mine and do likewise.

With another luckless crab caught, cooked, and consumed, I decided to try out my new hammock before retiring for the night. Lazily rocking myself while savouring an enchanting persimmon-tinted sunset (another joy of dwelling on this side of the island), once darkness had fallen I again had time on my hands to interrogate this deity I'd been muttering to. Once more, I challenged it to explain why I was the only person who'd lived to tell the tale (assuming it existed; and that I ever made it off this island to do the telling).

"There must have been hundreds of passengers aboard that flight who lived better lives that me," I petitioned it aloud, "And who ought to have at least merited a token acknowledgement on your part of their faith and their goodness. So why did you not answer their prayers? Why did you not spare them?"

Maybe the old saying about the 'good dying young' rang true. In which case, I sneered, maybe this deity had determined that I should live to be a hundred; and spend the next sixty years of that lonely life slowly going mad in this place!

"Look, I understand if you think I'm just a miserable shit who doesn't deserve to be shown mercy. I understand if you want to make me suffer for destroying my marriage and leaving Emily behind in England. But why banish me to this remote place? All you've achieved is to separate an eight-year-old child from her father – a child who, at this moment, is probably distraught over his death. Can't you see: You're punishing her, not just me!" I raged tearfully. "So answer me this: if it's true what they say about you – that 'God is love' – then what kind of 'loving God' are you that you would make my daughter suffer in that way?"

There was no reply. I'd been foolish to believe there would be. The supposed 'God of love' – like the moon and the constellations above me – was deaf to my despair. All was silent apart from the distant crashing of the surf.

"Of course, if you do exist, it would be nice if you introduced yourself!" I grunted in a further parting sneer.

Again, there was no reply. Otherwise, I feared there would be many more such nights like this to come – lonely twilight hours when I could reflect upon just what a wretched shit I was.

7

*"It happen'd one day about noon… I was
exceedingly surpriz'd with the print of a man's
naked foot on the shore, which was very plain to be
seen in the sand. I stood like one thunderstruck; or
as if I had seen an apparition."*

Robinson Crusoe

I slept better in my new and more permanent shelter – despite that sleep being disturbed by another overnight storm. Therefore, after breakfast, I decided to explore the island again, this time its northern reaches. Off I set, attired in my boots, my T-shirt, and my tanga briefs – three of the only five garments I possessed. Not that I anticipated requiring more formal dress. It was obvious by now that the island was uninhabited. Today, I was going to have a go at catching a bird to supplement my meagre diet of crabs and coconuts, scheming as I walked about how I would do this.

Indeed, were it not for the diet and the loneliness, I could get use to my new home. With its wide blue skies, warm breeze, pristine beaches, and the total absence of cars, bars and other raucous intrusions of noisy civilisation, in any other context this place would be the kind of sleepy exotic retreat that people would pay good money to jet away to. Once more I fantasised about Anila; strolling along its bleached white sands, hand-in-hand with her – both of us naked as the day we'd been born – pausing only occasionally to make passionate and unhurried love.

"Dream on, Smithy!" I sang wearily to the azure sky above.

Otherwise, the scorching tropical sun reminded me that my clothes were not a wholly superfluous intrusion, despite having taken to discarding them completely when pottering about my camp. What's more, after further walking and daydreaming I was to find they might be required for reasons of modesty after all. For there, stretching in a line from the forest to the water's edge and back again were fresh human footprints. My God, I was not alone in this place after all!

I stared up and scanned the tree line. There was no one to be seen. As I trotted gingerly up the beach in pursuit of the trail, my delight turned to intrigue upon examining those footprints more closely. Halting and planting a Timberland alongside one it was apparent that whoever this unexpected barefoot companion was, he possessed smaller feet that me. Considerably smaller, in fact – like a child's.

Recommencing my investigation, I arrived at the treeline, where the trail disappeared into the forest and became harder to follow. A troubling thought then occurred to me: what if, rather than a child, those prints belonged to a pygmy adult. I'd read somewhere about a small, coral-fringed island in the Andaman Sea that was inhabited by stone-age aborigines – a fierce, xenophobic tribe that had defied all attempts at ending their isolation from the rest of humanity (and who had dealt murderously with visitations by outsiders, intentional or otherwise). Perhaps I'd been wise not to call out and announce my presence to whoever had deposited those prints.

Gazing about the sun-dappled glade, my adze gripped tightly in my hand, for a tense moment I was unsure whether I'd landed in paradise after all. And yet how to explain all those other finds on the island that pointed to periodic occupation by outsiders? How to explain that, despite three days spent wandering its length and breadth (frequently chortling at the top of my voice) I'd encountered not a single human being – much less a band of irate natives chasing after me with bows and arrows?

My intrigue deepened. I pressed into the forest to follow those footprints as best I could, eventually to discover that they terminated in a clearing, where a small green pod sat camouflaged in the undergrowth. Like some curious time capsule that H G Wells might have dreamed up, this pod not only had a door but windows too – small glass portholes that were even so opaque with grime. I tiptoed over one of the guy wires that anchored the pod to the forest floor and peered through one.

It was a toss-up who was more freaked by whom: me upon being confronted by a startled brown face; or that brown face upon suddenly being confronted by a startled white one. We both flinched and drew away from our respective sides of the glass.

Stumbling onto my haunches – and with my adze at the ready – I caught my breath and scanned the forest in case the sudden commotion had alerted its companions. Satisfied there was no one about, I tiptoed up to the door, upon which was affixed a small label that bore the baroque inscription: *'Property of the Australian Government – Director of National Parks. Permitted dwelling under the terms of the Environment Protection and Biodiversity Conservation Act 1999'*. More intrigued than ever, I twisted the handle and pulled the door open.

There inside, huddled in the foetal position beneath the window, was a little girl who was dressed in flowery leg-ins and a bright tangerine-coloured top, its short frilly sleeves exposing a pair of match-like brown arms. As I stooped and curled my head inside, the diminutive figure whimpered and pressed herself tighter against the off-white fibre-glass walls of this pokey little bubble, clutching at something she was concealing from me.

"It's alright. I'm not going to hurt you," I insisted, placing my adze down and crouching alongside the child to dispel any suggestion of hostile intent. Gently I ran my newly-free right hand along her bony little shoulder.

"Look, I'm sorry if I startled you just then. You see, I came ashore a few days ago," I continued, unsure whether addressing her in English was the best way to make myself understood.

That said, a soft smile is a soft smile in any language and so I offered her one of those instead. In response, she glanced up at me through a pair of frightened eyes before concluding that I indeed presented no threat. Tentatively, she offered me a timid smile of her own.

"I apologise, sir – for stealing your things," she snivelled.

I was amazed: the girl spoke English! What's more, her cherubic little face was familiar.

"Steal? My things? But they're not… Hang about! I recognise you!" I then ventured in surprise.

The little girl swallowed nervously and realised that my face too was familiar – despite three days and nights of unshaved stubble and a windswept suntan.

"It is, sir. I remember you. You said I had a pretty name." she reminded me, those cute brown eyes that had been screwed up in terror, then doleful with remorse, now widening with relief.

"Preema?" I ventured again, expelling breath.

Beyond that, words truly did fail me. How on Earth had this delicate little child managed to escape the plane; then survive a perilous crossing of shark-infested ocean; and finally traverse that treacherous reef to make it ashore to safety? And, to cap it all, to then stumble upon a wildlife ranger's cabin that, from an initial glance around, I could see was stocked with sufficient provisions to tide her over until the said ranger returned to discover that a brown-skinned Goldilocks had been snaffling his food, sitting in his chair, and sleeping on his camp bed!

Though cursing under my breath that I hadn't stumbled upon this Aladdin's cave full of bounty before I'd gone to the trouble of constructing my shelter, it soon became apparent that this stuffy, claustrophobic little pod was only ever intended for emergency use – presumably in the event that a sudden change in the weather or the sea state rendered it too dangerous to cast off from the island. Examining the items Preema had eaten and discarded – a packet of Arnott's arrowroot biscuits and a can of SPC fruit salad in juice (for which she'd managed to work the can opener) – her diet appeared to be hardly more varied than mine. Thankfully, she hadn't attempted to light the small camping gas stove and risk blowing both herself and the pod to kingdom come.

Rummaging further, I opened and perused the ranger's log book, which I found on a shelf next to some other books, which – as well as an illustrated guide to the plants and wildlife of Indian Ocean islands – included a collection of dog-eared paperback novels with which to pass the boredom of being holed up in this plastic hovel. Friday, February 21st 2014 read the last entry he'd penned in it – over a fortnight ago; and prior to that Thursday, September 5th 2013.

It was interesting too to learn that this island had a name and that it had been designated a 'national park'. Not that I could say I'd ever heard of it. Indeed, leafing through the pages it appeared that the ranger made only infrequent visits here – mostly to undertake observations of the flora and fauna. In addition – and precisely because it was a protected wildlife habitat – another document I perused informed me that *'landings on the island are prohibited without the express permission of the Director of National Parks, Parks Australia, GPO Box 787, Canberra, ACT 2061'*. So while it was supremely encouraging to learn that Preema and I would be rescued at some point, it was less so to be informed that we might be in for a long wait.

"Phew! It's hot in here," I puffed, placing the log book back on the shelf – for despite being in the shade the pod was dank, stifling and humid. "So is this where you've spent the last three days?" I quizzed her.

"Yes, sir. I have," she nodded, as if ashamed.

Otherwise, snuffling again and reverting to her diffident taciturnity, I sensed she was not going to volunteer me any details of how, when or where she'd turned up on the island. Then again, what child in her situation wouldn't abjure conversation! After all, she'd witnessed a truly terrifying air crash that had claimed the lives of both her parents; and then endured days and nights of further terror at sea, which (if anything like my own experience) must have been traumatic in the extreme for such a helpless and uncomprehending youngster.

"So how did you manage to get here?" I probed even so. "I thought I was the only person who'd escaped that plane alive."

In response, she offered me those same melancholic eyes. Maybe that revelation would have to wait. For now, it was sufficient that I gain her trust and assure her that the worst of her ordeal was over. Instead I rose to my feet and rummaged for things that would be of use to us while we sat out our stay: there was a wind-up torch that worked; a first-aid kit containing bandages, plasters, scissors, and rudimentary medicines and ointments, as well as sunblock; there were screwdrivers and a pair of pliers. There was even a wind-up transistor radio which, when tuned-in, picked up a static-laden broadcast of Pharrell Williams' *'Happy'*. Grinning and dancing my head from side to side to the beat, I elicited a grudging smile from my audience of one.

Alas, absent from this treasure trove was another sort of radio – a short-wave two-way set that might have enabled me to make contact with someone. However – along with as much of the food and bottled water as I could carry – I scooped these items into a shoulder bag I unearthed in another cupboard. However, it was when I at last stretched out my hand to bid Preema join me that I was to discover the most prized find of all.

All the while I'd been interrogating her and then raiding the larder – and especially when I'd first appeared at the door balefully wielding my adze – I'd had this nagging suspicion that she was hiding an object of some sort from me. Sure enough, as she too rose to her feet it became apparent what it was. In her hand she revealed a weapon of her own that she'd discovered here – a hefty, razor-sharp eighteen-inch machete!

"Bloody hell, Preema!" I gasped in shock, "You weren't really intending to slice my skull open with that thing, were you!"

For one mind-blowing moment I suspected she was – although she again struggled to articulate an answer.

"N-n-n-o, sir," she stuttered apologetically. "It's… it's to… to protect m-m-me… from the m-m-monster."

I must have shot her a suitably incredulous glare.

"The monster? What kind of monster? Do you mean a crocodile?" I gulped, alarmed that she was about to confirm that there was indeed a giant saltie lurking in that lagoon.

"No, sir. It is not a crocodile. This monster lives in the forest and comes out at night. It can climb trees too. I have seen it."

Who could say what terrors this poor child must have been tormented by, even once she'd survived her daunting journey to arrive here. Besides, with all those crabs combing the forest floor night time must have been unbearably spooky for a small child, alone by herself, and whose only sanctuary from those terrors was this miniscule fibre-glass bubble.

"Come on, Preema. Come with me and you can sit round a nice glowing fire; and eat something a bit more filling. You won't be on your own any more either. Instead you'll have me to protect you from 'the monster'," I beamed, though trying not to make light of her phobias. "And who knows: in a few days' time the man to whom this place belongs will come back in his boat to take us home."

"Will he be angry with me, sir: this man? For stealing his food?" she pleaded, still clutching that machete.

"No, Preema. I don't think he'll mind that you ate his biscuits!" I shook my head, touched by her innocence.

Otherwise, the hand of mine that was still beckoning I used to urge her to hand the machete to me to place inside the bag: one more valuable tool that I could find a use for.

However, before accompanying me she sauntered over to the ranger's bed and delved beneath the pillow, pulling out the only other possession she'd brought with her to the island (aside from the clothes she was standing up in): the hoodie I'd seen her don aboard the plane (and which, ironically given the sweltering ambient heat, was emblazoned with an image from that new Walt Disney movie 'Frozen'). Oh, and the pair of spectacles I remembered her stowing in the pocket of the hoodie. Curling them over her ears, she bodged them up her cute ball nose, tied the hoodie around her hips, and slipped her little paw in mine.

Closing the door of the survival pod behind us, Preema and I made our way to the beach, whereupon I paused to make a mental note of this spot (for I'd determined that the pod would serve instead as a storehouse for the remaining provisions that we were unable to carry). As I strolled back along those bleached white sands to my encampment – seeking to engage my new companion in reassuring small talk on the way – all the time I was attempting to get my head around how bizarre it was to be doing so hand-in-hand with a beautiful Indian after all (albeit most emphatically not the one I'd been fantasising about!).

* * * * *

If my tale of survival against the odds was nothing short of miraculous, then Preema Patel's was truly epic. Though she had no recollection of how she'd been spewed out through the exit door of what was left of the tail section of that airliner, incredibly she'd retained the presence of mind to pull the toggle on her life jacket once she had. Then, while splashing about in the darkness, she'd been bumped by one of those inflated escape chutes, managing to haul herself aboard and cling to it. Only by this nugget of good fortune had she been able to avoid encounters with the sharks that she too had witnessed circling her during the days and nights that followed.

Eventually – after drifting at sea exhausted, sunburned, half-starved, and badly-dehydrated – she'd washed up on the northern shore of the island, the chute having somehow been buffeted through the reef. Hence the shredded remains of the thing that I'd come across yesterday.

Furthermore, she explained how, in like manner to my first night ashore, she too had quenched an intolerable thirst by using her tiny hands to funnel as much of that rainstorm into her mouth as she could. The following day – dazed and bewildered – she'd chanced upon the survival pod. Like me too (though I was loathed to admit it), all this time she'd kept her spirits up by 'praying to God' that He would keep her alive in the face of such extreme adversity – albeit (and having finally managed to coax the full story out of her) she seemed to possess a bit more faith in who she'd been praying too.

As a reward for her candour and a salute to her fortitude, I served her a hearty meal of crabmeat and coconuts, which she wolfed down, thanking me with quaint and deferential politeness. We also treated ourselves to a can of SPC 'Aussie-made' baked beans heated up over the brazier (I'd decided to leave the Vegemite behind in the pod in the event of more desperate times. Hopefully, we would be long gone from the island before we were reduced to scooping at this foul stuff with our fingers!).

We chatted a while longer after the sun had gone down. Somnolence beckoning, I then chivalrously donated my palm-thatched shelter for Preema to sleep in while I nestled in the hammock instead. With plenty of timber left over from the demolished *ataps* and a wealth of tools now to hand with which to construct another one, hopefully the rain would hold off tonight and I could complete the task tomorrow.

Soon enough, a soft snoring emanating from within the shelter signalled that Preema was sleeping the slumber of the saved. Though the surprise discovery that I'd been blessed with a mate for the duration of my stay was without doubt a fillip to morale, it also left me a tad uneasy. While I rejoiced that this unseen deity had spared this cute and deserving innocent from among the passengers aboard my flight, I still mourned that a different Patel of the feminine gender had not been spared as well. Did this deity perchance possess a sense of humour? Was it perhaps trying to tell me something – for it was impossible to behold this comically sweet eight-year-old girl and not be reminded of another, lighter-skinned eight-year-old girl back in England?

Otherwise, I tried to visualise what other challenges her presence would throw up? Not the least was the cultural one. Sure, it was fortunate that she spoke excellent English. However, she was Indian and spoke it with a pronounced and endearing lilt. Even were she not a child, I knew there were going to be times when we would each find ourselves glancing at the other with either amazement or incomprehension.

It was fortunate too that she was of an age when children no longer require constant supervision lest incorrigible curiosity lead them into naive (and possibly fatal) mischief. Indeed, as I remembered her father exulting, Preema gave the impression of being a remarkably bright and personable child – notwithstanding that lingering wariness on her part about opening up to a stranger. I guess I would have to keep probing with small talk, patiently coaxing her to offer further insights into who she was and how she'd come to be aboard that flight.

Set against all this was the fact that she obviously lacked the physical strength to do other than fetch or carry small items; and certainly not the brawn and stamina required to hunt and bring down an animal for food. Neither would she possess the maturity with which to conduct profound conversations about life and love. Regrettably – unlike an older, curvier, and more astute Patel aboard that flight – there was no prospect of me being able to reflect in any meaningful or intimate way upon the wonders and pitfalls of human sexuality!

Talking of which, kids grow up fast nowadays (or so Leanne was always waxing rueful). And although at present Preema was only a skinny little lass with a flat chest, before she knew it puberty would be upon her – and with that, periods. My God (I really did beseech the Almighty in earnest that night): please don't let me be the one who has to explain to her about periods (a task that, apropos the other eight-year-old-going-on-sixteen girl in my life, I was more than willing to delegate to my ex-wife)! It was another good reason to hope that we would be rescued from this island sooner rather than later.

However, on that score the news was more depressing. With bantling snores still drifting from that shelter, I reached down and grabbed the wind-up radio, cranking the handle as stealthily as I could so as not to wake the slumbering newcomer. Lowering the volume, I pressed it to my ear. Twiddling with the tuning dial, I flitted across the stations before finally alighting upon an English language news channel.

> *"... At his press conference today, the premier of Western Australia, Colin Barnett, said Troy Buswell had resigned following the accident involving his ministerial car. However, he further announced that his treasurer and transport minister – who is no stranger to scandal and controversy – had been admitted to hospital several weeks earlier following a mental breakdown..."*

The signal reception was far from ideal. I stood to my feet and drifted onto the beach to see if moving away from the trees would improve it. I could also turn up the volume.

> *"... In other news, the hunt for the missing Airbus A380 is continuing. Naval and air forces from several nations have announced they are stepping up their search of the South China Sea following reports of wreckage being spotted off the Spratly Islands..."*

The South China Sea? There were no Australian national parks in the South China Sea, I raged aloud. Why on Earth were they looking for it there?

> *"... Radio contact with the flight – which was heading from Perth to London with three-hundred-and eighty-passengers aboard – was lost in the early hours of Friday morning shortly after it departed*

Singapore. The airliner then conducted a series of bizarre manoeuvres over the Andaman Sea before setting an easterly course towards Thailand, upon which radar contact was mysteriously lost..."

"Easterly? But we flew south!" I slapped my brow in despair. No wonder there had been neither sight nor sound of planes or ships scouring this particular corner of the Indian Ocean. How could the authorities have got it so wrong?

"... Greg Isherwood, an aviation expert, told ABC News Radio that it was possible that someone – not discounting a member of the flight crew – may have switched off or disabled the plane's ACARS system, the means by which modern commercial aircraft transmit automated updates to air traffic controllers. If so, then it would explain why the ACARS satellites were unable to track the flight..."

Could it get any worse? In his utter wickedness, Rick Mackenzie had made doubly sure that no one would ever find what was left of the plane after he'd crashed it. For the longer the actual location where it had gone down went unsearched, the more likely it was that the wreckage from it would either sink or be dispersed far and wide by powerful ocean currents.

"... Meanwhile, in a statement put out today, a Chinese government spokesman categorically denied that his country's armed forces had shot down the airliner for intruding into what China claims to be its airspace. The Spratly Islands are a cluster of largely uninhabited atolls, ownership of which is also claimed by Vietnam, the Philippines and Malaysia. Of late, tensions have been running high in the area following China's decision to construct a naval base on one of the atolls..."

I was on the verge of dashing the radio on the rocks in frustration. However, it was not just the senseless folly of doing so that arrested my hand. I caught the presenter breaking an equally shocking piece of news.

> *"... Finally, police in Western Australia have confirmed tonight that the naked body of a woman that was recovered from Fremantle harbour on Sunday is that of missing social worker, Willow Mackenzie. Thirty-three-year-old Mrs Mackenzie, who was last seen leaving her home in the Swanbourne district of Perth on Thursday night, is the wife of Richard Mackenzie – who was a member of the flight crew aboard that missing airliner. A police spokesman refused to rule out the possibility that the two incidents might be connected..."*

My blood ran cold. Whatever clues the police in Perth were piecing together at that moment, my worst fears about Willow's fate were all but confirmed: she'd almost certainly been murdered in a fit of jealousy by her deranged husband, who had then dumped her body before embarking on his suicide mission.

Switching the radio off, I drifted back to my hammock. I might indeed be in for a long wait to be rescued. The only consolation was that at least I would no longer have to wait alone. Wondering what the coming days, weeks – or even months – might hold, I peered inside the shelter at Preema, who was sleeping peacefully. In the soft glow of the fire, I gently ran my fingers through her unruly black mop, sweeping a lock of it from her face.

"I guess it's just you and me then, kid," I whispered resignedly. "Let's hope we can make this work, eh."

8

> *"Here was an undoubted testimony: that there was*
> *scarce any condition in the world so miserable, but*
> *that there was something positive to be thankful for*
> *in it… that we may always find in it something to*
> *comfort our selves from, and to set in the description*
> *of good and evil, on the credit side of the accounts."*

Robinson Crusoe

Sex with Miss Patel: it was what I'd been lusting for. Now, as we halted on the beach and I ran my hands along her bare, tawny shoulders, she glanced up at me with guilt-laden eyes. Reticent at first, even so she permitted me to draw her in and kiss her and to reach my hand down to fondle her…

Drat! My dozing dream about Anila was abruptly shattered by a frenetic scream filling my ears. Leaping from my hammock, I dived into my boots and raced into the forest to where – the afternoon before, and for reasons of privacy and hygiene – I'd set aside a spot where Preema could do her toileting. From the sound of her high-pitched squeals I feared my complacency about incorrigible curiosity leading the youngster into mischief was about to be proved ill-judged.

"Preema! What is it?" I cried upon spotting her standing there rooted to the spot – chewing the fingers of her one hand and nervously pointing to something with the other.

"The monster! The m-m-monster!" she quivered in terror.

I turned and nearly fainted myself. For there, spread around the base of a lofty palm tree was the most humungous crustacean I had ever seen. If the coconut crab I'd trapped the other day was large, then this one was truly gargantuan. With a carapace the size of a dustbin lid and a limb span that was wider than mine, it was in the process of legging it up the tree – for these otherwise shy creatures were rightly wary of humans (who'd hunted them to the verge of extinction on many tropical islands).

"It's alright, Preema, it won't hurt you," I insisted, squatting and hugging her tight.

"It's the m-m-monster I told you about yesterday," she sobbed.

"I'll grant you, it is rather a big one!" I conceded with some understatement, slipping free of her tugging at me and striding over to examine it.

With claws larger than my hands I was loathed to provoke it into employing them in anger, notwithstanding that the meat on it could keep us fed for a whole week. Instead, I kept a wary distance and permitted it to slowly haul itself up the tree.

"It is the same one. I am sure it is, sir. It comes out at night. It must have followed us here," Preema charged with fanciful innocence, hesitantly venturing to join me observing the crab clamber out of reach.

"I doubt it. It's probably a different one. But you're right: they seem to prefer scavenging at night," I bestowed upon her the benefit of my own observations while I'd been on the island.

"Perhaps we should give it a name," I added, hoping to dispel some of the dread this 'monster' had instilled. My gaze returned in time to observe her looking up at me in childlike astonishment.

"What do you suggest we call him?" I pressed her.

Slowly, the terror abated from her tear-streaked face.

"We should call him Uttal," she replied.

"Uttal?"

"Yes, sir. It means 'big' and 'strong' in my language. For God has indeed made him very big and strong so that he can climb trees," she enlightened me, our heads again tilting skywards as we watched him ascend higher still.

"So what language is that you speak?" I was eager to know once this morning's drama was over and we had tramped back to the beach.

"Gujarati, sir. Although I also speak Hindi. And English too, of course."

"Yes, you speak it very well" I couldn't resist noting. "Just as well really, because I'm afraid I don't speak any Indian languages

– although I did learn French and German at school. Not that I remember much of it!" I joked.

If the 'monster' that had freaked Preema posed no threat to her, the same could not be said of a more pressing matter that risked compromising her ability to survive on the island. Having observed my new companion's tiny bare feet tiptoeing through the undergrowth – and with a greater selection of tools now to hand – I knew I needed to turn my blossoming desert island D-I-Y skills to fabricating something else. In the meantime however, our encounter with the crab had served to break a bit more of the proverbial ice – as I now remarked to her.

"What does 'breaking the ice' mean?" she offered me that look of innocent incomprehension again.

"It means to… well, to say something funny or silly that helps people feel at ease in each other's company. Like when I asked you to give that crab a name. I guess had I been naming him I might have called him Clive."

"Clive? What does 'Clive' mean in your language, sir?"

"I don't know. But I once knew this boy at school called Clive Pearson. He was a big lad – and very strong with it."

"What? Bigger than you are, sir?" she marvelled, for, being six-foot from head-to-toe, I guess I too seemed enormous to her.

"Yes, even bigger than me," I explained. "So when I saw that massive crab I thought about Clive Pearson."

My absurd recollection elicited a chuckle from the little girl.

"That is very funny, sir. We shall call him Clive then," she insisted, at the same time poking those glasses up onto the bridge of her nose, from where they made her sweet brown eyes appear even larger than they actually were.

From the possessiveness she demonstrated towards those spectacles, I suspected she would struggle to see properly without them. As such, it was fortunate that she'd declined an offer by her mother to hold onto them for safekeeping during the flight. As with my Timberlands, even I couldn't gainsay that it was almost as if someone up above had determined that we should each depart that sinking airliner in possession of at least one personal item that would be essential to our survival on the island.

"Listen, Preema," I thought it moot to remind her again as we returned to the encampment. "You don't have to keep calling me 'sir', you know. I'm not your headmaster."

"Then what should I call you, sir?" she enquired.

I sat down opposite her and shot her an indulgent smile.

"Wes. You can call me by my name. It's short for Wesley."

"And what does 'Wesley' mean in your language?"

"Again, I don't know. I think my mom just liked the sound of it! Wesley was also the name of an Englishman who started some religion," I added.

"Yes, my father told me about this man," she surprised me with her reply. A clever child indeed!

"Anyway," I replied, hoisting her off her feet and plonking her inside the hammock, "right now I want you to stay here while I go and find some things that I need."

"What things, sir?"

"I'm going to make something – a little something especially for you," I teased her.

"Can I come with you and help you make it?" she insisted even so. "You have been so very kind to me, sir. Therefore, I would like to help you if I can."

"And help me you will. But first will you promise me you'll wait here and not get up to anything naughty while I'm away?"

"I promise," she smiled. "Will you be long?"

"Hopefully not. But I have to think a bit more about how I'm going to make it first."

"Will I like what you are going to make me?"

"I hope you will."

* * * * *

Leaving Preema behind, I headed back into the palm grove with the machete in my hand. What I was about to make would be rudimentary, but it would be a potential lifesaver nonetheless. With all manner of sharp objects littering the forest floor and jagged coral clinker littering many of the beaches – to say nothing of venomous cone snails that lay hidden in the shallows ready to inject their harpoon-like barbs into the soles of the unwary – it was vital that I protect those delicate little feet of hers with some form of footwear. But how to make shoes on a desert island?

In this respect, while holidaying with Leanne in the Far East we'd been party to an excursion to a local craft centre. All very 'touristy' I'd dismissed it at the time – the kind of thing one does to pass an afternoon when one's wife has grown bored of hanging around the hotel pool. However, the recollection of observing one particular craftsman in action set my mind racing. Locating just what I was looking for I began hacking off strips of bark from the base of a large palm tree, along with some leaf fronds too. Returning to the camp, all I needed to do now was try and remember what I'd been shown.

* * * * *

As I laid out the bark and bade her step onto it, the youngster was genuinely intrigued – more so as I took the scissors I'd rifled from the first-aid kit and scored around her right foot, repeating the exercise on a second strip of bark for her left. Then, taking the pliers, I nibbled away at both pieces until I had the soles ready.

While I was shaping them, I'd set Preema the task of pulling strands of fibre from the fronds I'd collected and making twine from them – a task to which she proved adept, smiling across at me and seeking my approval. In no time at all, I was ready to marry the soles with the straps she'd made, twisting holes in the bark with the screwdriver through which the twine could then be threaded. Hey presto – a pair of tough-wearing sandals fashioned from a palm tree!

"You are very clever, Mr Wez," she opined, stepping into her new shoes and lacing the straps around her ankles. "Thank you," she added while parading up and down in them.

I was thankful too: that they fitted snugly, but also that the kid had finally stopped calling me 'sir' (well, I guess 'Mr Wez' was an improvement!). I folded my arms smugly and took a moment to admire them and concur.

"Does this mean that I can now help you build your new house?" she looked up at me excitedly.

"You can indeed. First though, how about a bite to eat," I announced, lifting up from the trap a crab that had been residing there for safekeeping. "I'll get the fire going,"

"Must we always eat crab?" the inevitable question came – to which I harboured a degree of sympathy.

"No. Hopefully tomorrow I'll catch a fish. Until then, let us not be ungrateful for what nature has provided us with."

"But we could eat something from the Green House," she suggested, referring to the survival pod by the quaint and descriptive name she'd given it.

"I want to keep most of the tinned food there in reserve in case it's all we have," I assured her. "In the meantime, young lady, let me show you another clever trick: how to make fire."

Having grabbed some sticks and coconut husk, I bade her join me on the beach, where I demonstrated how to rub sticks together in the manner I thought I'd perfected. And rub… And rub… And rub… And… nothing! Meanwhile, Preema glaring across at me with a hint of bemusement was no less galling than knowing yet another waiting crab was probably scoffing too.

"Well, normally doing this will create sparks," I huffed, catching my breath. Meanwhile, I could feel that hot and intense morning sun on my back once again.

Very hot! And very intense indeed! With Preema waiting expectantly upon me, I looked up from rubbing and stared instead into those big brown eyes of hers, there to experience yet another remarkable 'Eureka' moment. I leaned forward to gently place my fingers upon the frame of her spectacles. With those eyes peering warily at them through the corners of the lenses, I then lifted them from her ears. Taking them to the tinder, I then trained them at just the right distance so that the beam refracted from that intense sun glowed bright and hot. I had only to wait a matter of seconds before the tell-tale trail of grey smoke was followed by a flame dancing into life. Hey presto – fire: the easy way!

"You know, Preema, the more I think about it, the more I'm coming to believe you and I were put on this island for a reason," I crowed, handing the spectacles back to their owner and carefully hurrying the flame back to the brazier.

* * * * *

Flippancy aside, I'd noticed that my new companion needed no chivvying on my part to show gratitude to Providence. With the crustacean cooked and served up, before Preema had placed a morsel to her lips she'd closed her eyes, placed her hands together, and offered up a silent prayer – presumably to the same deity her father had prayed to that night in the hope it might spare his family. I glanced at her uneasily when she opened her eyes. A generous soul might concede that at least his prayer had been partially answered.

"Do you always pray before you eat," I enquired.

"Yes. It is important that we say thank you to God for all the good things He gives to us," she asserted between mouthfuls.

I was genuinely at a loss for what to say that would not offend her. This pitiful little child, whose only crime was to board the wrong airliner on the wrong day, had lost both her father *and* her mother; *and* endured hell alone at sea; *and* cowered frightened and alone in some spooky forest hideaway. So how could she talk about this 'God' (whose existence her parents had presumably drummed into her) giving her 'good things'? What 'sin' had she ever committed to cause this callous deity to test her simple faith in this way?

I held my tongue. Maybe one day, when she was older and wiser and could think for herself, she'd realise (as I prided myself on having done a long time ago) that religion is a delusion; a poisonous mindset that inhibited people from taking control of their own lives. To be sure, the world was beset by evil – purposeful evil perpetuated, among other things, by religious intolerance; but random evil too (like psychopathic airline pilots plunging their planes into the sea) that this 'God' she worshipped seemed incapable of staying. And yet when something as chance and banal as a miserly crab and coconut lunch offered Preema a smidgin' of solace, her religion dictated she must ascribe such 'goodness' to the power and forbearance of that same 'God'. If this deity really did exist then it struck me his game was very much 'heads I win, tails you lose'.

* * * * *

After sitting out the hottest part of the day in the shade, as promised – and now that she was properly shod – I permitted Preema to help me strip some more timbers from the derelict *ataps* and to haul them back to the encampment so that I might construct a second raised shelter.

"I must say, Preema, you make an excellent Girl Friday," I chortled, for knocking those timbers together and thatching the roof proved so much easier with an extra pair of hands.

"What is a Girl Friday?" I should have anticipated the inevitable, puzzled reply. I shot her a doting smile.

"It's a female version of a Man Friday."

That quizzical look lingered as she bodged her spectacles back up her nose and awaited further explanation.

"You see, Friday was a character in a story called 'Robinson Crusoe'. It was written many years ago by an Englishman called Daniel Defoe. I used to read it as a boy when I was your age. It's an account of a man who was a castaway."

"What's a castaway?"

"It's a term for someone who finds themselves stranded all alone on an island."

"Like we are?"

"Yes, like we are. Anyway, Robinson Crusoe was all alone on his island. He ended up waiting twenty-eight years for a passing ship to rescue him."

"My Goodness, Mr Wez. That is a long time. I do hope we don't have to wait that long?"

"Me too!" I puffed. "However, while he's waiting, one day he spots a boatload of Indians coming ashore on his island..."

"What? Indians like me?" she evinced surprise.

"Well, no. These were a different sort of Indian – not like the ones who come from India."

"I thought all Indians came from India," she sank her chin in her hands, her hopeful grin having turned to perplexity again.

"Anyway, as it turned out, these were not nice Indians. In fact, they'd arrived on the island to sacrifice one of their friends – to kill him and eat him so that they might appease their god..."

What does 'appease' mean?"

"Er, it means to try and make an angry god, er… well, not quite so angry," I fumbled.

"Why was God angry with them?"

"I don't know, but they seemed to think he was," I fumbled a little less patiently. "Anyway, where was I?"

"Those nasty Indians were going to kill their friend and eat him because they thought their god was angry."

"Yes, well, anyway, Robinson Crusoe saves this poor Indian from being killed. In return, the man agrees to become his helper. And because he landed on the island on a Friday, Robinson names him Man Friday."

"In the same way that we named that crab Clive because he is big and strong – just like your friend?"

"Yes, I suppose. Anyway, what I was trying to explain is that it's because of that story that today we use the term Man Friday to describe someone who is really helpful to another person."

"Am I really helpful to you, Mr Wez?"

It was a moment of beautiful, innocent accord that touched me with the strange sensation that perhaps I'd been washed up in this place with the right Miss Patel after all.

"Very helpful," I acknowledged as she held steadied another timber for me to hammer into place.

* * * * *

The levity of our daytime discourses couldn't wholly disguise the trauma Preema had been through – that we'd both been through. With the sun going down on Day Five on our involuntary island adventure, I was again lazily rocking myself in the hammock while pondering the absurdity of it all. Meanwhile, from within her shelter my diminutive companion was muttering in her sleep, as if troubled by nightmares of the things she'd witnessed. Upon her stirring from a particularly vivid flashback, I rose and wandered over to hush her and bid her close her eyes again.

"I want my mommy," she sat up and snivelled drowsily. "I want my daddy too."

"Shhh! You go back to sleep, eh," I counselled softly, trailing my fingers through her sable mop. As I did, I halted to brush away a tear of my own – having longingly recalled those times when I used to similarly hurry Emily to sleep.

"Do you think Mommy and Daddy are still alive too? If so, do you think God will help them find me?" she implored, tearfully flopping back onto her side.

"Maybe. But you mustn't worry yourself about such things."

It was a meaningless platitude. But what else could I say? Maybe, in time, it would fall to me to disabuse this credulous little soul and explain to her that clinging to such hope was futile. Her parents were dead: I had witnessed that with my own eyes. And the god in whom she was still naively placing her trust wasn't going to bring them back to life. Not now. Not ever.

And yet I couldn't escape an awful awareness that telling her the truth would be no less cruel and callous than perpetuating the fiction that there was a fairy tale land in the sky where we would one day meet up again. As I recalled, Robinson Crusoe had convinced Friday to turn from his heathen ways and convert to Christianity. How ironic therefore that here I was contemplating how I might persuade 'Girl Friday' to lay aside her touching piety and embrace my cynical brand of atheism.

Yet to what hope could I point instead? That death was final? That there was no afterlife? Nor were there going to be any great rejoicing reunions in the sky with those we loved and missed? That there was nothing left for her to do except treasure the memory of her parents and the time they'd spent with her?

I tossed some more driftwood into the brazier to keep the fire alight a while longer – maybe in the hope that a passing ship would indeed spot it. However, there'd been no ships today, yesterday or the day before that. For all I knew there would be none tomorrow or the day after either.

Retiring to my own newly-completed wood-and-thatch shelter, I lay back on the palm fronds and thought of Emily back home in England. Like Preema, I wondered if, at that moment, she too was missing the father she feared she would never see again – as well as whether she might also be calling out to someone greater than herself in the hope that, crazy as it sounded, that someone might answer her prayers.

9

*"What need I ha' been concern'd at the tediousness
of any thing I had to do, seeing I had time enough to
do it in? Nor had I any other employment if that had
been over, at least that I could foresee, except the
ranging of the island for food, which I did more or
less every day."*

Robinson Crusoe

"So where are we going today?" the questions were coming thick and fast.

"Like I said, I want to see if we can catch something other than crabs to eat."

"But you said we were going to catch a fish. I was quite looking forward to catching one with you."

"Well, yes, I know. But I thought perhaps I'd try my hand at catching a bird instead."

"A bird?" her voice rose an octave in incredulity.

Unsure whether she was dismissive or horrified, I glanced down at her as we advanced towards a clearing in the forest. The machete in my hand was glinting in the sun.

"Yes, a bird. You know, CAW! CAW!" I teased her, flapping my elbows in an impersonation that owed more to the *'Chicken Dance'* than to the island's more graceful avian occupants.

"You're funny, Mr Wez," she laughed, though this time I detected a sardonic hint to her amusement.

We arrived at the shore of the lagoon to observe that this strange body of water was alive to the sounds of birds of all sizes and varieties coming and going from the foliage that fringed it. Among that number (and having retrieved and perused that handy wildlife guide) I counted terns, frigate birds, common noddies, and those comical red-footed boobies.

Meanwhile, this gay cacophony had induced a silent awe in Girl Friday that afforded my ears a moment of respite from her questioning – for, not unlike my Emily, Preema had well and truly set aside her initial diffidence and revealed herself to be an incorrigible chatterbox. Verbal diarrhoea almost! Oh well, Smith: did that toying deity not catch you the other day begging him for human company!

"Anyway, why the squeamishness?" I called back to her, "After all, we've got to eat to survive – and meat is very nourishing. Lots of protein," I insisted. "For a healthy body."

Then a salient thought struck me. I turned to her again.

"Go on. I suppose you're going to remind me that you Hindus don't eat animals," I was tempted to scoff.

"It is true, Mr Wez: many Hindus do not eat meat. But I am not a Hindu," she informed me matter-of-factly.

"Oh," I fumbled. "I'm sorry. It's just that I thought…"

"You thought that because I come from India I must be a Hindu," she pre-empted my unfinished sentence.

"Well, most people from India are. Aren't they?" I shrugged before returning to the point.

"Anyway, look, where's the problem? It's not pork. And you Muslims eat chicken, don't you?"

"But I am not a Muslim either," she countered.

"Sikh…?" I tried again, wincing feebly.

She shook her head most adamantly.

"Buddhist…?"

Through those spectacles, she stared at me in a way that suggested she was revelling in my failing guesswork. As I'd feared might happen, sooner or later the rock of peculiar Eastern customs had collided head on with the hard place of pragmatic Western presumption. However, aided by another of those heart-meltingly innocent smiles, she finally put me out of my misery.

"I am none of those religions, Mr Wez. My parents were Christians. And so am I."

That was me told!

"I see," I mused, observing the pride with which Preema was beaming as she announced this revelation.

Be careful what you wish for, Smith: it brought to mind that other idle request I'd made: that the supposed 'God of Love' introduce himself. Might this small, but highly intelligent youngster perchance be the vehicle for that epiphany!

"Did I say something wrong?" she enquired, picking up on my unease.

"No," I shrugged nonchalantly. "I just never particularly thought of Christianity being an Indian religion."

"There are many Christians in India. Besides, Christianity is a religion for all people, from whatever country they come from."

I grinned uneasily again, eager to change the subject. Fortunately, my pious Girl Friday was astute or gracious enough to recognise my awkwardness, offering a hiatus from further discourse with which I could ponder the more pressing matter: how to execute the task we'd set out to accomplish.

* * * * *

To be sure, I'd observed on previous occasions how tame the birds on this island were – a consequence (or so I assumed) of there being no natural predators here, as well as only infrequent contact with humans. Therefore, having instructed Preema to wait quietly further back while I snuck up on them, it was perfectly possible to get right up close to one of those booby birds that was roosting in the shrubbery.

However, my closet veganism inconveniently surfaced again. With the inquisitive bird almost eyeball-to-eyeball with me, it felt almost obscene to slay such a sentient and trusting creature. Any second now I was also expecting that precocious little companion of mine to call over and tell me that she'd given it a name; and to remind me that, under Australian law, it was probably a protected species of wildlife too! I gripped the machete and made ready to grasp the bird's neck with one hand while swiftly slitting its throat with the other. And yet despatching a docile booby was a different proposition to slaying a truculent decapod. All the time the bird was blinking serenely, staring back at me with the kind of dreamy contentment that was almost calculated to induce me to loosen my grip on that machete.

I couldn't do it. Well, at least not with an eight-year-old girl looking on from just a few metres away. Instead, for a moment I was tempted to reach up my free hand and trail it along the bird's soft brown plumage. However, possessed of a nifty nine-inch bill, I reasoned that even this dopey specimen's forbearance had limits. And I valued my hand! Therefore, I drifted away and left it to roost in peace – for now, at least.

"Couldn't you catch it, Mr Wez?" the avalanche of questions resumed.

"I could, but…" I said, dithering. "Look, perhaps you're right. Let's try a spot of fishing instead, shall we."

And with that, we forsook the relative tranquillity of the sheltered lagoon, Preema trailing after me as I advanced back through the forest towards the roar of waves breaking on the reef.

* * * * *

"Did you catch fish when you were a boy too, Mr Wez?"

If I thought I was in for a peaceful afternoon with which to reacquaint myself with a forgotten childhood pastime I was sore mistaken. While my ever-clacking companion was sat on the sand, looking on while swishing her legs in the lapping waves, I'd explained to her how I'd come to be in Australia (or at least the sanitized version of my story that was suitable for young ears!). However, while I was wading thigh deep in the stretch of water between the reef and the shore Preema progressed to interrogating me about my childhood too. In between answering her questions, I endeavoured to scoop up the fish that were darting between my legs, using the piece of net I'd discovered the other day.

"Yes, I used to fish a lot," I called back impatiently.

"Where did you fish?"

"Oh, lots of places; but mostly in the local canal. There was one not far from where I lived. Me and my friends would gather on the banks scooping sticklebacks into our nets."

"What's a stickleback?"

"Damn you!" I muttered under my breath as one of its Indian Ocean cousins annoyingly slipped my grasp.

"A stickleback is a small fish that lives in lakes and canals in Britain. We used to catch them and put them in a jar."

Glancing up, I awaited the inevitable remark about how out-of-practice my skills had become since. Instead I spotted Preema peering into the empty artillery shell case I'd discovered further up the beach and which I'd filled with sea water to detain the solitary tiddler I'd snared so far. Into it she dipped her hand to chase its occupant around the sides.

"Just remember what I said, Preema," I cautioned her. "Don't you go playing with those rusty munitions. Fortunately, this one is spent. However, the others may contain explosives that are very dangerous – even after all these years. I suspect they were stored here in case the Japanese tried to capture the island... during the Second World War, that is."

"But why did they leave them here if they are dangerous?"

"Oh, I don't know. Perhaps someone just forgot about them."

"Rather like someone has forgotten about us?"

Just then I spotted a larger and more promising fish edging closer to my feet. Slowly and stealthily, I slid my hands back into the water and manoeuvred to close the net around it.

"Wey-hey! Gotcha!" I crowed, hauling it from the water and hurrying back to the shore with the fish wriggling in my grasp.

"Bravo, Mr Wez. That is a big one!" Preema rose to her feet and cheered, doing a little dance around the old shell case as I dumped the fish inside it. "Does that mean we don't have to eat crabs anymore?"

"Well, at least tonight we won't."

Indeed, maybe not for a while – for I had still not given up hope of catching and serving up one of those meaty seabirds.

* * * * *

With two more large fishes netted, the afternoon we'd spent fishing proved a most productive use of time. With evening drawing in, the brazier was lit, and our catch was cooking nicely on the wooden skewers I'd balanced on the rim of it. While I split open some more coconuts to provide the side dish (as well as the nearest thing to a cocktail to complement our evening meal), I delegated Preema with the task of turning the skewers at regular intervals to ensure our supper wasn't cremated.

"So how come your parents were on that flight to England?" I decided to do some more interrogation of my own. "After all, I thought you said you hailed from India."

"I do, Mr Wez. I come from Gujarat. It is a large state by the sea. My parents were born there too. Gujarat is also where Mr Mohatma Gandhi was born. He was a very famous Indian who helped my country win its independence from you British – or so my father told me."

It was an interesting historical footnote which Preema recounted with pride – even if it didn't answer my question. However, glancing up from rotating those skewers she read my mind, brushing a shock of sable hair from her eyes.

"However, now I live in England," she elaborated.

"Really?" I expressed surprise.

"Yes. For the last year my parents have been living in a house in Birmingham. I enjoy Birmingham very much. It is a wonderful city, with so many exciting things to see and to do."

"Then it's a small world," I marvelled. "You see, I come from Solihull – which is not far from Birmingham. My parents still live there – in a house near the canal that I told you about."

"How amazing is that, Mr Wez. I like living in Birmingham because it means I am able to see my big sister too."

"So you have an older sister?" I cocked an eyebrow again.

"Yes. Her name is Ramila. She is nineteen-years-old and is studying to be a doctor at the university there. Ramila is very clever; and she is very beautiful too."

"Just like you then!" I felt goaded to charm my little friend. Upon which Preema's proud smile drooped.

"I miss my sister, Mr Wez. Now that my parents are gone, she is all I have left – apart, that is, from my grandparents in India. Do you think I will ever see her again?"

"Of course, you will," I assured her – a hope upon which she could be more confident. "And your grandparents too."

"Anyway, that still doesn't explain how you came to be on a flight from Perth," I reminded her again.

"My father was a minister," she explained.

"What? A government minister?"

"No, silly," she chided me. "A Christian minister. He was very well known in India, where he travelled to lots of places telling people about Jesus. He also travelled to many other countries in the world telling people about Him too – including to your country, Mr Wez. His name is Paul Patel and he was a very famous evangelist. An evangelist is a man who tells people all about Jesus. Perhaps you have heard of my father."

"I can't say I have," I shrugged – warily and ironically given my distaste for 'religious charlatans'.

"A few years ago, some Hindus in my country said they didn't like what he was preaching. In Gujarat they even passed a law to stop people like my father telling people about Jesus; or showing them how to give their lives to Him. Therefore, he moved to England with my mother, my sister and I. In England they do not persecute Christians for telling people about Jesus."

"And Perth?" I chivvied her again, determined to get to the bottom of this bizarre story.

"My father was very famous in Australia too, where he preached in many churches and at crusades. Crusades are big occasions where lots of people come to hear about Jesus," she added, presuming I'd not heard of the term. I doffed to remind her to rotate those skewers.

"However, this time he decided to take my mother and I to Australia with him. I enjoyed Australia. It was fun. We saw koala bears and lots of kangaroos. And we drove across the big bridge in Sydney," she enthused, digressing again. However, lest the childlike glimmer in her eyes glow too brightly, reality intruded again. Her smile drooped a second time.

"The last crusade my father preached at was in Perth – in a big sports stadium there. There were lots of people there that night, Mr Wez. My father spoke very powerfully to them. He asked them what they would do if they died tomorrow and had to give an account of their lives to God. At the end many of those people were crying and came forward to give their lives to Jesus.

"Then the following night we boarded that plane to London..."

I looked on while the loquacious little girl paused to draw breath. The pitiful gulp that followed stood in for recounting those final fateful hours before her parents were to be rudely spirited away to give account of their own lives to this same God who her father had preached about so powerfully.

"I'm sorry, Preema. I didn't mean to make you feel bad about what happened," I stood and apologised, resuming the rotating of the skewers for her.

"It is okay, Mr Wez. I know you did not mean to... And anyway, somewhere in England you have a daughter who thinks you are dead – just like my sister thinks I am dead."

It was my turn to draw breath and gulp.

"You're a very brave little girl, Preema. Your mother and father would have been very proud of you. And your sister will be proud of you too – when we finally leave this island and return to England. And that is what we will do – you and I. But to do that, we must be brave; and we must be strong."

I stared down at doleful eyes that dipped and which were yearning to release tears. However, gulping again, she drew those eyes up to me and forced another smile.

"I will try, Mr Wez. I will pray to Jesus and ask that He will help me. I will also pray for you, Mr Wez; that He will help you too – for you are a good man. So good that you must be an angel... one with a man's body: someone who God has very kindly placed on this island to look after me."

I pursed my lips and nodded in humility. Someone up above definitely had a worryingly bizarre sense of humour!

10

"As soon as I saw but a prospect of living, and that I should not starve or perish for hunger, all the sense of my affliction wore off, and I begun to be very easy, apply'd my self to my works proper for my preservation and supply, and was far enough from affliction at my condition as a judgement from Heaven, or as the hand of God against me. These were thoughts which seldom enter'd into my head."

Robinson Crusoe

Having given her instructions about what to do and what not to do while I was away, after breakfast I left Preema behind at the camp and headed back into the forest – this time determined to return home with the prize of something more substantial to eat.

Swallowing any scruples (and away from the glare of a pair of outraged young eyes) it didn't take long for me to select a victim, taking advantage of the bird's tame disposition to lure it within my grasp, overpower it, and throttle it. However, I can't deny the queasiness I felt at having slain such a beautiful animal. Even so, I suspected the ease with which the regrettable deed had been accomplished would be a diminishing asset: with its mates looking on in horror it would not take long before their latent wariness of human beings returned. Stuffing the kill in my bag, I accepted that future attempts at catching birds on the island might not be quite so straightforward.

Before heading back, I decided to explore the lagoon some more. The wildlife book I'd retrieved from the survival pod had given me a valuable heads-up on the island's flora too. For example, from it I'd discovered that the leaves of those *Pisonia Grandis* trees that flourished here were edible and had long been a staple in the cuisine of Indian Ocean islanders. Likewise the fruit of the *Pandanus tectorius* tree. Meanwhile, the tea shrub *Pemphis acidula* that grew around the lakeshore was renowned for its hardwood properties and had consequently found use in the construction of their dwellings. More intriguingly, the octopus bush *Argusia argentea* possessed medicinal properties that could be used to treat a variety of ailments and bacterial infections. The African cabbage plant *cleome gynandra* similarly possessed both edible and medicinal properties. As well as the main course already in the bag, I plucked handfuls of leaves and shoots from each of these plants with a view to further exploring how I might vary our diet.

It was while surveying the forest that I thought I detected a humming sound in the distance. I cocked an ear. It was a plane – the first one I'd heard since arriving on the island! What's more, it was heading my way. Making haste to a small clearing I arrived just in time to witness the grey outline of a reconnaissance aircraft swoop low overhead, the Royal Australian Air Force 'kangaroo' roundels visible on the undersides of its wings.

"Here! I'm here!" I cried, waving my arms above my head for all I was worth – regardless of whether I could possibly be heard above the roar of its four, prop-driven engines.

There was no way of knowing whether anyone aboard had spotted me. However, I was aware from the lingering drone of those engines that the plane was circling to make a second pass. There was only one thing for it: to make for the beach as fast as I could, where – clear of those accursed trees – I could hopefully make myself more visible to its crew.

Alas, the treeline was further than I thought, my passage hampered by the tangled undergrowth. By the time I'd reached it and could race out onto the sand, the lumbering Lockheed Orion had already overflown me and was banking to head south. Again, I couldn't be confident its crew had spotted me. Again, I cussed at having been in the wrong place at the opportune moment.

It quickly became evident it wasn't going to undertake a third sweep of the island. Both sight and sound of it faded. My only hope was that Preema too had heard the aircraft approach and had raced out onto the beach where she might have been spotted.

Otherwise, what to make of this welcome visitation? On one hand it was tempting to believe it was a herald that the search for the missing airliner had now been widened. Then again, the fleeting and almost cursory nature of the overflight suggested either the crew weren't seriously expecting to find traces of either the plane or its passengers on the island; or that they'd been conducting a purely routine patrol of the area.

Drifting down to the water's edge I stared out at a horizon that was again devoid of shipping. Wherever this place was, it confirmed my hunch that it must exist at the very extremity of Australia's maritime territory. More to the point, I'd chopped up the remains of that floatation chute to which Preema had clung to make my hammock, as well as to waterproof the roofs of our shelters. I cursed that, had I possessed the presence of mind to have spread it out on the beach and tethered it with rocks it might have at least alerted the reconnaissance crew to the possibility that someone had made it ashore. As it was, I accepted that I would have to make our encampment much more visible from the air in the event of further overflights.

Even more dispiriting was that that survival chute had been the only piece of wreckage I'd come across during my sojourns around the island (the absence of which was likely another reason why that Orion hadn't bothered to loiter). It was as if what had remained of that mighty airliner had been consumed by the ocean.

Well, almost. Aside from one of its chutes and two of its passengers, that afternoon another little reminder of the doomed flight unexpectedly caught my eye while I was journeying back around the wild, northernmost tip of the island. Spotting it washing back and forth in the surf, I waded in and scooped up the colourful little cube, stuffing it inside my pocket.

* * * * *

"Are you impressed, Mr Wez?"

I'd returned from my trek to find Preema playing on the beach, excitedly showing off to me the large castle she'd busied herself constructing from wet sand exposed by the retreating tide. Along with moats and channels, she'd decorated it with an assortment of shells, driftwood and other bits-and-bobs she'd found, topping it with a flag made from a small palm leaf.

"Yes, very pretty," I commended her. "But like I said, you just be careful what you're picking up off the beach – especially those sea shells," I added, not wishing to dampen her enthusiasm.

"Did you see that plane, Mr Wez?" she further enthused.

"Yes, I did. More to the point, did the people on the plane see you?" I was anxious to know.

"I don't think so. I was lying in your hammock," she confessed with contrite eyes. "I'm afraid it had gone by the time I rushed out to see it. Though I waved and waved, it did not come back."

It was as I'd feared: the reconnaissance flight had returned to base oblivious to the fact that someone was here.

"Did you kill anything?" she enquired, pointing to my bag and rising to accompany me as I strolled back to the camp.

"I did," I confirmed, though loathed to reveal what was inside.

"I do understand why you have to kill animals, Mr Wez," she acknowledged even so.

Flitting between subjects, she pressed me again. "Do you think that plane flying over means someone is looking for us?"

"I hope so."

"It's nice being on this island sometimes. But I do hope we're not going to be here for much longer. That's why I decided to make that sandcastle: so I wouldn't have to think about all the bad things that have happened to me."

"Well, I've got something for you that will hopefully also take your mind of them," I offered her a tantalising smile.

"You have?" her face lit up.

I delved into my pocket and drew out what I'd found.

"My Rubik's cube! You found it!" she hopped from foot to foot as I presented it to her. "Thank you! And thank you, Jesus too: for helping Mr Wez find it," she beamed up at Heaven.

"Yes, it was rather a coincidence," I tempered her ecstatic thanksgiving. "However, it would have been better still had something more substantial from the plane made its way ashore – something large enough to be spotted from the air, for instance."

"Yes, our camp is hidden by all these trees. Perhaps that's why the people on the plane didn't spot it."

"Well," I said, ruffling her hair and smiling mischievously, "once we've dined that's something I intend to put right. And you, Preema, can help me."

* * * * *

Once I'd plucked it, undertaken the icky (if necessary) job of removing its innards, and then roasted it over the brazier, the bird I'd caught tasted divine. Why, even my diminutive 'dinner guest' ventured me tongue-in-cheek compliments about my culinary expertise.

Consuming it in the shade of lofty palms, between mouthfuls we both gazed out across those paradise sands and the azure blue sea beyond them. Admiring them, it was possible to concede that there was indeed an upside to being marooned here. As such – and with Preema once more entertaining herself on the beach – I slunk back into the hammock to savour the bliss. Occasionally glancing up to observe her tiny hands digging furiously in the sand, I was tempted to offer my civil engineering expertise to supplement her valiant attempt to protect her castle from the advancing tide. Instead though, I wound up the radio, extended its aerial, and lay back to find out what was going on in the world that lay beyond our idyllic shores.

> *"... Commenting on the unemployment figures, Prime Minister Tony Abbott said that, with forty-seven thousand new jobs created last month, the economy was now performing much better than it had under Labor. In response, Opposition employment spokesman, Brendan O'Connor – campaigning today in the Senate by-election in Western Australia – seized on the rising number of lay-offs in the mining industry to remind voters that the state now had a higher rate of unemployment than New South Wales, something he claimed would once have been unthinkable..."*

Perhaps I'd picked the right moment after all to take up that job offer in Canada. I permitted myself a self-satisfied smile – only to have it rudely erased by a reminder of why I would not be heading to British Columbia any time soon.

> *"... A Chinese government spokesman today confirmed that the huge search operation it has been co-ordinating with other navies in the South China Sea has failed to locate any wreckage from the Airbus jet that went missing last week. Neither has it been able to establish any clues to the whereabouts of the plane's vital 'black box' flight data recorder..."*

Why were the authorities still looking in the wrong place, I seethed! However, as I listened further there was hope at last that someone might have sussed out the truth.

> *"... While a spokesman for the airline dismissed suggestions that the missing jet could have continued flying for several hours after air traffic controllers lost contact with it, in an article in yesterday's* 'Wall Street Journal' *a group of aviation experts claimed that automated Inmarsat broadcasts sent by the plane suggest it had instead flown south from its last reported position, into the Indian Ocean.*
>
> *"Meanwhile, police in Singapore have confirmed that two Iranian passengers who boarded the flight there using stolen British passports were most likely asylum seekers attempting to gain entry into the United Kingdom. A spokesman for Interpol also confirmed that the airliner's disappearance is not considered to be a terrorist incident..."*

I switched off the radio to ponder what I'd picked up from these bulletins so far. Of course, the sixty-four-million-dollar question was whether, with their combined search efforts having drawn a blank, those governments might be ready to consider this alternative theory. It was a process not aided by the inference that, geopolitical rivals one and all, they remained extremely reluctant to share intelligence with each other – including whatever their military radar networks might have gleaned regarding the whereabouts of the missing jet.

By the time I re-joined her on the beach, Preema's once-impressive sandcastle was succumbing to the waves now lapping around it. Instead – and with this welcome development in mind – I summoned her attention for a new and more pressing beachside task for which I now required Girl Friday's assistance.

* * * * *

"What are you trying to spell out, Mr Wez?" the customary barrage of questions resumed.

Having joined me in gathering up and hauling the largest rocks her tender frame could carry, time and again she deposited them on the sand in the spots where I instructed her, having by now correctly deduced that a word might indeed be taking shape.

"We're positioning them to spell S-O-S," I replied, having dumped the one I'd been lugging and pausing to mop my brow and gather breath, ready to fetch another.

"S-O-S?" she quizzed, employing one of her sticklike arms to mop her own forehead. "What does that mean?"

"It's the internationally-recognised signal that someone is in distress. If we can make the word large enough, then maybe the next time a plane flies over the pilot will spot it and report that someone is on the island waiting to be rescued."

"Oh, I see. That is very clever. But what do the letters S-O-S stand for?" she pressed me further.

Oh, I don't know. Somebody once told me it stands for 'save-our-souls'. It's the letters that sailors used to tap out over their radios in Morse code when their ships were sinking."

"My father told me that only Jesus can save our souls," my helpmate twittered, brushing her hair from her eyes.

"Well, maybe people were more religious back then," I offered an anodyne reply. "And while nobody uses Morse code any more, the letters S-O-S are still widely understood."

Preema's ostensibly innocent remark was one of several idly scattered asides by which she'd subtly drawn the conversation back to what her father had done for a living before his own soul had been abruptly carted off. My response was yet another gentle hint that I was becoming uncomfortable with her childlike piety. Indeed, it was starting to grate on me.

"Are you religious, Mr Wez?" she continued to pursue this line of guileless curiosity as we gathered up more rocks.

"No, I'm not," I said, trying not to sound curt.

"I am," she chortled proudly. "I believe in Jesus. It is why I pray to Him; and why I go to church every Sunday."

"Oh really," I hummed, pointing out a modest-sized boulder that I thought she could comfortably carry while I stooped to lift the larger one posited next to it.

"Yes," she puffed, hugging it to her chest. "While my parents listened to the pastor, I attended the Sunday school classes, where I learned lots of stories about Jesus; about how he made many sick people better; how he made blind people see; and how He even made a dead man come back to life again."

"Is that so," I hummed testily.

"Yes. And I learned all the stories that Jesus told people about Heaven and how they can get there. *'For God so loved the world that He gave his one and only Son, that whoever believes in Him shall not perish but have eternal life'*. See, that's from John's Gospel, Chapter Three, Verse Sixteen. It is the most famous verse in the Bible – or so my Sunday School teacher told me," she recounted as we walked, adding that *"'For it is by grace you have been saved, through faith—and this is not from yourselves, it is the gift of God – not by works, so that no one can boast'*. That's another famous verse – from the Book of Ephesians. It tells us that, even though we often do many naughty things that stop us getting to Heaven, God will let us in if we believe in Him.

"I know many more Bible verses, Mr Wez," she puffed once she'd deposited her contribution to my latest wheeze for effecting rescue. "I won first prize in my Sunday school class for remembering verses from the Bible."

"Let me guess: another Bible?" I tried not to sneer.

"Yes, it was. A children's Bible – with pictures that show the many miracles that Jesus did."

"Yes, well. I suppose it helped having a dad who made a living preaching from the thing!" I remarked acidly.

"*'Salvation is found in no one else, for there is no other name under Heaven given to mankind by which we must be saved'*," she continued like some wound-up clockwork toy, oblivious to my ill-concealed sarcasm. "That's from the Book of Acts, when Peter, one of the disciples, was told to stop telling people about Jesus. Just like people in my country tried to stop my father telling them that they should not bow down and worship Kali, Vishnu, Shiva, or silly gods that look like elephants; but they should instead bow down and worship only Jesus."

Upon which, I'm afraid my patience snapped. Having dumped another heavy rock in the sand, I flopped my throbbing hands on her shoulders and swivelled her about to face me.

"Look, kid," I hissed, "do you think we can just call a halt to all this yacking on about Jesus."

At first the brainy Bible student whose sinuous frame I was clutching stared up at me as if to protest. Then her mien of indignant *amour propre* settled into one of crestfallen dismay.

"I'm sorry, Mr Wez," she said. "It's just that I thought you would like to hear some of the many Bible stories I've learned. I won first prize in Sunday School for remembering them," she commended herself again.

Had this sanctimonious God-botherer been a guy of my own age and build, I was sure I would have thumped him. However, an eight-year-old girl? And one possessed of an artless, angelic little face that was looking up at me as if it was about to moisten with tears? Instead, without her needing to mutter another word it was the heathen glaring back at her who felt chastened.

"No worries," I tapped her cheek, as much to dissipate my remorse as to assure her of my continued affection.

"Look, I'm sure your father was a good man and that he meant well," I acknowledged as graciously as I knew how. "But, well... often people have their own ideas about who God is and how to worship him – like those people in India who got angry with your father. Meanwhile, many people in the West – where I come from – no longer believe there's even a God out there to worship.

Either way, it's not always appreciated when men like your father go around drumming their own religious beliefs into people. As you get older, Preema, you'll hopefully understand that."

She smiled wanly but appeared to accept my soft-spoken admonition – for now at least.

"But you won't get angry at me for praying – and for thanking God for the nice food you cook; and the lovely little house you very kindly built for me?" she craftily availed herself of those big, artless eyes, enquiring politely.

I sighed again and shook my head.

"Of course not," I assured her. "If that's what you believe, then I promise I won't get angry with you."

"And you won't mind if I pray for you too, Mr Wez?" those eyes fluttered again as she probed my indulgence further.

I smiled and shook my head again.

"On the contrary, I shall be honoured that you consider me worthy of a mention," I noted jovially.

Relieved that little matter was settled, we could instead resume the job in hand and continue to hunt together for sizeable rocks with which to spell out on the sand our ongoing predicament. Hopefully, we would henceforth avoid further misunderstandings about what constituted the permissible bounds of articulating our respective religious (or irreligious) beliefs.

11

"What I had received by the good instruction of my father was worn out by an uninterrupted series of seafaring wickedness, and a constant conversation with nothing but such as were like my self, wicked and prophane to the last degree. I do not remember that I had in all that time one thought that so much as tended either to looking upwards towards God, or inward towards a reflection upon my own ways."

Robinson Crusoe

Preema had been the first to spot it. Quite early in the morning, with the sun only just up, she tugged me from my slumber to hurry me down onto the beach, pointing out a small grey shape that could be discerned balancing on the horizon.

"It's a ship, Mr Wez!" she hollered.

It was indeed. And from the shape of the hull and the superstructure, it was a warship too – making haste in a northerly direction.

"Do you think the people on board can see our sign?" Preema continued to dance about excitedly, pointing over her shoulder to the huge letters we'd spelt out with rocks.

I wanted to sound upbeat. However, the ship was too far away – and the message set at too oblique an angle – to possibly be spotted from that distance. What's more, even if I was able to relight the fire in time and have smoke billowing from it, it was unlikely it too would be spotted before the ship had hurried past the island. Our only hope was that the vessel might launch the helicopter in the hangar at its stern, perchance to overfly the island on another routine patrol. However, it didn't. Instead, within a few minutes it had disappeared over the horizon – and with it another fleeting opportunity for rescue.

* * * * *

The day we spotted that warship would mark the anniversary of my first week ashore. It would be the last time in a while that we would spot any kind of activity off the coast or in the air. Gradually, the realisation sank in that, if we were going to be rescued, it would not be any time soon. Psychologically, I tried to temper our hopes by directing our thoughts instead upon the bread-and-butter business of staying alive. Thankfully, the huge Airbus had come down where it had, rather than continuing farther south towards the frigid environs of Antarctica.

Pretty soon our lives would settle into a routine – albeit one governed not with precision by clocks, but by the more leisurely stations of the sun. For example, upon its rising we would each attend to our ablutions, Preema having come to regard the occasional lurking presence of Clive the Coconut Crab in her toileting spot less with horror and more with grudging affection. Perhaps giving our fears names had helped after all.

For my part, I was more relaxed about her venturing in the forest alone knowing there were no snakes or other deadly creatures on the island (or so that wildlife book informed me). Meanwhile, in the absence of a reliable source of fresh water, the washing of our bodies and our clothes invariably had to be done in the sea – although I was concerned that too much exposure to salt water not only risked bleaching them (Preema's dayglo top and flowery leg-ins were already losing their sheen), but also coarsening our skin. Therefore, locating some more large plastic pop bottles that had washed ashore, I sliced the tops off them and positioned large leaves around them to funnel into these receptacles as much water from passing rain squalls as I could.

The next daily task I would detail Preema to undertake was to gather firewood while I chopped open coconuts and prepared for cooking whatever hapless crab had stumbled into the trap overnight. After breakfast, we would attend to any repair tasks that required our attention before setting off on another exploration of the island to locate further useful items from the remains of previous settlements here.

Preema meanwhile needed no encouragement to plonk her bottom inside the cockpit of that old Zero fighter – like me, there to pretend she was flying it. Those imaginary dogfights would continue when I chased her up and down the beach with my fingers and thumbs looped over my eyes like flying goggles, pretending to machine-gun her as the laughter flowed over her shoulders. Such moments of levity made the inevitable tedium of long days so much easier to bear.

Returning to camp just as the sun was at its fiercest, we would pass the hottest part of the afternoon in the welcome shade of those palm trees. Sometimes we would slumber. Sometimes we would talk. Sometimes I would read a few more pages from those paperback novels that the ranger had rather thoughtfully left behind in the survival pod. Sometimes Preema would play with her Rubik's cube, having first challenged me to twist and turn it so thoroughly that it would keep her occupied for a while. However, in the end there was never an occasion when this sharp-witted child didn't successfully return the colours to their correct positions. By which time the station of the sun hinted it was time to hunt or fish for the evening meal.

At the close of each day of our surreal incarceration we would invariably sit together around the brazier. Suffice to say, the romance of it all – gazing out upon dreamy or dramatic sunsets while sharing the touching (and frequently comical) adult-child camaraderie to be had chatting around a roaring fire – could never entirely banish from our thoughts the knowledge that we were both apart from (and almost certainly dead to) our grieving families; nor that, by some incredible and unspoken miracle, we'd survived traumatic experiences that, by right, should have broken us. Consequently, once night had fallen and it was time to retire to our respective shelters there would be further tears. As I laid my head on the pillow I'd fashioned from what was left of my old life jacket I would sometimes detect Preema snuffling in her shelter as she quietly petitioned her God.

It would prompt me to switch on my phone and briefly scroll through those photographs of Emily, quietly shedding tears of my own as I struggled to make sense of how my life had panned out. Whatever my protestations to the contrary, for the first time since my own brushes with almost certain death the week before, I worried that I was becoming partial to discovering more about this 'Jesus' fellow that Preema had set me thinking about.

* * * * *

"Look what I've found, Mr Wez," my slumber was disturbed by her excited call. Lifting myself from my hammock, I watched Preema approach and wandered what useful inanimate object she'd stumbled upon while venturing up the beach. Instead, it appeared she'd caught something to eat.

"What the...? Where on Earth did you find that?" I frowned in disbelief. There certainly wasn't much meat on it! What's more, I suspected to devour it was not her intention.

"By a nest; up the beach. The big one was picking on the little one, trying to kill it. Meanwhile, the mother was just sitting there watching it being bullied and doing nothing to protect it. It was horrible, Mr Wez. I had to save the poor thing."

In between Preema's hopeful appeal to my better nature, the tiny, naked chick she was cupping in her hands was twittering feebly. She held it up for me to take a closer look.

"And what do you suppose we do with this thing?" I eyed her up and down, incredulous.

"Feed it. And look after it. Then maybe it will grow strong and will fly away and have chicks of its own."

There was a naivety in her suggestion that was touching – even if she would countenance no cautioning that, deprived of its mother, its chances of surviving were as pitiful as its treatment by its sibling. I was no ornithologist and possessed no knowledge of how to hand-raise a seabird chick. However, I could tell from the way she was staring at me expectantly it was going to be yet another skill that I would have to hastily acquire.

"Look. It is so small and helpless, Mr Wez; and cute too. It is why I have named it Babo: which means 'cute' in my language."

The cupped hands that permitted me to behold this find reached up a little further to bid me cup my own and take it from her. This I reluctantly did, thinking how bizarre it was that, while those same hands had been busy slaying its cousins for food, they were now being asked to nurse this rescued hatchling.

And so it was that our camp would acquire its third (and most unlikely) occupant – albeit a very demanding one: from now on every few hours each of would take turns to chew on pieces of crab or fish meat which we then plucked from our mouth to feed into Babo's gullet via the straws I'd fashioned from palm leaves.

* * * * *

Availing myself of the information in the wildlife book enabled me to identify Babo as the offspring of a masked booby bird and to understand why his older sibling had (with his mother's tacit consent) ejected him from the nest. Unlike the more populous red-footed boobies on the island (which nested in the trees and laid only one egg), ground-nesting masked boobies often lay two eggs in hollows in the shingle. However, the reality of finding enough food means that parents are only able to successfully rear one chick. Invariably, some crude instinct will goad the older and stronger hatchling to eject the younger and weaker one from the protective shade of its brooding mother, leaving it to wither in the sun or be carried off by circling gulls.

Such brutal siblicide was Darwinian 'survival of the fittest' at its most raw. And yet here we were interrupting that law by rescuing one of its casualties. It recalled Nietsche's condemnation of Christianity for extolling and perpetuating weakness – contrary to what nature intended. But then, as Preema dolefully implored, the alternative was to have left poor little Babo to perish.

Contrary to my protestations of its foolhardiness, our act of Christian compassion seemed to be working. Far from expiring, Babo responded well to our care – even if his intense feeding regime required me to wake during the night to attend to it! If someone had told me I'd somehow end up becoming the reluctant surrogate parent to a booby bird I would have laughed aloud! It was yet another reminder that my time on this island was challenging so many of my assumptions about life.

* * * * *

By perusing that wildlife book I'd also established that the island on which Preema and I were involuntarily ensconced was only a mere fifty kilometres or so from civilisation – being the uninhabited outcrop of an archipelago that was both Australian external territory and a popular tourist destination. It was therefore doubly surreal to visualise these pampered sightseers downing their snags and vodka kamikazes while not too far away a pair of bedraggled plane crash survivors were butchering seabirds for sustenance while swigging rainwater from washed-up pop bottles. As time wore on, it rendered it more baffling still that the authorities on the main island remained unaware of our presence. In part, I guess it was explained by the protected status of this place as a wildlife sanctuary, but also by the difficulty of undertaking treacherous crossings by boat when sea conditions all too frequently made landing here impossible.

As if to demonstrate how fickle the weather could be, one morning we awoke to a full-blown storm heading our way. Soon enough, the sea had turned a convulsing slate-grey and the trees around us were flexing and flailing. There was little else to do that day except hunker down in our shelters and listen to the rain pounding upon the roof. On such dismal days, hope could so easily turn to despair knowing that freedom lay just over the horizon – so close and yet so maddeningly out of reach.

However, that passing storm was a salutary reminder too that the cyclone season was not over yet and there was always the possibility that one might yet chart a course in our direction.

* * * * *

When studying for my 'A' levels as a young man, I'd hung around with a gang of mates, one of whom was studying to be an electrical engineer. I recall him one day explaining to us how he'd transformed an old transistor radio into a transmitter set simply by fiddling with a few wires inside it. At the time we'd pulled his leg for being something of a nerd. How I wished now that I'd paid attention to how he'd done it. Instead, I was insufficiently confident to prise open the back of my wind-up radio and fiddle myself – and thereby risk jeopardising my only means of keeping abreast of what was going on in the world.

Each evening while Preema was nursing Babo or playing with her Rubik's cube, I would wind it up; either to listen to music playing on the main island's radio station (for which the signal was strongest), or to tune in to more distant stations if atmospheric conditions permitted. Invariably though, it would be the English language news channels to which I would return.

It was from these that I would learn during that second week that the authorities had switched their search efforts at last from the South China Sea to the Indian Ocean. However, relief on my part would be short-lived. Having poured over the flight's automated Inmarsat messages (which Rick Mackenzie had been unaware were still transmitting data back to Airbus engineers in Europe), aviation experts announced that the jet could have remained airborne for several hours after contact with it had been lost. While that left one massive arc of potential crash sites to investigate – ranging from Kazakhstan in Central Asia over to Zanzibar off the coast of Africa – they'd reached the conclusion that the most likely outcome was that the plane had flown south.

In the light of this, Canberra had directed its air and naval forces to co-ordinate an international search effort covering a huge swathe of the southern Indian Ocean. It was a bleak corner of the world renowned for both its sheer remoteness and its mountainous sub-Antarctic seas. Not for nothing did official bulletins emphasise that the likelihood of finding survivors in such a cold, desolate place was virtually nil.

However, hopes of locating the jet itself were raised when, two weeks after its disappearance, the Australian military reported that satellite imagery had identified what appeared to be aircraft debris adrift over two-and-a-half-thousand kilometres south-west of Perth.

Once again, I was reduced to tearing at my hair in frustration. How could the best minds in aviation investigation not know that the plane they were hunting for had actually come down thousands of kilometres further north? In a world where modern GPS technology can plot the movements of every mobile phone user on the planet, how could one of the largest commercial airliners to ever take to the skies – packed full of sophisticated electronic gadgets – simply vanish without trace?

* * * * *

"Why do you keep staring at those leaves, Mr Wez?"

Sat on my haunches, I looked up with the sprig poised in my hand and offered Preema a jaded expression. In my despair, perhaps she thought I was tempted to smoke them!

"You know, the more I think about it the more I'm sure your parents gave you the wrong name," I stared her out and mused.

She nudged her spectacles back up her nose, behind which those big brown eyes of hers were now swimming in puzzlement like fish in an aquarium.

"Yes. They should have called you 'Why?' Or maybe 'What?' Or even 'How?' Do you never stop asking questions?"

"My father used to say to me that you will never understand anything if you don't ask questions. It is what Jesus tells us to do in the Bible too: *'Ask and it will be given to you; seek and you will find; knock and the door will be opened to you'*," she responded with both a handy quote from Scripture and her by-now familiar cocky cheerfulness.

"Look, if you must know, I intend to become a guinea pig."

"A guinea pig?" she appended her reply with another question mark. "That's a little furry animal. My best friend at school in England has two of them that she keeps in her garden as pets. She used to take them out of their cage and let me stroke them. So are those leaves that you are staring at magic, Mr Wez? Will they make you turn into a little furry animal too?" she enquired with singsong amusement.

I glared at her again, convinced she was winding me up.

"You really can be an annoying child sometimes!" I muttered with faux exasperation before explaining that "I don't mean literally! To be a 'guinea pig' is an expression we British use when someone offers themselves to take part in an experiment. In this instance, I'm going to lick this leaf."

I could tell from her askance frown that I might just have well have smoked it – perchance upon inhaling its aroma to be magically transformed into a 'little furry animal'.

"Look, pay attention," I thought I might as well make use of her impish curiosity to demonstrate what I had in mind. "This leaf is from the Pisonia tree – which, as you might have spotted, grows in abundance on this island. I'm ninety-nine percent sure it's edible. If so, then it can make a useful contribution to our diet – like sprouts and cabbage, a valuable source of fibre and vitamins. Didn't your mother ever lecture you about the importance of eating your greens?"

"We Indians don't eat sprouts and cabbage; but we do eat lentils and beans. We eat rice too; and herbs and spices. I enjoy cooking," she assured me with a winsome smile, "I used to help my mother prepare all these things when we lived in India. However, when we moved to Birmingham she bought them in packets from the supermarket instead."

"Yes, well, unfortunately I've yet to spot the local Waitrose around here," I quipped. "However, we do have plenty of Pisonia trees. And you are going to help me cook Pisonia leaves. First, however, I want to make sure they are indeed safe to eat. Therefore, as a wise Australian man in the bush once showed me, first I'm going to lick this leaf and then wait. If, after a few hours, I fall sick then I will know instead that it's poisonous. However, if I exhibit no ill effects then I will proceed to devour the whole leaf. Again, if I exhibit no ill effects then we can be confident that these leaves are safe to eat."

"You are very clever, Mr Wez. And very brave!" she chuckled drolly. "But I also want to be brave. So shall I lick one of those leaves too?" she offered, reaching over to pluck one.

"Whoah! No. You mustn't," I slapped her fingers playfully. "You see, I need you to be what is called the 'control' in this little experiment. After all, if you lick it and we both then fall ill then how will we know it's the leaf that caused our sickness and not something else we may have eaten?"

"Oh, I see. But if you fall ill and die what will happen to *me*?"

It was an apposite question, for which those bright enthusing eyes dipped. Then, as if fearing more earnest censure on my part, she looked up and reminded me again.

"I know you don't believe in God, Mr Wez. And you don't like me talking about Him. But every night I thank Him that He has sent you to look after me now that my parents have gone to be with Jesus. You have taught me so many important things," she insisted. "How to make fire; how to get water from coconuts; how to feed little Babo; and even how to make string from palm trees so that you can tie my hair up," she said, swinging her head sideways to proudly show off her new pony-tail.

I was genuinely humbled. And there was me thinking how amateurish was this first attempt at ladies' hairdressing (certainly when compared to how masterfully I remembered Leanne used to braid and bow Emily's hair into cute little pigtails).

"Every night I pray that He will look after you too, Mr Wez – so you will be able to carry on teaching me important things; but also so you will one day you will see your daughter again in England. She is very lucky, Mr Wez: to have a father who is so brave and clever like you are; but also so kind and so caring too."

Not for the first time one of Preema's touching and sincere compliments had, without her realising it, brought me to the brink of tears. This time her words were more clawing for being so at variance with the truth. How could she know what a poor excuse for a father I'd in fact turned out to be; a man who, for all his undoubted good intentions, had ended up impatiently sacrificing his marriage and his family for his ambitions; a man for whom, at any given moment, his career rung on the company ladder had mattered more than being there for his wife and child; a man who had derived his thrills from the cut-throat business of managing multi-billion pound mining operations on other continents, forsaking time in his daughter's company. *'For what profits a man if he gains the whole world but loses his own soul?'*

* * * * *

Boiling them up over the brazier in empty baked bean tins, over the coming days Preema and I cooked and ate the leaves of the Pisonia tree. And while I can't say they were the most delectable things I'd ever tasted, thanks to those rudimentary survival skills I'd imbibed from my bush-trekking adventures in Australia (as well as to Preema's continued prayers, I would tease her) we both lived to tell the tale.

I had no idea how much longer I would be compelled to endure this sometimes cruel, sometimes comical exile. However, with each passing day it was becoming more humbling and instructional, as well as strangely enriching and humanising. Who would have credited that the unwitting instrument of this long-overdue catharsis in my life would turn out to be a sassy and inquisitive little Indian girl whose simple faith was bugging me.

12

*"One morning early, when lying in my bed, and
fill'd with thought about my danger from the
appearance of savages, I found it discompos'd me
very much... My business was by all possible means
to conceal my self from them, and not to leave the
least signal to them to guess by, that there were any
living creatures on the island of humane shape."*

Robinson Crusoe

It had appeared at first light on a morning when overcast skies
and a lack of discernible breeze meant the sea was becalmed
enough to make a landing possible. It was Preema who had first
alerted me to the presence of a ship, having run back up the beach
from where she'd spotted it.

"Do you think it has come to take us home, Mr Wez?" she
panted. "I tried waving to it, but there is no one onboard to see
me. It is a bit of a tatty ship though. In fact, it could do with a new
coat of paint."

Whether it was that pertinent observation or some nagging
sixth sense, but I had the distinct impression that the sudden
appearance of this grey, rust-streaked and anonymous-looking
vessel might not be the unalloyed good news we'd been praying
for. Riding at anchor upon a glasslike sea just beyond the reef, I
could discern no signs of activity on its decks. And with no flag
hanging from the mast it was impossible to be certain of its
nationality. The best deduction I could make was that it might be
an illegal fishing vessel, which (from entries in the ranger's log) I
knew occasionally visited this remote spot to repair and revictual.
Such activity constituted the principal threat to the island's
wildlife and might have been the reason why that RAAF
reconnaissance plane had buzzed the island a while back.

"Shall we light the fire so that they can see us? I can run down to the shore again and try shouting at it if you like," my eager, prepubescent companion was urging.

I frowned anxiously. Then, after pausing for reflection, I draped a protective arm across her shoulders.

"Let's wait and see if anyone does appear on deck first, shall we," I cautioned. "Then we can decide what kind of welcome we want to extend to our visitors."

* * * * *

Rather than stoking the fire as suggested, I instead took the precaution of extinguishing it, kicking over the brazier and smothering the embers with sand. I also instructed Preema to gather up all the useful implements we'd acquired – the tools, the first aid kit, the radio – and hide them somewhere deep in the forest. Meanwhile, I unhooked the hammock and emptied the palm fronds from the shelters. Satisfied our encampment looked as if it had been abandoned – and armed with that mean-looking machete – I ordered that she wait with me behind the treeline.

"But what about Babo?" she stared up and enquired.

"I glanced down at the tweeting chick rocking from side to side in the nest I'd made for him from the old ammunition case I'd found (and which we'd stuffed with palm fronds).

"Well... Just hide him somewhere for now. In the forest maybe," I replied in a fluster.

"But the crabs will eat him," she pleaded.

"Maybe they will. But we can't take him with us," I insisted.

When at last a member of the ship's crew deigned to greet the morning, all my worst fears were confirmed. This swarthy, gangling figure idly lit a cigarette before training a pair of binoculars upon the shoreline. Rather than waving to him, we ducked out of sight. Even at this distance, a naked eye could spot the automatic assault rifle that was slung across his shoulder.

"Why does that man have a gun, Mr Wez?" Preema's latest question came in a whisper laden with misgiving.

"I don't know. But I suspect he's not looking to be our friend," I shuddered, subconsciously pressing her head a little lower behind the screen of foliage.

For several more minutes this lone figure scanned his surrounding while dragging on his cigarette. In particular, he seemed intrigued by the stones we'd laid in a pattern upon the beach. I wondered whether he understood the significance of the letters they spelled out. Soon enough, up popped a second figure – also sporting an automatic weapon. Upon being offered a smoke, he muttered something to his buddy. However, from their obsidian complexions and the glottal harshness with which I heard them conversing, I suspected these guys who'd come calling were not fishermen at all; they were pirates!

As if to remove all doubt, suddenly a portal on the superstructure burst open and out onto the prow stumbled a light-skinned woman in torn garments, and who was being pursued by another member of the crew. Furthermore, from the manner in which she was gasping pleas for mercy I suspected she'd failed to perform to her assailant's satisfaction – whatever manner of sexual humiliation he derived that satisfaction from. Aided by the intervention of his comrades, he quickly had her rounded up.

"What are those men doing to her?" Preema trembled, this time her question devoid of innocent curiosity. "Are they going to bring her ashore to kill her and eat her: like Friday in that 'Robinson Crusoe' book you told me about?"

"Let's hope not," I snarled.

I gripped her shoulder to reassure her, for even at her tender age she knew perfectly well that this was not how grown men ought to treat a helpless member of the weaker sex.

With each imploring wail, the woman settled into her brutal subjugation. Once her assailant had had his fun, it was the turn of his mates to slap her about and penetrate her. Grinding my teeth with righteous anger, I hauled Preema's disbelieving gaze away and shielded her ears. Otherwise, with these thugs preoccupied, I sensed it was time to steal ourselves away in the forest until they'd departed our peaceful shores.

However, as I hauled the sobbing child to her feet and led her away, the intruders had one final indignity to bestow upon their captive. Startled to discover that there was still some fight left in their pint-sized plaything, she so enraged a goon who was attempting to have his way with her that he snatched back his weapon from a comrade and pumped a round into her.

Preema instinctively screamed in terror. More ominously, her cry prompted one of the thugs on deck to glance over his shoulder as if to catch from whence the scream had come – even as his attention was quickly re-engaged by another altercation that was now breaking out aboard ship.

The skipper of this motley gang emerged on deck, livid to encounter this summary despatching of what may have been their last bargaining chip for extracting a ransom from the owners of whichever passing ship they'd dragged the woman from. Briskly pressing my hand to Preema's mouth, the last thing I caught sight of while hurrying her out of sight was the skipper and his insubordinate crew member haranguing and jostling each other.

* * * * *

In the time it took for the ringleader of this outfit to rustle together a landing party, Preema and I made ourselves scarce. With a bit of luck, the pirates would make only a cursory foray on the island. Long enough maybe to restock their larders and be gone before the Australian military discovered their presence.

Lowering one of the ship's boats, its coxswain steered a course through the reef and eventually leapt out into surf that was shallow enough for him and his armed cohorts to drag the boat ashore. Thereafter, hidden away in the dense forest we could only listen out for their sporadic banter as they scoured the beach before venturing inland. Soon enough, I could detect the tone of wary curiosity in their voices as they must have discovered and ransacked our encampment. Hopefully, they would conclude that whoever had built it had, like them, visited the island only fleetingly before sailing off to other parts.

Eventually, their voices grew more distant. Perhaps having stretched their legs and rounded up what they needed they'd made haste back to their vessel.

"Is it safe to come out yet, Mr Wez?" Preema enquired in hushed tones.

"Shhh! I'm not sure. Better that we wait – just to be certain they've gone."

For a second time that day my gut instinct was correct: while most of the landing party had wandered off up the island, the sudden cracking of a tree bough alerted me to the presence of a straggler. I pressed Preema's face to the ground and tapped my lips with my forefinger. If ever there was a time for her to demonstrate what a big, brave girl she was (and a silent one at that!) it was now. Maybe now she could understand why we'd had to abandon the chirping Babo for the duration.

Preema smiled feebly and joined me listening out for a pair of callused feet that flopped in a pair of badly-fitting espadrilles as they sounded a passage towards us. A little further and the lone goon suddenly halted. Through gaps in the undergrowth I could now more clearly observe this sable-skinned individual – as well as the clunky great AK-47 he was wielding. From the way his eyes were warily scanning the forest while his bony fingers fondled the trigger maybe he sensed someone was lurking nearby. I just hoped he wouldn't spot Preema's dayglo orange top through those same gaps in the foliage.

There ensured possibly the longest thirty seconds of my life, for I was silently praying with the same urgent intensity that Preema was. Satisfied that he was perhaps imagining things, the lad's glower seemed to abate. So much so that – the nervous tension having gotten to him too – he then propped his rifle against an adjacent palm trunk and loosened his trousers.

Suddenly, terror on my part morphed into utter incredulity. Whatever this teenager had devoured for breakfast had clearly gone straight through him! To a cacophony of bubbling farts, he was now expunging the lot from his bowels! I was forced to gently steer Preema's eyes away for a second time.

All the time this surreal scatological encounter was being played out my other hand was ready on the machete. I'd witnessed what his mates had done to that pitiful young woman. Righteous anger welling afresh, I nestled Preema a little closer to me. I was determined that this was one diminutive little lady he would not be snatching without a fight.

What's more, if I was swift enough I would surely never have a better opportunity to slay this crapping Boy Wonder before he could grab that rifle again. However, lest this temptation to strike pre-emptively get the better of me, the stillness was suddenly broken by a loud crump that emanated from further up the island (and which set every bird in the trees to flight). When their frantic cawing subsided, it was the agitated cries of his comrades that was instead carrying in the distance.

The lad sprung to his feet, hauling his pants back around his unwiped arse. Grabbing his rifle, he hurried after the commotion.

"What was that, Mr Wez?" Preema whispered, questioning me again now that the immediate danger had passed.

"It was an explosion," I craned up and proffered, my forehead puckering in genuine puzzlement. Perhaps the Aussie navy had showed up after all – and in the nick of time too.

With an instruction to Preema to remain concealed, I gingerly rose to my feet to sneak a view of this one-sided skirmish. For if the good guys really were shelling the beach then their opening shot must have been both accurate and sobering. It sounded like it had put this roguish gang of mariners to flight without the need to fire off a second one.

* * * * *

As I'd feared, the visitors had trashed or carried off those bits of our encampment that we hadn't been able to spirit away beforehand. However, at least with my invaluable collection of tools safe the shelters could be repaired.

Revenge though would be to be present to witness this band of savages being rounded up (and if Preema and I could cadge a lift back to civilisation aboard whichever of Her Majesty's Australian warships had brought their reign of terror to an end, bring it on!). I carried on through the forest, keeping far enough back from the treeline to avoid being caught in any crossfire. Soon enough I was able to glimpse the pirate landing party through gaps in the trees.

However, to my surprise, there was no warship patrolling offshore; nor any posse of marines steering a passage through the reef to apprehend them. More chillingly, upon counting I spotted that one of their number was absent – although not the one with the dicky bowels, who'd by now re-joined his febrile colleagues on the beach. Even as I lingered for a better view, I swallowed hard and peered over my shoulder into the forest behind me – machete at the ready.

I soon realised that it was their skipper who was missing – or rather that it was bits of him that were missing. For there, surrounded by his mortified cohorts, his limbless and lifeless torso lay where it had landed in a swathe of blood-drenched sand. From the gouge in the beach a short distance away – and apropos why I'd warned Preema against playing in this spot – I could see exactly what had happened. Somehow their leader had accidentally detonated one of the rusting artillery shells that had been dumped here (and which accounted for the explosion).

By now, the earlier cloud was lifting. Along with the sun breaking through, a stiff breeze was picking up. Alas, with nothing more that the horrified landing party could do for their skipper, one of their number crossed his arms upon his chest and offered up a brisk prayer. Thankfully, they then hurried into their launch, carrying what goodies they'd amassed and making haste back to their creaking hulk before the roughening surf stranded them on the island too.

* * * * *

Suffice to say, it was with relief that Preema received the news that the baddies had weighed anchor and departed with their tails between their legs (albeit with their erstwhile skipper's severed legs still at either end of the lonely beach on which he'd been summoned to meet his maker). However, the incursion had shaken her up badly. Therefore, I took time out that afternoon to nurse away her tears and shore up her frayed nerves. The process of consolation was aided by the discovery that Babo had thankfully managed to survive his concealment in the forest. The process of feeding and cooing over the hungry chick soon banished the child's anxious snuffling.

Otherwise, before the sun went down there was a far more loathsome task that I begged my leave to attend to. Returning to the spot where the raiders had come ashore, I gathered up their leader and hurled what remained of him into the surf in the hope that the retreating tide would carry off these gruesome reminders of the visitation for the sharks to dispose of.

Thereafter, I trudged a little further up the beach – both to dissipate my own belated trauma and to check on the survival pod. To my horror, I discovered that the goons had trashed that too, as well as pilfering its stocks of tinned food and bottled water. Hence our precious stock of emergency supplies was gone. Along with them too had disappeared the medicines I'd kept stored there. The swines had even made off with the camping stove! Meanwhile, shredded about the floor were both the ranger's log and those paperback novels that I'd yet to get around to reading. From now on, whatever we would need to get by as castaways – to sustain, to heal, or to entertain ourselves – we would have to find in the forest, on the beach, or in the shallows that fronted the reef.

It was while tidying the place up that I spotted another book that had somehow been spared their wanton vandalism (and which I bent down to pick up from the floor).

"'The Holy Bible – placed by The Gideons'," I surveyed the gilded title on its otherwise anonymous wine-red cover.

It was by now too gloomy in the unlit pod to undertake even a cursory perusal of it, though from a brief thumbing I could tell it had probably never been read. Presumably, the ranger had been presented with it; or had purloined it from some hotel he'd visited. Perhaps indifferent to its pearls of wisdom himself, he'd even so left it behind to amuse the next member of the parks team to find themselves holed up here. That said (and squirreling it away under my arm), I could think of at least one young castaway who would likely make use of it.

* * * * *

On my return to the camp (and with dusk drawing in) I was to make one final harrowing discovery. With the tide having turned, the partially-clothed body of the woman who the pirates had raped and murdered had washed ashore, having been tossed overboard upon their departure. Dragging lazily in the surf, as if by some miracle it had been spared the depredations of the sharks and (save for that gunshot wound) was remarkably intact.

Grabbing it by the arms and hauling it up the beach, upon turning the corpse over it was possible to make out that the bitsy young lady had been of Oriental origin – Thai, Filipino, Malay, or Chinese: who could say. Indeed, was she the scion of some wealthy Asian shipping magnate who just happened to be in the wrong place at the wrong time when one of Daddy's vessels had been hijacked? Or maybe she hailed from some unsung coastal village and had been snatched by those goons the last time they'd put ashore. Or just some lowly guest worker in the Middle-East – a maid or a nanny, perhaps – who (courtesy of the vicissitudes of human trafficking) had had the terrible misfortune to wind up the plaything of a gang of gun-toting maritime crooks.

All I knew for sure was that this was a terribly undignified end to her short life. Whoever she was, this poor young thing didn't deserve to die this way – unloved, unmourned and unremembered. Trusting that the 'loving God' who'd earlier spared his holy scripture from desecration might also (for one night at least) spare her mortal remains from the attention of those emerging crabs, I crossed her arms over her chest, whipped off my shirt to cover her face, and wiped the tears from my eyes. Tomorrow, when daylight returned, I promised her I too would return to arrange for a proper burial. It was the least I could do.

13

*"Having now brought to mind a little relish to my
condition, and given over looking out to sea to see if
I could spy a ship... I began to apply myself to
accommodate my way of living, and to make things
as easy to me as I could."*

Robinson Crusoe

*"The LORD is my shepherd; I shall not want.
He maketh me to lie down in green pastures.
He leadeth me beside the still waters..."*

Having been up since the crack of dawn excavating the grave, laying her body to rest, and then covering it over – and with nothing more substantial with which to accomplish this invidious task than my trusty adze – I seized the opportunity of Preema reading those words aloud from the Gideon Bible to close my eyes and gather together my thoughts.

*"... Surely goodness and mercy shall follow me all
the days of my life: and I will dwell in the house of
the LORD for ever."*

"Amen," her dulcet voice appended the verses, an expectant pair of eyes duly glancing up at me.

"Amen," I cocked an eye in her direction and mumbled obligingly.

Thereupon, Preema knelt in the sand to lay a small posy of flowers she'd picked from the forest beside the wooden cross that I'd made and planted atop the grave. Committal service concluded – brief and simple though it was – after a moment of silent reflection we turned about and she permitted me to lead her back to the camp for a well-earned breakfast.

"Thank you, Mr Wez," she commended me along the way.

I proffered an inadequate sigh. "It's the least we could do for her. Poor soul."

"No, I mean thank you for finding this Bible. And for kindly giving it to me," she said by way of clarification.

Another sigh cloaked me fumbling for something to say.

"Well, at least it's come in handy this morning," I eventually muttered, in return commending her oratorical skills. A preacher in the making – just like her late father, I joked lamely.

"So where's it from – that passage you read?" I enquired, pointing to the Bible she was clutching protectively to her bosom.

"It's the Twenty-third Psalm," she chortled as if it was self-evident. "It was one of the psalms I had to learn to win first prize in Sunday school. That's how I knew where to find it. But it is also one of the most well-known passages in the Bible."

"I thought it sounded familiar."

"You've read it then, Mr Wez?" her eyes lit up.

"When I was young: at school, that is. We used to have this RE teacher – Mr Blount – who took great pleasure reading the Bible to us. Not that we thirteen-year-olds used to pay much attention. We were too busy flicking elastic bands at him when he wasn't looking!" I recalled with droll delight.

"But you should read the Bible too, Mr Wez. I'm sure you would enjoy it. There are many verses like those that encourage us to trust that God will give us good things in our lives."

I tutted – ostensibly to humour my wishful companion; but also drawing upon that same deep reservoir of cynical unbelief that had witnessed me torment the bullish Mr Blount; and nowadays to erect a similar mental wall that served to deflect Preema's hortatory sermons.

"It is the Word of God, Mr Wez. My father used to tell me that if we read the Bible we will hear God talking to us. That way we can live good lives so that people will see that Jesus lives in us."

"Yeah, well. Maybe one day," I fobbed her off.

Though by now she knew better than to weary me by regurgitating those bits of her old man's sermons that had lodged in her memory, still Preema had an uncanny knack of judging just the right moment to let slip a nugget of testimony that would set me thinking again – as had this morning's homily.

Now that the dust had settled on the previous day's hair-raising events, I was again mulling over the paradoxes of my castaway adventure so far. For example, though all night long I'd been cursing a God who could permitted evil men to slay a helpless young woman, I couldn't help marvelling at the miracle of timely deliverance that had even so spared Preema and me from a similar fate. It seemed to follow a pattern: life-threatening plight befalling us from out-of-the-blue – yet without fail being narrowly averted by some similar inexplicable, nick-of-time deliverance. For example, the plane that Rick Mackenzie had intended should be our tomb had spun about and broken apart upon hitting the water – and yet we had been counted among the few passengers who'd survived the impact. In my case, because some sixth sense had alerted me to take up the brace position without waiting for the announcement; in Preema's, because the large, enveloping seat she'd been strapped into had shielded her tiny frame and prevented her neck and limbs from being snapped by its force. And even though I'd cursed at having been ejected into the ocean shod in a pair of cumbersome lace-up boots, those same boots had proved of inestimable worth, both for throttling sharks and clambering to safety over a jagged coral reef.

It was extraordinary too how we'd both been washed up on a remote, uninhabited island possessing not a single essential survival aid – only to discover that previous visitors had left behind a veritable treasure trove of discarded equipment and supplies. And most intriguing of all: how come the Miss Patel with whom I now found myself strolling along its shores had transpired to be not the ravishing sex kitten in whose company I'd fantasised about spending time, but rather a weeny eight-year-old Bible basher whose sapient insights were remorselessly chiselling away at my cynical unbelief – even as I feigned to dismiss them?

* * * * *

Following the pilfering of that stock of tinned fruit that I'd been sparingly dipping into, it was fortunate that I was to discover an alternative source of Vitamin C for our diet (or rather Preema had accidentally discovered it when she'd picked those flowers to place on the lady's grave). More commonly known as a species of pawpaw, the *Carica Papaya* tree was a native of Central America that had been introduced to the island by previous visitors and had thrived in its dry, sandy soil. After performing the customary lick-of-the-tongue test, it had proved safe to eat. Furthermore (as that invaluable wildlife book had informed me), ripe papaya fruit could be eaten raw or unripe pods cooked, while Indian Ocean islanders traditionally ground up its seeds to spice their meals.

So it was that on another pleasant, balmy evening Preema and I were finger-picking at barbequed seabird and mashed-up papaya, washing it down with the customary coconut water. What's more – luxury of luxuries – we were now able to enjoy it while sat on rough-hewn stools around a rough-hewn table, all of which I'd been able to knock together using palm trunks, planks from the *ataps*, and the *ad hoc* carpentry skills I'd acquired.

"Tastes good, eh? You like it?" it was my turn to proudly fire off a few questions.

With a mouth stuffed with what her hand was scooping from her plate (an item of 'crockery' I'd also fashioned from left-over pieces of timber!), she nodded her head in affirmation.

"You know, it looks like we may be on this island for some time before the ranger returns. In which case, we really need to think about resuming your education," I noted matter-of-factly in between my own mouthfuls.

Again, a concurring nod of the head stood in for a fulsome reply. Not that I thought for one minute she'd beg to dissent. While most children would have been relaxed about skipping school for a month to frolic on the beach and learn exciting survival skills, I knew from our conversations so far that this astute little lass regretted not being able to show off her commendable erudition to her teachers and her classmates.

"But how will you teach me, Mr Wez?" she eventually enquired upon swallowing. "You are not a teacher."

"I can teach you about the things I know: geography, history, and science, for example. And I can help you further develop your reading and writing skills too," I insisted.

She proffered me a knowing smile, having sharpened them up herself from the reading material to hand – principally that Gideon Bible she'd taken to treasuring. In this respect, maybe it had come in handy for other things too. During our afternoon siestas, I would periodically find myself being roused in my hammock by a prodding finger pointing out some archaic or convoluted word for which she required pronunciation and enlightenment: 'yokefellow', 'ambassage', and 'malefactor', as well as 'effeminates', 'whoremongers' and 'circumcision'.

I must confess that explaining those latter words required some self-conscious verbal somersaults on my part. It left me wondering whether this so-called 'Good Book' was entirely suitable reading for an eight-year-old girl whose mother and father (I imagined) had otherwise not been the most open and forthcoming of parents when it came to discussing sex.

Meanwhile, there were other words for which she'd sought my counsel which, though I understood the everyday uses for which they were employed ('atonement', 'justification', 'remission'), I struggled to explain to her in the context that the men who'd written the Bible had no doubt intended. One tongue-twister in particular – 'propitiation' – completely foxed me. I made a mental note to run it past the dictionary app on my phone next time I switched it on.

Otherwise, any hope of protecting her innocence had, I feared, been well and truly shattered by the events of the last few weeks. To the trauma of losing both her parents had been added the desolation of being cast adrift at sea and then washing up alone on a deserted island (though not so deserted that she hadn't run into an axe-wielding Englishman prowling about in his underpants!). She'd then witnessed a harrowing rape and murder carried out by armed pirates, thereafter coming within an ace of being abducted by them herself. What more could Yours Truly fumbling to describe what little boys had done to their choppers possibly do to quicken this roller-coaster ride into adulthood into which Preema Patel had suddenly found herself strapped!

"Do you think we will ever be found, Mr Wez?" she had that glimmer of doubt in her eyes again. "By nice, friendly people, I mean. People who will help us go home to see our families?"

"We will – one day soon," I assured her, even so reminding her that "But now we know that not every boat that sails these waters is crewed by 'nice, friendly people', next time you spot one anchored offshore make sure you tell me first, won't you."

She nodded, chastened, scooping some more pawpaw.

"In which case, why don't we build a boat ourselves, Mr Wez – from all these trees on the island? Then, like Mr Noah and his wife and his sons – and all the animals too – we can escape aboard it. I'll help you build a big boat, Mr Wez – just like Mr Noah did. If you want me to, that is."

It was a kind and sincere offer. However, how could I tell her that even were my rudimentary carpentry skills up to constructing something seaworthy – and my even more threadbare navigation skills up to skippering it – the wind and the prevailing currents would almost certainly carry us away from the other islands, further out into open ocean. That's assuming the reef or the treacherous swell beyond it didn't cause it to flounder first.

"I miss my sister, Mr Wez. I wish she was here with me; or that I was back in England with her. Or better still, that we were both back home in India, listening to my grandmother and baking cakes with her," she sighed instead upon being politely informed that her brainwave was a non-starter – regardless of what this 'Mr Noah' had supposedly done in the Book of Genesis. "My grandmother is very wise and taught us lots of wonderful things. We used to stay with her whenever my mother was away from home with my father on his crusades."

"It sounds like your old man was away a lot," I put it to her – aware that the life of an itinerant evangelist was hardly conducive to the kind of stable family set-up that born-again Christians supposedly prized.

"He was... Often... All over the world... But then it made the moments when we were together more special. I have lots of happy memories of my father. I especially loved listening to him practising his sermons. He knew the Bible very well, Mr Wez – much better than I do. And he spoke so boldly too. It is why so many people found Jesus whenever he preached to them. I know I will always miss my father – even though you are very kind and helpful to me, Mr Wez. In fact, you are almost like a father to me too – if such a thing was possible."

Flattered though I was to be riding so high in her estimation, I was conscious how, on previous occasions, maudlin reminiscence of her deceased parents had ended up plunging Preema into bouts of most 'ungodly' despondency.

"Yes, well. I hope I can live up to his example," I said, attempting to inject some welcome levity into the conversation.

"Tell me about your daughter, Mr Wez," she then veered that conversation in a new and unexpected direction. "You too must have so many memories of happy things you did together."

Where to start? We had indeed done many things together – when we were a family, that is. I similarly treasured memories of Leanne and I watching Emily riding her first tricycle to the park; or being woken on Christmas mornings by her peering around our bedroom door screaming excitedly that Father Christmas had been; memories too of Leanne and I holding hands and gazing at each other in amused and knowing pride when Emily made her thespian debut in the nursery school play. All these and more I now recounted to my enchanted listener as she carried on shovelling pawpaw from her plate.

"I'm afraid I wasn't always a very good father to her though," I confessed as despondency gripped me instead. "I could have done so much more – for Emily; and for my wife too."

"But what could you have done, Mr Wez? You are such a kind man," she unwittingly damned me with her praise.

To which I summoned a mangled smile.

"Sometimes, kindness isn't enough – or rather the occasional acts that pass for kindness aren't when you're a very busy man with an important job. You say you were often apart from your father, Preema. But at least your father and mother loved each other and, with you and your sister, were a *family*. I'm afraid at times I behaved in ways that meant that, in the end, Emily's mother didn't want to be married to me anymore and the family we created broke up. You see, Emily's mother and I are divorced. We no longer live together. Meanwhile, Emily lives with her mother. It's why I've been living on my own in Australia these last three-and-a-half years," I admitted, certain that, nowadays residing in the West, my young confidante would have had cause to hear the words 'separation', 'divorce', and 'single parent' mentioned somewhere, either at school or on television.

"Oh, I see," she said, nudging her spectacles up her nose before staring at me regretfully. "But you still see Emily, don't you? You showed me those happy pictures of you together in Australia… on your phone," she reminded me.

"Yes, I still see her – from time to time. But when you live apart from your child the relationship you have with them is never the same again. Something has changed, though you can never quite put your finger on what it is. For instance, you're no longer there when she has things she wants to tell you or show you right away – like having made a new friend; or getting a good report at school. And even though there is Facebook, and Instagram, and Skype, it can never be a substitute for actually being there alongside your child. Soon enough, you find yourselves becoming strangers; and by the time you do get to see each other again the moment of excitement at making a new friend or getting a good school report has passed."

"But it doesn't mean Emily doesn't love you. Do not think like that, Mr Wez. You will always be her father; and a father is very important to any little girl. He is the one she will always turn to when she has important questions she wants to ask about the world," she insisted with the maudlin voice of experience.

"That's very kind of you to say so, Preema. However, I failed her mother too," I continued, fumbling to describe the pain and the hurt that adults often inflict upon each other in a way that an impressionable child might understand, as well as the mistakes they make that compound it. "I chose other priorities in my life over being there for my wife. And when we did finally go our separate ways I foolishly thought that loving another woman would make up for the way I failed to love Leanne. But it never can. Maybe that's why I'm destined to be exiled here – on this island – and to maybe end my days here," bitter despondency really was tainting my contribution to our discourse, "so I can never break the heart of another woman again."

I was conscious that I'd said too much. I'd clumsily and unthinkingly ventured into affairs of the heart, the caprices of which Preema would discover for herself in the fulness of time (but had no need to worry her little head about just yet).

"*'For what profits a man if he gains the whole world but loses his own soul?'*," I suddenly and inexplicably found myself blurting out as if to release the dam of my smouldering regret.

Instead Preema just stared back at me, mystified.

"It's from your Bible," I enlightened her. "I'm afraid it's the only verse I can remember, though I haven't a clue which book you find it in. It means you can think you have everything in life – a great job, a big house, a nice car, expensive holidays, money in the bank – and yet the most important thing of all slips unnoticed through your fingers. And then you wake up one day and realise it's gone. Maybe that verse is apt. Maybe this God of yours has made it my punishment to have cause to remember those words for the rest of my life."

I was conscious that my bitterness was morphing into arrant cynicism again – and even snide hostility towards the religion that my companion had put her childlike trust in. However, rather than taking offence, she instead offered me an empathetic smile.

"But God does not punish us, Mr Wez. My father used to tell me that when we find ourselves in bad situations and we think God has deserted us, He is instead using our unhappiness to teach us new things – about ourselves, but also about how much He loves us. Maybe the bad things that have happened to you – your wife divorcing you; being apart from Emily; meeting this other woman who you thought you loved but didn't really; and now being stranded on this island with me – these things are all part of God's plan, Mr Wez: to show you how much He loves you; and to teach you how to trust Him too."

That was one bold assertion for a callow eight-year-old kid to make about the hard-bitten unbeliever she now fixed her guileless brown eyes upon. Lest I build her hopes up that – in the manner of her late father (and by a similar slight of verbal sophistry, with a few apposite scriptures tossed in) – she might cause me to be 'born again', I rose to my feet and thrust my empty plate at her.

"Here! You can wash up. Meanwhile, I'll go take a walk up the beach and find some more wood to toss on the fire," I suggested impatiently.

Though I could see she was taken aback by my barely

suppressed anger, I turned and stormed off, trudging after some place well out of earshot where I would be at liberty to volubly curse both *her* God and *my* foolish candour. Besides, if I could keep that brazier roaring through the night then, who knows, the flames might indeed attract the attention of a passing ship – with luck, this one crewed by 'nice, friendly people'.

* * * * *

> *"Projected results from the Western Australia federal Senate election re-run suggest the Liberal Party has comfortably retained two seats, while Labor, the Greens and the PUP have one each. The Australian Electoral Commission has been sharply criticised over the debacle, having declared the previous contest void after almost fourteen-hundred votes went missing during a recount. However, a spokesman insisted that voters could be confident every effort had been made to ensure the veracity of the result this time around..."*

Same old, same old: life was carrying on as usual back in Oz – as indeed it was elsewhere in the world as the sun was going down on Day Twenty-Eight of us being castaway on the island. Listening in on the wind-up radio, neither had it gone unnoticed that the news story I had a vested interest in had been slipping further down the order of bulletins with each passing week.

> *"... A navy spokesman today confirmed that a thirteen-minute pulse detected by one of its sonar vessels could have been emitted by the underwater locator beacon fitted to the Airbus's 'black box' flight data recorder. With the battery life of the device thought unlikely to exceed thirty days, search teams are now racing to establish its precise location before worsening weather in the southern Indian Ocean forces them to abandon efforts to recover it.*
> *"Retrieval of the 'black box' should enable air*

*accident   investigators   to   piece   together   what
happened to the airliner during its final hours...* "

I shook my head and ground my teeth in despair. Whatever had emitted that strange underwater ping, it was not the plane that Rick Mackenzie had crashed into the sea thousands of kilometres further north. Meanwhile, the fire in the brazier was roaring away, but with both the horizon and the sky above it devoid of anything that might report the strange fiery glow emanating from this otherwise deserted island.

I glanced over to observe Preema was lying on her front inside her shelter, delving into that Bible again – chin propped in one hand while sucking on the thumb of the other. I sniffed icily: surely it was not possible to read its tiny print with only the dancing amber glow of the fire for illumination. Perhaps this demonstrative act was a sulk: a way of letting me know that she was unfazed by my frostiness. Perhaps, in her mind, I was now to be counted among those other 'wicked men' in her native India who had persecuted her father for preaching about Jesus.

To be sure, relations between us had become progressively more strained even before I'd confronted her the other evening. Though remaining superficially polite and deferential towards me, it was not difficult to detect the censure that lurked behind those gawky specs. For my part, I was becoming ever more irritated by little things she said or did that might once have amused me but now grated instead – and not just her propensity to seize upon any excuse to preach the Gospel at me.

I guess it was inevitable that things would turn out like this sooner or later. Maybe the tribulation of being thrown together so dramatically and intimately was giving way to the tension that came with being cooped together on little more than one square kilometre of sand and palm trees. Suddenly – and notwithstanding our fraught encounter with those pirates – being castaway was no longer the gripping, death-defying adventure it had once been and was beginning to feel more like the prison sentence it really was. Meanwhile, the very chores that assured our comfort and welfare – washing; gathering firewood; repairing stuff; finding things to cook and eat; even listening to that confounded radio each night –

only served to make it more so.

In the time I'd been rocking myself in the hammock and contemplating these things, I noticed Preema had laid aside that Bible and had curled up and drifted off to sleep. Perhaps our imprisonment was as hard on her as it was on me – maybe more so, involving as it did such a premature introduction to some of the less savoury aspects of adulthood.

"Mr Wez?" I heard her pipe up.

"Uh-uh," I acknowledged her perfunctorily.

"Are you still angry with me?" she ventured with a voice that was enchantingly probing in a way that only a child's can be; and yet also subtly conveying resolution in the event of rebuff.

"No, Preema. I'm not angry with you. And I'm sorry if I've made you think that I was."

"Mr Wez," she piped up again after a pregnant pause.

"Yes, Preema."

"Goodnight... And God bless."

The crafty little moo! You'd need a heart of stone not to smile.

"Goodnight, Preema... And God bless you too."

14

"I frequently sat down with thankfulness, and admir'd the hand of God's providence, which had spread my table in the wilderness. I learn'd to look more upon the bright side of my condition, and less upon the dark side, and to consider what I enjoy'd, rather than what I wanted; and this gave me sometimes such secret comforts that I cannot express them... All our discontents about what we want appear'd to me to spring from the want of thankfulness for what we have."

Robinson Crusoe

In the days that followed, I would opt to spend more time by myself, where Preema's more annoying little quirks wouldn't bug me. I'm sure she preferred it that way too. With a further stern admonition to watch out for deadly cone snails along the shore, each day I was content to let her venture from the camp on her own. So after morning chores, followed by an hour or so spent in 'class' (where I rather amateurishly attended to her schooling), I would then take myself off to the north side of the island, where the hunting and the fishing always seemed more profitable.

Congratulating myself that I was becoming ever more adept at surviving on this remote speck, I thought I might try my hand at clothes-making too. The garments we'd come ashore in were by now distinctly threadbare after near-constant wear followed by washing in the sea and drying on the line I'd strung between two palm trees. During that time (and because the ambient temperature – even at night – seldom dipped below the mid-twenties centigrade, rendering them both superfluous and uncomfortable), I'd decided to slice off the legs of my denim jeans. Having retained the discarded material, I'd pondered whether, by using coconut twine as thread, I might be able to recycle it to make a skirt for Preema (whose own leg-ins were looking similarly tattered).

Hence on my travels today I called by at the survival pod to see if it was feasible to similarly employ the blankets on the camp bed. Upon holding them aloft and examining them, I felt sufficiently confident of my novice dress-making skills to resolve to collect them on my return journey and to make kitting out the youngster in a new outfit my next big project.

Such 'projects' – whether using the tools I'd amassed and the materials to hand to make palm leaf sun hats, palm frond parasols, ironwood ladders, or coconut shell beakers – not only enhanced our ability to sit out our exile but passed the time too. It also kept the mind more productively engaged than on endlessly contemplating how on Earth we'd ever get out of here. I discovered too that it afforded me a healthy sense of self-reliance – as if to demonstrate to Preema that not every good thing we had was the gift of a benevolent God; but rather that we were doing what human beings had done for millennia: employing our dexterous hands and our highly-evolved brains to adapt to our environment and thrive.

Another joy of not having Preema about was that I was able to wander these pristine beaches in my birthday suit. In this respect, a further joy of inhabiting an island heaving with palm trees was that there was an abundance of the staple ingredient in natural coconut oil sunscreen. Leanne used to swear by it. Having used up the supply of sunblock from the survival pod, after trial-and-error experimenting with various methods of extracting it from the flesh of coconuts I could now confidently step out into the midday sun without fear of my arse being scorched.

Another thing I had determined to do was take some photographs of our island paradise – to be able to look back upon with fondness once we finally made it home. Surprised at how well the battery in my phone was holding its charge, I would switch it on periodically to snap images of our camp, the survival pod, the lagoon, the seabird colonies, as well as Babo the rescued booby bird chick and Clive the giant coconut crab (who from time to time could still be found loitering around Preema's toileting spot). Oh, and not forgetting the obligatory selfies! It was obvious too that no such electronic photo album would be complete without shots of the island's magnificent beaches. Today I was adding to the collection, marvelling that these wondrous white sands were home to nobody else on Earth except us.

Of course, there's something therapeutic about the sea that means, no matter how long you dwell beside it, you never tire of its ceaseless rhythm. Wading stealthily in the shallows while patiently scouting for a fish to spear, it was possible to further experience this sensation of being at one with nature – rather as I imagined our hunter-gatherer ancestors once had. Watched over by those wide blue skies and that mighty, thunderous ocean, one could all too readily perceive how twenty-first century man – in his quest to tame nature and to remove its inherent danger – had so sanitised his life that he'd bled it dry of the essential challenge that made it worth living.

It also explained why so many folks in the affluent West sought to replicate those absent primeval thrills by engaging in extreme sports and other high-risk pastimes. For what fulfilment was there to be had microwaving cellophane-wrapped edibles one has shopped for online when compared to the prize of patiently and skilfully trapping one's own prey to cook and eat? What joy was there to be derived from project-managing multi-million-pound engineering schemes when placed beside the achievement of hand-crafting simple, everyday items that transformed a beachside camp into a home-from-home? And likewise, when it came to something as elemental as the call of nature, how could crapping in an opulent bathroom that boasted gold-plated fittings, soft toilet tissue, and multi-channel television ever compare to the raw thrill, out here, of just spreading your legs, admiring the seabirds soaring overhead, and letting gravity do the rest? Oh, and swishing your arse in the sea afterwards?

Apropos this sensation of lost innocence regained brought to mind those unforgettable closing scenes from Nicholas Roeg's film *'Walkabout'*. As I did, I waxed lyrical to myself about whether – once safely back home in Anglo-Saxon suburbia – there would come a time when I too would fondly look back upon idyllic moments like these and pine that I might return to the island again.

* * * * *

Carried away by this blissful ambience of peace and wholeness, it was mid-afternoon by the time I'd ambled back to the camp with fish on a skewer, those blankets under my arm, and a warm glow in my soul. However, there was no sign of Preema.

Weary from my peregrinations in the sun, I sliced open a coconut to wet my pallet, thinking I'd rest for a while before taking a stroll down the beach to see if I could catch up with her. Before slinking into my hammock however, I first picked up the Bible from inside her shelter, where she'd left it. Lazily, I leafed through the opening page of *'The Epistle Of Paul The Apostle To The Romans'*, where the writer talked about 'this gospel' being *"the power of God unto salvation to everyone that believeth; to the Jew first, and also to the Greek. For therein is the righteousness of God revealed from faith to faith: as it is written: the just shall live by faith."* Elsewhere, this Paul geezer spoke of those who 'professing themselves wise' (though revealing themselves instead to be 'fools'), pursued *"uncleanness through the lusts of their own hearts, to dishonour their own bodies between themselves."*

I smirked. Wading through the stilted, seventeenth-century idioms, I could understand enough of 'The Apostle's' drift to suss out that he was most likely referring to me.

I snapped the book shut. Sliding it back inside Preema's shelter, I decided to forego my siesta and find out where she'd gotten to. Traipsing southwards along the beach to where that old Jap fighter lay half-buried in the sand, I wondered whether she might be playing make-believe aviators again. However, with no sign of her there, I pressed on around the headland.

As I did, a white shape caught my eye some distance out to sea. It was a yacht tacking through the waves, heading away from the island with its sails unfurled. Fearing the craft was by now too far away for anyone aboard to possibly spot me – much less catch me hailing them – even so I ran down to the water's edge and waved my hands above my head, hollering for all I was worth.

However, the craft carried on sailing further out of sight.

"Mr Wez! Mr Wez! Thank God you are here! Where have you been?" I turned to witness Preema emerging from the dunes, her sandals flicking up sand as she hurried down the beach to join me.

"More to the point, where have *you* been?" I cussed. "And did you not think to tell me there was a boat off the island?"

"I looked for you but could not find you. And anyway, you told me not to wave at strange ships," she hauled in a breath and reminded me, "so I hid from them. I have been hiding in those trees all afternoon while they were here."

"Here? What? You mean the people from that boat came ashore?" I exclaimed, my mouth dropping open.

"Yes, it dropped its anchor beyond the reef, where some of the people aboard jumped over the side – with masks on their faces and flippers on their feet and tanks strapped to their backs," she gesticulated excitedly.

"Meanwhile, the others came ashore and lit a fire and cooked some food," she pointed further up the beach to where a jumble of bottles lay scattered around the fire's extinguished remains. "Then the men and women who were swimming under the water came ashore to join them and eat the food they had cooked."

It sounded like the yacht had borne a party of divers here, almost certainly to explore the wreck of that old German warship that had long since broke apart on the reef and settled in shallow water a few hundred metres offshore. They may or may not have had official permission to land on the island, though from Preema's description of the party and the kind of activities they'd gotten up to I suspected it was the latter case.

"I thought they might be pirates too, Mr Wez – searching for hidden treasure," she exclaimed, still betraying a quaint, old-fashioned notion of how pirates made a living nowadays. "Therefore, I hid from them. However, after they had eaten the food and drunk lots of beer, some of them entered the forest to go to the toilet – just like that nasty pirate did that we hid from the other day.

"Then, later on, two of those people – a man and a woman – came into the forest again. The man led the woman to a spot near to where I was hiding. Then he started doing things to her – like what we saw the pirates do to that lady we buried. I thought he was going to kill her too, Mr Wez; because even though this woman didn't fight him she was making lots of strange noises while he was doing them – like he was hurting her. But when he'd finished doing those things they kissed and cuddled, and she looked very happy. And then they returned to the beach and got back into their boat with their friends and left the island."

I was flabbergasted. You just couldn't make this up!

"And you witnessed all this?" I shook my head appalled.

"Yes. I was very frightened, Mr Wez. I thought any moment those people would see me and be very angry. Did I do the right thing, Mr Wez? By hiding and not letting them know I was spying on them?" she pleaded.

"I'm pretty sure those people weren't pirates, Preema," I said, squeezing her shoulder. "They were most probably just young people visiting the island on their holidays."

"Oh, I see. So should I have told them about us?" she enquired dolefully, the penny having dropped.

She would be kept waiting for my reply. Wandering among the detritus of the tourists' abandoned barbie, I surveyed and kicked about small, but emblematic remains of a civilisation it seemed like an eternity that I'd left behind: bread rolls, salad, half-munched chicken drumsticks, beefsteaks, cigarettes, and bottled beer. Of the latter, I stooped to collect up one that looked like it had barely been touched.

It really did seem like forever since I'd last swigged an ice-cold beer (though this one had heated up in the sun in the time that had passed since its owner had discarded it). However, from the corner of my eye I spotted the captious glare of a brown-skinned moppet who was waiting to see if I would draw it to my lips. Instead, reluctantly, I made do with a sentimental sniff of the bottle's contents before pouring it into the sand in an act of self-denial masquerading as outrage.

"The inconsiderate so-and-sos! They might at least have taken their litter home with them," I scowled. "No wonder some parts of this beach look like a tip."

Otherwise, I stretched out an arm to draw her to my side as we walked back to the camp. Though it galled, I joked to the youngster that I appeared to have been hoisted on the petard of my own well-meaning instruction to her – for as well as Preema having forfeited more of her threadbare innocence, a priceless opportunity to alert the world to our plight had also been missed.

* * * * *

By the third week of April, deteriorating weather in the southern Indian Ocean had put paid to the last frantic efforts to locate the remains of the huge airliner. Aviation experts acknowledged that by now – over six weeks having passed since the plane went missing – any debris from it would have become water-logged and sunk. In addition, with the battery expired on the flight's 'black box' flight data recorder all hope of retrieving it had been lost too. The search operation – which had cost millions of dollars, combed countless square kilometres of sub-Antarctic seas, and involved ships and planes from several nations – had drawn a blank and was to be dramatically scaled down. The disappearance of that fateful flight – which had claimed the lives of four hundred passengers and crew of many different nationalities – remained a mystery.

Neither was there any hint that aviation investigators were prepared to entertain the possibility that the plane might have crashed elsewhere, relegating such talk alongside the inevitable conspiracy theories that were being bandied about. Some of the more outlandish of these included the plane having been shot down (accidentally or otherwise) by any one of the rival nations of South-East Asia; that it had been electronically hijacked by the Russians in some bizarre game of brinkmanship with the West and then flown to a remote airfield in Central Asia; or even that, having been physically hijacked by Islamic terrorists, it had been shot down by the US military, who feared it was being employed for a suicide attack on their huge Indian Ocean base at Diego Garcia. Either way, it was rumoured, the precise circumstances of its disappearance might never be revealed.

It was depressing news – compounded by the fact that Preema and I would glimpse no further sightings of boats or planes in the weeks that followed. Neither did the ranger seem in any hurry to return and check up on his patch. Twenty-eight years Robinson Crusoe had been a castaway; and while I was confident we wouldn't have to wait anywhere near as long to be rescued, I can't deny there weren't times when I feared boredom, despair, disaster, or the travails of getting on each other's nerves, would finally get the better of us.

However, such introspection would soon be eclipsed by more ominous news which I began to pick-up on the wind-up radio. Just when it looked like our time on the island might pass without encountering one, the Bureau of Meteorology in Melbourne announced that a weather front was massing in the eastern Indian Ocean – which it soon upgraded to the category of a tropical storm. In the days that followed the barometer plummeted precipitously and the storm was upgraded still further. It now had a name too: Cyclone Kiona was on its way and heading straight for us.

15

*"Then I cry'd out, 'Lord, be my help, for I am in
great distress'. This was the first prayer, if I may call
it so, that I had made for many years."*

Robinson Crusoe

Like a harbinger of an impending apocalypse, the first thing we
noticed was an increase in the ambient humidity. Soon enough,
the sun had disappeared behind an ever-darkening mass of cloud.
The cyclone would soon be upon us – even as I hoped that, being
unpredictable things, it might yet veer away from the island.

Otherwise, I decided that the best option for riding it out would
be to decamp to the survival pod. Robustly-constructed from
weather-proof fibre-glass and well-tethered with steel guy cables,
it was also located in as sheltered a spot as one was likely to find.
To this end, all morning Preema and I had been shuttling back
and forth to it, carrying with us our most valuable items –
including the fresh water we'd amassed in as many receptacles as
we'd been able to lay our hands on. We paused only to watch in
awe and dread as an onshore swell began to drive waves almost
up to the tree line of the beach. Indeed, those thunderous breakers
reminded me all too well that, with nowhere on the island rising
to more than a few metres above sea level, the inevitable storm
surge would pose as big a threat as the wind speeds that were
predicted to exceed two hundred kilometres-an-hour.

As the hours passed, to that roughening sea and strengthening
wind would be added a hard, driving rain. Having emptied the
camp of the things we needed, I decided the time had come to
hunker down in the pod for as long as it took for Cyclone Kiona
to do its worst. It was going to be a very long, anxious night.

* * * * *

"Come on! It looks like it's arrived!" I cried out.

Within minutes what had been a strong gale had accelerated into a tempest of such ferocity that even standing up was a challenge, much less walking. I turned to chivvy Preema, who was plainly struggling to do just that. Just as I was about to take her hand and assist her, a gust lifted her bodily off her feet and dumped her in the sand a few metres away. Attempting to scramble onto all fours, her first instinct was to chase after the Rubik's cube she'd been clutching in her hand (and which was now hurtling away down the beach).

"Leave it!" I bawled, grabbing her arm and hauling her away.

Though she mounted a token protest, glancing back over her shoulder she realised that it was tumbling away too fast to possibly catch up with. Meanwhile, all around us, tall palms were being pressed almost horizontal and their branches torn away.

"I'm scared!" she squealed to make herself heard above the din of howling wind and sheeting rain.

Though it had been a close call, we arrived at last at our spherical bolt-hole in the forest. Grasping the handle to the pod, I hauled open the door and urged the terrified lass inside. Shutting it behind me immediately eliminated the wind and reduced its deafening roar to a subdued moan, permitting us to sweep wet hair from our faces and catch our breaths.

"How long do you think we will have to stay in here, Mr Wez?" said Preema, resting on the edge of a camp bed that was now denuded of blankets (and which left me wondering whether I'd been too hasty cutting them up).

"The weather people said the cyclone is quite slow-moving," I replied, winding up the radio and trying to get a signal in the face of both the abysmal atmospherics and the 'Faraday cage' effect of the pokey little pod. Having scanned back and forth across the airwaves in vain, I gave up and put it away.

"I'm guessing we might be here for a while. Still, not to worry: we've got food, we've got water, we've got shelter – and we've got each other. Oh, and we've got Babo!" I consoled her, brushing a hand over one of her wet cheeks to direct her gaze at the bird chirruping from beneath the bed. "You've also got a change of clothing," I added, reaching up the bed and unfolding my first-ever attempt at dress-making.

I turned away as Preema stripped out of her soggy tangerine top and peeled off her well-worn leg-ins, slipping her head inside the dress I'd made for her and hurrying it past her waist. As on other such occasions, this gracious act of chivalry on my part was one of the more comically heroic charms of having to share one's island with a bashful young lady.

"Yeah, well. Prada it most definitely isn't," I conceded as she twirled about in the frumpy concoction. I wondered what her elegant and accoutred namesake who'd flown in Business Class would have made of it.

"It is very smart, Mr Wez. But it is a bit scratchy," she qualified her praise, shuffling to get comfortable in it. "But what are *you* going to wear?" she then posed the obvious question.

I feigned to glance about before returning my gaze to her.

"I don't know. I guess these things will just have to dry on my person," I replied resignedly. However, I was already shivering. I rubbed my upper arms in a gesture of bravado – even as I sensed it was going to be a very uncomfortable night too.

"I can read you a story if you like," Preema then volunteered, ducking under the bed to retrieve her Gideon Bible (one item she'd made sure to gather up on our first shuttle trip between the camp and the pod).

I felt my nostrils dilate with equal resignation, declining to sit down on the bed beside her in my ringing wet shorts. Instead, I drew up the ranger's folding chair and wound up the torch so that she could make out the print in the gloom. Besides – and in the interests of keeping morale up – how else were we going to pass the next twenty-four hours in the absence of either radio reception or Preema's beloved Rubik's cube? After stealing an anxious glance at me, she opened the book out and found the verses she was looking for. Bodging her glasses up her nose, she began reciting them in earnest (and in the same lyrical, childlike prose that had no doubt helped her win first prize in Sunday school).

"And the same day, when the evening was come, He saith unto them, 'Let us pass over unto the other side'. And when they had sent away the..."

"Mul-ti-tude," I proffered upon being directed to the word she was struggling with, pedagogically running a finger across each syllable for her instruction.

"... Multitude, they took Him even as He was in the ship. And there were also with Him other little ships. And there arose a great storm of wind, and the waves beat into the ship, so that it was now full. And He was in the hinder part of the ship..."

The joys of the Authorised King James translation! She paused and looked up at me expectantly again.

"That's the stern – the back end of the boat," I enlightened her.

"... Asleep on a pillow: and they awake Him, and say unto Him, 'Master, carest thou not that we perish'? And He arose, and rebuked the wind, and said unto the sea, 'Peace, be still'. And the wind ceased, and there was a great calm. And He said unto them, 'Why are ye so fearful? How is it that ye have no faith'? And they feared..."

"Ex-cee-ding-ly," I obliged again. "That means: greatly."

"Exceedingly, and said one to another, 'What manner of man is this, that even the wind and the sea obey him'?"

It was a well-known, if improbable tale: Jesus snatching forty winks while all around Him a tempest was raging (which, if it was anything like the one that was at that moment buffeting the pod, really was improbable!). His terrified disciples are then amazed, when, upon being prodded, He utters three perfunctory words and the sea is calm again. However, if recounting this passage from Matthew's Gospel helped calm the jitters of a frightened little girl, where was the harm? Meanwhile, I wasn't the only one to glance up with a start when the crack of an adjacent tree being snapped was promptly followed by the almighty thud of its trunk crashing to the ground (the tremor from which transferred through the floor of the pod – causing Babo to flutter about with anxiety).

"Blimey! That was close," I interjected, rising to my feet to peer through the grimy port hole. However, all was darkness outside.

From the juddering of the pod and the singing of its guy cables I reasoned the cyclone was unleashing its full fury upon us. I just hoped those cables held. I fretted too that the surrounding trees – though nowhere near as tall and hefty as those beachfront palms – could quite easily smash a hole in the pod (and in our skulls with it!) if their creaking and breaking boughs were flung at it with enough force. Wake up, Jesus – wherever you are, I tittered to myself uneasily.

"Mr Wez," Preema nervously petitioned my shadow as it paced about inside the darkened pod, "What do *you* do when you're frightened."

"Oh, I don't know," I mumbled with the impatience of one who had weightier things on his mind just then.

"I sing when I'm frightened," she proffered. "Do you mind if I sing now?"

"If you must," I grunted again, still straining to observe the chaos that was enveloping the forest outside.

"*Jesus loves me this I know, for the Bible tells me so,*" she demonstrated like so (and in the same sweet, angelic voice with which I'd caught her tootling spiritual ditties to herself on previous occasions), "*Little ones to Him belong, they are weak, but He is strong... Yes, Jesus loves me... Yes, Jesus loves me... Yes, Jesus loves me... The Bible tells me so.*"

If ever there was a moment when the absurdity of where I was and the words I was being accosted with finally began to make some kind of sense this was it. For even as Cyclone Kiona was rattling the pod for all it was worth – and as the child continued to nervously warble that chorus – I swallowed hard and had that same terrible sense of imminent mortality that I'd experienced when the airliner I'd been aboard had plunged into the sea; and that I'd been similarly overcome with later on that day when that huge great shark had circled menacingly.

Just then, a loud zinging noise preceded the whipping and puncturing of the pod's fibre-glass sides: one of those guy cables had snapped. Babo squawked! Preema screamed, jumped up, and instinctively launched herself at my shadow, finding and burying herself in my arms! Instinctively too, I clutched her tight.

"Oh, God! Oh, God!" I found myself imploring the deity who I couldn't see, but whose mercy some similarly primeval instinct urged me to seek out – wherever He was.

"We're going to die, Mr Wez! We're going to meet Jesus!" Preema sobbed, clinging to me as the soughing wind forced its draught through the tear in the pod.

Any second now I fully expected the remaining cables to snap as well. If that happened, then – like that bright-coloured cube that had been seized from Preema's grasp – there would be nothing to prevent the pod (and us with it) from tumbling to the beach to be consumed by those mountainous seas.

"No, we're not," I hushed her, directing her to sit down beside me on the bed. However, my assurance was at stark variance with what I was telling myself at that dreadful moment. Perhaps this really was the end.

What a way to die, I found myself pondering again. The only consolation was that, this time, at least I wouldn't die alone. However, it was uncanny – as if yet again I'd felt compelled to put aside all those haughty pronouncements I'd made about self-reliance and embrace a better way; a way of trust and faith in this incarnate 'Son of God' who Preema was calling upon (and who alone, I prayed, could bid the storm cease).

"*Jesus loves me this I know, for the Bible tells me so,*" she was meanwhile warbling tearfully, "*Little ones to Him belong, they are weak, but He is strong...*"

* * * * *

Jesus might have been relaxed about storms because He had power over them; however, it was sheer nervous exhaustion that eventually drove Preema to lie down in the darkness on that single bed, snuffling and sucking her thumb before finally falling asleep. Meanwhile, sitting on the floor beside her while resting my head upon the arm I'd propped upon it, with my other hand I trailed my fingers through her damp hair, still quietly petitioning that God in His mercy would permit me to see my own daughter again. In time, the winds outside eased and I too could slumber.

* * * * *

"You stupid, stupid child!" I bawled with a start – jolted from a nightmare I'd been having about the time I'd torn into Emily over some trivial mistake she'd made.

Troubled upon recalling my terrifying loss of self-control, I rubbed the sleep from my eyes and was overcome by the peacefulness all around me. The wind had died. It was light outside. What's more, Preema was no longer asleep beside me; and the source of that glinting daylight was the door to the pod, which lay open.

Lifting myself to my feet, I poked my head through the portal to survey the scene of utter devastation all around – even as the morning sun was bizarrely shining down through a patch of bright blue sky. And though the remaining guy cables had thankfully held, it was as if every single tree had been either uprooted, snapped, or stripped bare of branches. At first dumbstruck by the power of nature to wreak such havoc, it was with gathering unease that I stepped outside, quickening the pace and racing through the forest.

"Preema…! Preema…!" I cried, vaulting over debris as I went.

There was no sign of her.

Finally, I arrived on a deserted beach upon which those mountainous breakers were still billowing. Anxiously, I glanced up and down it before eventually spotting her some distance away, staring up in wonder at that blinding sun. I called out again while hurrying over to join her.

"Look, Mr Wez. Jesus has heard our prayers. He has made the wind stop. And now He is making the clouds go away so that the sun can shine again," she insisted, cupping a delicate little hand to her eyes and jauntily pointing up to it with the other.

I confess that, for a moment, I too was utterly transfixed by its welcome brilliance – as well as by the swirling tunnel of cloud that, stretching up tens of thousands of feet almost to Heaven itself, was truly breathtaking to behold. Meanwhile, here we were like the Israelites in the Old Testament – tiny specks of humanity gazing up in awe at this truly Biblical demonstration of an omnipotent God reasserting His power and dominion over nature.

However, I was not so in awe that I couldn't discern that the breeze was picking up; nor that this phalanx of swirling cloud was edging ever closer to us.

"This isn't the answer to prayer, Preema," I insisted. "We're in what's known as the 'eye' of the cyclone – the small area of calm in the centre of its mass. And that there is its wall – the deadliest part of any tropical storm," I trembled, shaking my head in horror and subconsciously reaching across to grab her arm. "Come on, we've gotta' get back to the pod. Now!"

The wind was already gusting again as we raced back up the beach. Furthermore, with the treescape kaleidoscopically jumbled up by Cyclone Kiona's devastating power, it was almost impossible to make out where the path was that led back to the pod. In vain, I dragged Preema along the remains of a forest trail, clambering over broken trees along the way only to realise it led nowhere. All the time the wind was strengthening, the skies were darkening, and the sun had once more disappeared.

"Mr Wez, you're hurting me!" Preema squealed as, like a ragdoll dragged along behind me, I hurried her this way and that. Then I felt the tug on my arm as her hand was wrenched from my grasp. I turned to discover that she'd tripped over debris and had landed heavily.

"You stupid, stupid child!" I cursed above the howling gale.

I reached down to seize her arm again. However, she screamed in agony and clutched it to her side, pushing me away with her good arm. Realising what I'd done, I bent down and insistently scooped the distraught child into my arms, lifting her and running with her – though I had not a clue where I was running to. With each jolt of movement, she squealed and sobbed.

Then – the real miracle of that day – the emerald green shell of the survival pod presented itself at last. Stepping over the last few fallen trees as the screaming winds once more made pressing forward virtually impossible, I yanked open the door and deposited her upon the bed inside.

With the relative tranquillity afforded by being sealed inside our sanctuary again, I could observe more fully that, whatever injury Preema had sustained during that fall, she was in considerable pain. Though she continued to fight my attempts to release her grip on her lower left forearm, I eventually coaxed her to let me examine it. It didn't look good. The purple coloration of bruising was already advancing up it from just above her wrist. What's more, I suspected the glow I felt emanating from her perspiring forehead was not solely attributable to exhaustion from running through the forest. The little girl was in shock.

"I'm sorry, Mr Wez. I didn't mean to be a stupid child," she panted tearfully.

"Shhh! I'm sorry too, Preema. It was very wrong of me to call you that," I begged, removing her glasses and nursing her head against my chest.

For the first time during the storm, the screaming wind and the rain hammering against the pod became of little import to me – even as I had speculated whether Hell itself could unleash fury as violent of the wall of the cyclone that was now passing over us. I was resigned that it would do to us what it willed; and that if those guy cables did finally fail, then strangely – and for the first time too – I felt ready to face the God to whom I even so made another heartfelt plea to keep us safe.

This strange, imputed sensation of calm enabled me to concentrate on tending to Preema's arm. I asked if she could wiggle her fingers; to which, she replied, she could – though not very well and it hurt to do so. There was also a noticeable bowing of her forearm that suggested a break had indeed occurred.

Leaving her on the bed for a moment, I stretched across the floor to nudge Babo out of the way and locate the first-aid kit that we'd brought back from the camp. Opening the box, among the jumble of plasters, bandages and what-nots I located the small pamphlet that gave advice for treating the most common emergencies. Thumbing past pages on what to do in the event of concussion or snake bites, I scanned down the instructions about broken limbs.

It was as I'd feared. Though mercifully she hadn't sustained an open break, she'd almost certainly sustained either a partial or a complete fracture. All the tell-tale signs were present: the bruising; the swelling; the wooziness; the hot, throbbing brow – even as the rest of Preema's body felt cold to the touch. And though the bone was not showing through the skin, the possibility of the break becoming infected could not be ruled out.

It was the scenario I'd been dreading most: one of us sustaining a serious, life-threatening injury – and with no hope of accessing professional medical care.

"Will I be alright, Mr Wez? My arm is still hurting," she looked over at me and pleaded.

"I think so, Preema," I said, glancing up from the manual. "But it looks like you've broken your arm."

"Will you be able to mend it for me?" she snuffled pitifully.

I was cut to the quick by an overwhelming sense of my own impotency. What could I say? And what could I possibly do? I was not a doctor; and in the absence of an X-ray machine I had absolutely no way of knowing what was going on beneath my patient's glowing bruise. All I possessed was a flimsy first-aid pamphlet and faltering confidence in my ability to carry out its elementary instructions. Oh God, I called up in my helplessness. Oh God, please help me.

Concealing my own tearfulness from her, I wound up the ranger's torch and feigned to further study the manual, demonstratively flicking the pages. Behind me, I heard Preema cry out in pain as another spasm coursed through her arm.

'Administer pain relief as necessary', the pamphlet advised. However, the painkillers I'd kept stored in the pod had all been pilfered by the pirates. All I had to hand to offer any kind of relief were a few aspirins that had been kept in the first-aid box. In the glow of the torch, I strained to read the label on the carton: 'Do NOT administer aspirins to children under twelve unless *prescribed by your doctor'*, it cautioned. Oh God, please help me, I glanced up to Heaven again.

The pamphlet meanwhile confirmed something I already knew: that to avoid deformity, it was vital that the bone be reset at the earliest opportunity. Therefore, I would have to find some means of holding her arm rigid. But there was nothing in the pod from which to fashion a splint. A tree branch or two would suffice if I could use those bandages to strap them to her swollen limb. But how to get hold of branches in the middle of a raging cyclone – even though at that moment, perversely (and as if in mockery of me), dozens of them were bouncing off the carapace of the pod as Cyclone Kiona whipped them from the trees?

"Mr Wez," I heard her whimper again.

Switching off the torch, I returned to comfort her.

"Shhh! I'll make sure you get better," I spoke in soft, lachrymose words as I nursed and kissed her perspiring brow.

A weary, resigned smile flitted across her face. Perhaps she knew I was struggling to believe my own words.

"I know I am safe with you, Mr Wez. You have always taken care of me. And I know Jesus will help you to take care of me again – and show you how to make my poorly arm better."

16

*"Though I could not say I thank'd God for being
there, yet I sincerely gave thanks to God for opening
my eyes, by whatever afflicting providences, to see
the former condition of my life, and to mourn for my
wickedness and repent."*

Robinson Crusoe

If the initial devastation that Cyclone Kiona had wreaked was sobering, the havoc I would survey upon re-emerging from the survival pod was even worse. The forest had been decimated, with uprooted trees and snapped trunks wherever one turned. The storm surge too had completely remodelled the beach, removing the sand escarpment along the western side of the island and exposing the roots of those trees along its edge that the ferocious winds hadn't already felled.

The surge and the winds had also obliterated our camp, smashing the table and stools, ripping apart the shelters, and burying the clearance in which they'd sat in a layer of sand and shredded foliage. Meanwhile – and as if to mock any feelings of control I felt I'd reasserted over my life – my beloved hammock had been torn from its tethers and shredded.

Rebuilding the encampment would be a mammoth task – even were I able to call upon Preema to assist me. However, though I'd managed to settle her – enabling me to venture from the pod and see what could be retrieved of our belongings – neither the pain nor the swelling had abated. There was no way she would be able to perform even straightforward tasks unless I could fix her arm. Until I did, there would be no choice for us but to carry on sharing that claustrophobic little pod – getting by on our drastically reduced rations. It brought home – if ever I needed reminding – that, for all the idyllic moments that imprisonment here had afforded us, the island remained a bleak and lonely place where nature and the elements were ever ready to spring nasty surprises; a place where no man should ever be so smug or complacent to think his destiny is entirely in his own hands.

* * * * *

As well as searching for something to catch, kill, and eat, it was the task of fixing that arm that had impelled me to venture out, both to collect up suitable pieces of timber to bind it up and to find some means of relieving the wracking pain Preema was in. Tramping the shores of the lagoon, I stumbled upon just what I was looking for: a perfect specimen of the genus *Argusia argentea* – otherwise known as the Octopus bush.

Maybe it was because it was short and squat that this diminutive and peculiar-looking tree had survived the worst ravages of the cyclone. Thank God it had. The medicinal properties of its green, spiralling flowers with their white-tipped stigmas (resembling the ligulas of an octopus – hence the name) – might just hold the key to ameliorating the poor girl's discomfort. Taking a handful of them, I savoured their faint perfume before placing them into my bag.

Of course, I was only too aware that I ought really to perform the 'tongue test' first – and on myself at that, just to be absolutely sure. However, in view of the urgency of stabilising her condition, I would just have to forego that formality, trusting instead that the information I'd gleaned from that wildlife book was correct. Beyond that, it would be down to my judgement about the correct dosage to administer – assisted by nothing more than faith that it would work.

Watched over by clear blue skies in which a benign sun was once more shining, I glanced up to Heaven to exercise that faith: for what I was about to do would either cure the child or kill her.

* * * * *

"... Although Cyclone Kiona has caused extensive damage on Pulu Pajang, thankfully no fatalities

occurred. The Bureau of Meteorology attributes this to the eye of the category-five storm veering north of the Cocos Islands shortly before it struck.

"Meanwhile, in other news, at a press conference today Prime Minister Tony Abbott announced that the huge search operation for the Airbus A380 that went missing on March 7th has officially ended. During the last six weeks fifteen ships and thirty aircraft from seven countries have combed almost five million square kilometres of the southern Indian Ocean.

"Mr Abbott confirmed that, while Australian naval forces will be withdrawn, commercial survey ships will continue to scan the seabed with sophisticated sonar devices for as long as weather in the area permits, insisting that, 'We owe it to the families and we owe it to the world to do whatever we reasonably can to get to the bottom of this mystery. We won't let them down'."

* * * * *

"What are you going to do with those sticks, Mr Wez?"

I guessed it was an encouraging sign that my little companion had recovered at least some of her loquacity (as well as her penchant for firing off never-ending streams of questions). Perhaps the rosmarinic acid in those flowers I'd pestled for her to swallow was working after all.

"I'm going to strap them to your poorly arm so that the break in the bone will heal and you can use it again."

I hoped. It was certainly going to be a daunting task. In the first instance I had to coax the wary child to offer me that bruised limb, which she was still clutching protectively. However, having brushed up on the procedure and talked her through it by means of the illustrations in the first-aid pamphlet, she relented. Grimacing in trepidation, she allowed me to open the arm out. Thereupon, I presented her with another, smaller piece of wood. As instructed – and like a heroic scene from a war movie – she opened her mouth so that I could insert it between her teeth to bite upon, for not even the pain-killing properties of the Octopus bush were going to wholly assuage the next few minutes of agony. With everything now in place, I was ready to commence the most invidious task of all: resetting the broken bone.

To say I was winging it was an understatement. I'd never attempted anything like this before, had no training in the procedure, and was only too aware that if I messed it up I risked complicating her injury even further. Accompanied by another silent prayer, I inched my fingers into place and pressed hard. Upon which, Preema unleashed a full-on shriek that was muffled only by that stick she now sank her molars into.

"It's coming... It's coming..." I spoke encouragement to her.

Finally, I managed to knead the limb so that it looked more or less straight. Taking the larger bits of timber that I'd chopped to size and laying them against her wounded forearm, I gestured for her to employ her free hand to hold them in place while I draped the bandages around them. Satisfied the arm was trussed up tightly – though not so tight that it would cut off the circulation of blood – I reached up to remove the bit from her mouth and mop her clammy brow with an off-cut from the bed linen.

"There. Better?"

She gulped and nodded, seeking to put on a brave face.

"Now lie down and relax and try not to move it. It may take a few weeks for your arm to heal fully. But the good news is the bones of children are so much suppler than those of adults. So it should heal without any complications."

Yeah, Smith, keep telling yourself that! I fired off a smile in the hope she wouldn't see that I was as hopeful about this hasty, impromptu repair as she was. It reinforced my conviction that the only way of ultimately assuring the little girl's welfare was to get her off this island. Maybe the ranger would advance the date of his return to check on how the island's wildlife had fared at the hands of Cyclone Kiona.

* * * * *

"Leave it!" I bawled, grasping her arm and hauling her away. Though she mounted a token protest, glancing back over her shoulder she realised that it was tumbling away too fast to possibly catch up with.

"Daddy, you're hurting me!" Emily squealed as, like a ragdoll dragged along behind me, I hurried her back to the car park. Then I felt the tug on my arm as her hand was wrenched from my grasp. I turned to discover that she'd tripped over her flip-flops and had landed heavily on the tarmac.

"You stupid, stupid child!" I cursed while all around me startled beachgoers gazed on in dismay. I reached down to seize her arm again.

However, she screamed in agony and clutched it to her side, loosening her grip to push me away with her good arm. Realising what I'd done, I bent down and insistently scooped the distraught child into my arms, lifting her and running with her to the first-aid station. With each jolt of movement, she squealed and sobbed.

"I'm sorry, Daddy. I didn't mean to be a stupid child," she panted as the lifeguard bade me lay her down on the table. As I did I glanced up and spied Leanne's accusing glare.

"Shhh! I'm sorry too, Emily. It was very wrong of me to call you that," I begged her forgiveness, nursing her head to mine.

* * * * *

The nightmare woke me with a loud, disconcerting start. So loud that in the half-light I spotted Preema attempting to prop herself up on the bed to see what the commotion was. She clutched at her trussed-up arm the instant that she did.

Rising from the floor of the pod, where I'd been slumbering, I hushed her and pressed her supine again, checking that the splint was still in place. It was vital that she avoid applying sudden force upon that arm. What's more, it was still hurting, leaving me to agonise whether I dare up the dose of that Octopus bush pestle. Brushing a hand through her hair to hurry her back to sleep, I was eventually able to settle back down in the spot on the floor where I'd been sat. Babo waddled back up to nestle down alongside me.

You stupid, stupid child: over and over those words kept resounding in my head as I rested it wearily against the side of the pod and trailed a hand through the bird's feathers. And all because, having dawdled on the walk back from the beach (and ignored my instruction to both hurry up and keep a grip on it), Emily had dropped her beach ball, only to see it promptly lifted by a gust and sent hurtling from her grasp. My response had been to abandon all self-control, bawling at the broken-hearted four-year-old and angrily dragging her back to the car.

Looking back with chastened hindsight, it was yet one more incident that had sealed a reputation on my part for impatience and irascibility – of the kind that all-too-frequently manifested itself in a vile, explosive temper. You see, it was not just my daughter's innocent *faux-pas* that had occasioned that rebuke: in the process, she'd interrupted me answering an important phone call too; which, in turn, had prompted her aggrieved mother to question why I felt the need to be taking business calls when we were supposed to be on holiday. Her pertinent observation that day had earned her a profane, expletive-laden tongue-lashing too – one more milestone on the road to Leanne realising that she could no longer tolerate living with me.

'For what profits a man if he gains the whole world but loses his own soul?' If there was one thing that being marooned on this island had afforded me, it was having copious amounts of time on my hands to ponder over forty years of corners turned, roads taken, and mistakes made. The more I recounted them the more I'd come to mourn the more regrettable ones I'd turned, taken or blundered into. Of course, on the surface my life had proved an exhilarating success story. However, behind the scenes I'd forfeited the things that, I now realise, mattered far more; things that worldly success can't always buy.

Above all, being a castaway had left me with a deeply troubling awareness of my many shortcomings as a human being (and especially as a husband and a father); and that there was nowhere left for me to run and hide from them – literally or metaphorically. Furthermore, the longer I'd been forced to take time out in involuntary introspection the more I'd found myself arraigned by feelings of unworthiness because of them. It was a disturbing emotion that I'd never experienced before. Prior to my fateful exile, I'd prided myself on being one of those guys who made his own luck. It had rendered me serially intolerant of lesser mortals – whether members of my family or people I worked with – for whom luck did not always smile so benignly. Meanwhile, if misfortune did knock on my door (for example, in the shape of a messy separation and divorce), I would pick myself up, dust myself down, and get on with life, assuring myself that – by making a bit more luck – the hurt or disappointment I felt need only be transient.

Yet look at me now – at my wit's end, reduced to tearfully praying to a deity I couldn't see over the fate of a little girl who'd completely up-ended all those proud assumptions. A little girl who, it felt, had been parachuted into my life not only to confront me with my shortcomings – my tenuous relationship with my daughter of the same age included – but perhaps to point out a means by which I might also atone for them. It almost certainly explained why – notwithstanding a desire to demonstrate simple human compassion towards that little girl, who, for all her quirks, I'd grown immensely fond of – fixing that broken arm of hers had become a consuming obsession: a vicarious act of atonement for other things, if you like.

* * * * *

Over the days that followed, the calenture and the swelling began to subside and Preema's arm appeared to be on the mend. By the following week she was feeling chipper enough to emerge from the pod herself, her arm strapped in the splint and borne in the sling I'd made for it from offcuts of those sliced-up blankets.

Although two weeks had passed since the cyclone and still there was no sign of the ranger returning, on the anniversary of our second month marooned on the island there would be another brief, early morning overflight by an RAAF reconnaissance plane. Though the din of its approach roused me from my slumber I emerged from the pod too late to do other than wave impotently at it as it sped away. What's more, with our camp flattened and the storm surge having obscured those rocks on the beach with which we'd spelt out our predicament, I doubted its crew would perceive anything was amiss. To the authorities in Canberra this place remained a distant, uninhabited outpost – albeit one upon which nature was busy recovering from a devastating weather event.

Fed up with dossing down with Babo on the floor of the pod, I decided I would rebuild our encampment. As well as providing a greater measure of comfort in the sticky tropical heat, it would also keep me occupied and assuage the frustration I felt that yet another opportunity for rescue had eluded us. Would we ever get off this wretched island!

Rebuilding the camp helped keep Preema occupied too. Not physically, for though that arm was healing (and she could wiggle her fingers without it hurting) it was too early in the process for her to do much more than sit and observe me at work. Meanwhile, with that chirpy demeanour and cheeky smile having returned, I took comfort in the knowledge that she was most definitely 'on the mend'. As if to remove all doubt, she was once again assailing me with questions and observations.

17

*"How frequently, in the course of our lives, the evil
which in it self we seek most to shun, and which
when we are fallen into it is the most dreadful to us,
is oftentimes the very means by which we can be
rais'd again from the affliction we are fallen into."*

Robinson Crusoe

"If you're right – and there is no God, Mr Wez – then it doesn't matter if you don't believe in Him. But if *I'm* right – and there really is a God in Heaven – then because I believe in Him I will go there. But you will go to Hell instead because you don't."

My ears were being chewed again. However, after eight weeks of planting seeds in the fertile furrows of my mind Preema's preaching was nowadays less likely to draw my ire (not that I was enamoured with her blithe contention that I was destined for damnation!). Indeed, posing this classical dilemma was just the latest instalment in the eight-year-old's cunning, yet innocuous campaign to disabuse me of my lingering atheism.

"They call what you've just said Pascal's Wager," I noted, working out my irritation by hammering the planks of 'Sleeping Shelter Mark III' into place using the rusty nails I'd salvaged (and which Preema – squatting on her haunches beside me – was holding forth with her good hand for me to one-by-one take from her as I progressed along the shelter's resurrected frame).

"Who is Mr Pascal? And what is a wager?"

"Blaise Pascal was a French philosopher. A philosopher is someone who thinks a lot about life," I said, considering it wise to pre-empt the inevitable rejoinder, "And a wager is a bet – a gamble upon the outcome of something. If there is no God then, yes, why worry about Him? However, if, conversely, *you're* right;

then, having gambled by not believing in Him, I guess I might be in big trouble!

"Of course, your statement kind of assumes that God isn't smart enough to suss out whether a person genuinely believes in Him; or whether they're just a tyre kicker – hedging their bets to err on the safe side."

"A tyre kicker?"

"It's an Aussie term for someone who merely goes through the motions of showing an interest in something. As in a man who examines the tyres of a car he has no intention of buying. In the same way some people go through the motions of being religious without ever thinking seriously about spiritual things. Often they do so just to impress other people."

"Sadly, you are right, Mr Wez. My father used to tell me that many people pretend to be Christians – and even pray and go to church. But they don't really love Jesus and often do bad things. But I love Him. And I trust Him too," she was most insistent. "Or at least I try to. But then I know sometimes I do bad things too," she confessed.

I glanced up from hammering a nail, observing that her admission was accompanied by a dolefulness that I swore was defying me to pinpoint anything this gentle little girl could possibly have done that could even begin to compare with the magnitude of my own manifest failings.

"But how can you love a God who you can't see? And place your trust in Him too?" I fired back, resuming the task in hand.

Thinking I'd put my prepubescent interlocutor on the spot, I looked up again as she drew in her mouth pensively to ponder my question in earnest.

"But we do not always need to see things to believe that they exist, Mr Wez," she eventually replied. "I believe America exists – even though I have never been there and haven't seen it."

"Ah, but that's different," I reasoned. "You can believe that America exists because you can talk to Americans who tell you it does. And you can read about the place in books and newspapers and see it on television. And I bet you're going to tell me your father has preached there too!"

"Yes, he has. Lots of times," she said, loftily skating over my sarcasm. "But we can also read about Jesus in a book too," she then countered. "In the Bible there are many stories of people who talked to Jesus; and saw Him do miracles. People also saw Him die on the Cross; and talked to Him some more when He rose from the dead again. If television had been invented when Jesus had walked on the Earth then I'm sure we would have seen all these things on the news too."

This kid was not going to give up. But then, having foolishly risen to the bait, neither was I.

"But the Bible is a book written by men," I said. "Lots of men, in fact – some of whose stories contradict each other."

"No, Mr Wez. My father said the Bible is a book written by God. The men just wrote down the words that God told them."

I greeted her fanciful claim with the wriest of incredulous smirks. However, she had an answer for that too.

"My father told me that we know the stories in the Bible are true because – unlike other stories – the men who told them didn't hide the bad things that *they* did; but talked honestly about them; and about how God forgave them their sins."

Perhaps she could sense I still needed convincing. So – to my amusement (and straight off the top of her head) – she proceeded to orate aloud the words of one such man…

> *"Out of the depths I cry to You, Lord; hear my voice. Let Your ears be attentive to my cry for mercy. If You, Lord, kept a record of sins, who could stand? But with You there is forgiveness, so that we can, with reverence, serve You."*

"That's from Psalm One-Hundred-And-Thirty. It's another verse I had to memorise to win first prize in Sunday school."

"Yes, you're quite a little Bible scholar on the side, aren't you," I mused, eschewing further caustic put-downs. For a long, revealing moment our eyes locked. Preema must have sensed that the hard, outer shell of my disbelief was cracking.

"We also know the Bible is true because the men who wrote it told about things long before they happened," she continued. "For instance, the Prophet Isaiah told people that when Jesus came He would be 'despised and rejected'; that He would 'take up our pain' and 'bear our suffering'; and that He would be 'pierced for our transgressions' and 'crushed for our iniquities' – which my father told me are old-fashioned words for sin. But the Prophet also told us that 'by His wounds we are healed' – meaning that when Jesus died on the Cross He did so to forgive our sins. Don't you see, Mr Wez: all those words were written many, many years before Jesus was born; yet they tell us He would make a way for us to go to Heaven and, if we put out trust in Him, not to have to worry about all the bad things we have ever done."

What to say? This precocious seed had finally come up for air, permitting my chewed ears to recover. Meanwhile, lest she witter on, I was keeping in reserve the well-trodden arguments about the Genesis account of 'Creation' being blown apart by everything science had proved since about fossils and evolution.

"Tell me, Mr Wez: do you believe in love?" she digressed instead.

"You know I do, Preema" I sighed – even though love hadn't always been kind to me of late. "For instance, you know I love my daughter, Emily," I reaffirmed, cleaving to a more enduring example.

"Yes, of course. But I have heard you say many times that you haven't always been a good father to your daughter; that you left her behind in England to go and live in Australia; and that because of this she might not think you love her?"

Ouch! She was poking that neuralgic spot again – and which explained the hint of mischief lurking behind the ostensibly earnest smile she offered. My countenance must have darkened accordingly.

"But my daughter knows I love her because of the many little things we did together that demonstrated my love for her is real – and which hopefully outweigh the bad things I've also done. And anyway, what's any of this got to do with proving the Bible is true?" I curled an eyebrow at my interrogator.

"Well, in the same way that Emily sees the many good things you have done for her, I see the many good things that Jesus has done for me too – even though sometimes bad things happen," she riposted. "Like when I was all alone on the ocean, clinging to that raft; I prayed to Jesus and He brought me to this island. Or when that terrible storm struck; I prayed to Him and He spared us from the big waves and the fierce winds. And when I broke my arm too; I prayed to Him and He is now making it better again," she chirped, gesturing with her trussed-up left arm.

"Most of all, I was afraid that I would die if I was alone on this island all by myself. So I prayed and He sent you to find me. And even though you are sometimes angry with me, Mr Wez, you look after me and I know you will help me to one day return home to my family in India. That's why I thank God for you, Mr Wez: because *you* have been the best answer to prayer of all."

Another wry smile on my part greeted this touching, if wholly subjective claim. But then was it entirely without foundation? I recalled my own quiet, tentative prayers. And the times when I too had been tempted to view Preema and her presence on the island with the same fond thanksgiving.

I snatched another nail from her to demonstratively hammer into the plank, my silence a tacit admission that she might just be right. However, I wasn't ready to reveal to her just yet how, in my neurosis about things she was opening my eyes to, I'd taken to covertly delving into that Bible too when she wasn't looking. What, in Heaven's name, was happening to you, Smith?

* * * * *

"Look, Mr Wez! He can fly!"

He could indeed – though this was not the first time we'd witnessed young Babo take to the wing. After four months of patiently rearing him, he'd finally undertaken a handful of clumsy, exploratory flights – testing out the adult plumage he'd acquired. Soon he would be ready to strike out on his own. We could only hope that, now fully-fledged, he wouldn't return to seek out our company too often just because begging for scraps from our table was a less challenging enterprise than plunging into the waves at speed to fish for himself.

Because Preema had spent more time conversing with the bird than I, it was inevitably the sound of her voice that excited him most. Like so today, as we marvelled at him balancing upon the air currents that swept the breezy southern tip of the island. Soon enough he returned to perch in anticipation ahead of us upon the weathered wooden sign that informed the island's infrequent visitors about that sunken German warship that lay offshore.

Perhaps some innate sensibility rendered the creature unable to entirely forget or forsake the little girl who'd not only rescued him from rejection by his mother but had nursed him to the point where he was now able to seek out a playmate of his own kind. Today he seemed to have done just that. For there, swooping in to perch alongside him, was another juvenile booby bird that boasted a similar brown plumage to his own. At first wary of our approach, flapping his wings in agitation, his newfound friend was soon eager to understand what it was about this small human and her larger companion that Babo found so endearing.

"Isn't he a beautiful bird, Mr Wez. And to think: he would not have survived had I not picked him up and brought him back to the camp that day – to love and to care for him."

"Well, I think we can safely say he's grateful," I commended her, reaching out my hand for Babo to playfully nibble at with his bill. "Of course, I seem to remember Yours Truly having a hand in caring for him too!" I chided her with faux indignation.

She looked up at me with that percipient grin. Like so much else about our strange, yet symbiotic partnership, the challenge of rearing this abandoned seabird had strengthened bonds between us that not even our occasional fallings-out could erase. Knowing Preema Patel had truly been a blessing in my life – one that I was profoundly grateful for. She'd taught me so much about myself, as well as about the nature of compassion and the simple, protective love that an adult should always feel towards a child – whether one's own or someone else's. To be sure, our time together had also taught me about where that love had fallen down too – as well as the means by which I might yet make amends for it.

As we drifted away and left Babo to bond with his new friend, she permitted me to drape an arm across her shoulders. Upon which, she hugged my waist possessively – as if to reaffirm that gratitude for our time together was mutual.

"Why has the ranger not returned yet?" she enquired with an air of disappointment. "You told me that he would come back again to check on the island following the terrible storm. It is now two months since it struck and still he has not come back." she looked up at me again, this time with sadness in her eyes.

"I'm sure he will be back – soon. Maybe his boat was wrecked by the cyclone when it smashed into the main islands. According to the local radio station, the winds did quite a lot of damage."

I was conscious that I was making excuses. Four months had passed since the guy had last set foot here. Assuming he was preoccupied with tallying how the wildlife had fared on the main islands it might be at least another two before he returned again. Meanwhile – save for that solitary early morning overflight by the air force – we would go weeks without seeing either a plane or a ship; and even what specks in the sky or on the horizon we'd caught sight of were plainly not interested in us. It was impossible not to feel that the world beyond our shores had forgotten about this place.

* * * * *

As always, the prophylactic to dispiritedness was to keep ourselves busy. As such, the re-establishment of the camp was very much symbolic of a return to normality – insofar as being marooned on a desert island with a budding child evangelist could ever be regarded as a 'normal' existence.

However, the good news was that Preema's arm had healed sufficiently that I felt confident removing the splint from around it. Fingers crossed, she would suffer no lasting complications – though (like the cyclone that had ripped through the island) her injury had been a timely reminder of just how tenuous survival could be in such a remote place.

Otherwise, our daily lives soon settled back into their customary routines: mornings spent attending to domestic chores; followed by the furthering of Preema's education. Upon the conclusion of 'class', Preema would then hunt for firewood on the beach while I took myself off to hunt for things to eat. Afternoon siestas would be followed by the cooking and consuming of the main meal; and thereafter by another fireside chat around the brazier once the sun had gone down.

However, in other ways our sojourn on the island had changed. For instance, with June having given way to July not only had the dreaded cyclone season passed but so too had those monsoons and handy passing rain squalls. The dry season was upon us. For the next few months the only source of potable water to be had would be inside those ever-abundant coconuts we would gather. What's more, by now wary of my visitations to their nesting sites around the lagoon, it was becoming harder to come by fresh meat too. Long gone were the days when I could leisurely amble up to one of those roosting seabirds and just nab it.

Meanwhile, taking advantage of my newfound predisposition towards spiritual matters, Preema continued to subtly impress upon me the need to think seriously about my eternal salvation. In this respect, one of the more apposite metaphors she employed was to point to the care we'd lavished upon Babo – symbolic of the unmerited favour of a sovereign God towards His children. It did indeed seem a curious affair. Of all the birds I'd butchered out of sight for us to eat, why had we elected to lavish such compassion upon this one? Of all the people aboard that airliner, why had a sovereign God elected to lavish compassion upon us?

'If You, LORD, kept a record of sins, who could stand?' Certainly not a 'sinner' like me, I was coming to the uncomfortable conclusion (the sins of which if only my prepubescent listener knew the half!). *'But with You there is forgiveness, so that we can, with reverence, serve You.'* Maybe so: yet was I ready to surrender myself to the implications of publicly and unequivocally embracing that forgiveness?

Finally – and touching upon this – my nightly scanning of the airwaves brought home to me a no less sobering realisation: that having abandoned the costly maritime operation to locate it, the fate of that missing airliner had dropped out of the news altogether. Its disappearance looked set to remain a compelling, if unsolved mystery. How could such a colossal plane just vanish? What had become of it? And would the families of those who'd perished ever know for sure how or where or why their loved ones had vanished with it?

Likewise, the murder of Willow Mackenzie was old news too. Though circumstantial evidence (as well as the periodic ramblings of the conspiracy theorists) pointed to her husband's hand in her murder – as well as in the disappearance of the doomed flight he was aboard – the police had yet to come up with hard evidence that would remove all doubt. Her untimely demise too looked set to remain a compelling, if unsolved mystery.

Of course, there was one man who could point them to the truth about both enigmas. However, to the wider world – as well as to his own grieving family – that man's life had also ended tragically somewhere in the wilds of the southern Indian Ocean; as had that of a little girl whose late father had been one of India's best-known itinerant evangelists. Yet two people who had miraculously survived the flight's disappearance and who remained very much alive.

18

"Now I look'd back upon my past life with such horror, and my sins appear'd so dreadful, that my soul sought nothing of God but deliverance from the load of guilt that bore down all my comfort... And I add this part here, to hint to whoever shall read it, that whenever they come to a true sense of things, they will find deliverance from sin a much greater blessing that deliverance from affliction."

Robinson Crusoe

"... In other news, the Government today announced that Air Chief Marshal Angus Houston will head up the Australian contingent that will join the international team investigating the loss of Malaysian Airlines Flight MH17 over Ukraine last week. At least thirty-seven Australian citizens died when the Boeing 777 – which was en route from Amsterdam to Kuala Lumpur – was shot down by a surface-to-air missile believed to have been launched by Russian-backed separatists, who are fighting to wrest parts of the country from the pro-Western government in Kiev..."

"Keep still, Mr Wez," Preema broke to instruct me, surveying the set of nervous eyeballs I'd focussed upon the scissors. Though she was becoming a dab hand at it, I can't deny even now there weren't moments when my heart was in my mouth.

"You just be careful!" I muttered through a mouth that I'd scrunched-up to present my jutting chin for her attention. Otherwise, like an Australia that was once more in shock, I too struggled to take in news of this latest tragedy to befall a Far-

Eastern airline – and which had also claimed the lives of its citizens.

To be sure, with the only mirror we'd possessed having fallen and shattered in the survival pod while the cyclone was battering it (and with my phone's battery life too precious to switch it on for extended periods so that I might snip at it myself using its selfie camera), I'd since been presented with no choice but to permit Preema to undertake the regular task of keeping my hair and my designer stubble trim. I suppose, like Robinson Crusoe and other famous castaways, I could have just affected the bearded hippy look. However, I'd always loathed long hair and long beards and I wasn't about to fall in love with them now. Besides, if (as we were fully expecting) the ranger was about to turn up in his boat any day now, I wanted to at least look presentable for the occasion!

"I shall miss you, Mr Wez – when I return to India," she meanwhile tootled, perchance to shore up my frayed nerves. "You have become such a good friend to me that I feel I can tell you anything. Just like I can tell my big sister anything – even my biggest, bestest secrets."

"I'll miss you too, Preema," I said, humbled. "But we can still keep in touch. We can write letters; and send photographs of ourselves. Or, better still, we can Facetime each other. Then you can keep me abreast of how you're getting on at school.

"That's the wonder of twenty-first century technology. The world is so much smaller nowadays. It's enabled me to keep in touch with Emily on a regular basis," I recalled, wishing that my phone – if only for a few precious minutes – would pick up a signal so that I could talk to her again and imbibe her laughter. I tried to imagine her reaction when she saw me again in the flesh – a man brought back from the dead, as it were.

"Yes, we have this in India too. When I was in England I used to talk to my grandmother too using my father's mobile phone," she chuckled, grasping a piece of my fringe to snip at.

"Once upon a time – in Robinson Crusoe's day, for example; before the advent of cheap air travel – when someone travelled overseas it meant they had to say goodbye to their family for a very long time; possibly even for ever."

"That must have been very hard, Mr Wez. I really miss my family – especially my big sister. I could not bear the thought of never seeing Ramila again."

With the proximity of our faces as Preema snipped at another strand of my jet-black mop, I could sense in her eyes that she was still mourning the parents she *would* never see again – unless, of course, she was right about meeting them again in Heaven.

"You know – like you – the more I think about it the more I'm convinced that everything happens for a reason: the good things and the bad things too. Maybe the bad things do happen to make us better appreciate the good things we have," I ventured to suggest, though it seemed a meagre consolation.

"You and I have seen many bad things, Mr Wez. But we have also seen many good things too. And despite those bad things, I rejoice that God has looked after me; and you too, Mr Wez – even though you don't believe in him."

I studied those eyes again at close quarters as she glanced through her spectacles at me, angling for my reaction. However, I elected not to gainsay her observation. For it was true: as if by some miracle we had indeed survived the many ordeals and encounters that should, by right, have finished us off. To whom else could I possibly ascribe such blessing? It seemed too trite and churlish – even to an erstwhile 'unbeliever' like me – to ascribe everything to happenstance; or to good fortune; or to Lady Luck; or to any one of the other euphemisms by which human beings evade acknowledging that someone greater than themselves was directing their destinies.

Yet why would such a great all-seeing, all-knowing deity seek to favourably direct the destiny of such a hard-bitten man as I? And to what purpose? To that I still had no answer. Meanwhile, I was mulling over her guileless (if grammatically questionable) admission that she could tell me anything – including her 'biggest, bestest secrets'. Allied to these radio bulletins we were hearing about this latest mysterious air crash in Ukraine, might it just be an unwitting prompt from the Almighty that the time had come for me to speak frankly to my companion about a matter that was pertinent to another mysterious air crash: a matter that, until now, I'd kept resolutely to myself.

* * * * *

Later that afternoon, with the sun dipping, we were once more sat around the table I'd rebuilt, seated on the stools I'd similarly hammered back together. Furthermore, we were dining on crab meat, coconut white, and Pisonia leaves – again!

"It's something else I miss," my small companion opined at a point when a hiatus in the conversation had become sufficiently drawn out that it was obvious even the garrulous Preema Patel had run out of things to say. I looked up, suitably expectant.

"Proper food, Mr Wez. I'm tired of eating this. And I'm tired of drinking water from coconuts too," she said, the petulant edge to her voice suggesting even *her* gratitude to Providence had limits. *'And the people murmured against Moses, saying, 'What shall we drink?'* I was tempted to joke.

Flippancy aside, she had my sympathy. Almost five months we'd now been stranded on this island and still there was no sign of rescue arriving (though, as I reminded her again from time to time, Robinson Crusoe had been castaway for *twenty-eight years* – unlike us, most of it having had no other soul to converse with, save for a parrot!). Meanwhile, it was becoming harder to bear the long, hot days with nothing much going on. There's only so many times you can wander up and down an island that's barely more than a kilometre square *and* still discover new things. Preema too was making it obvious with each passing day that she was increasingly underwhelmed by the schooling I was wracking my brains to offer her.

The long, languid evenings were proving similarly wearisome (this close to the Equator darkness had invariably enveloped the camp by seven o'clock). Having despaired of spotting the lights of passing ships we'd likewise exhausted reminiscing about our families or fantasising aloud about all the things we would do when we did eventually make it back to civilisation. Meanwhile, the crackling of the fire and the endless caressing of the waves upon the beach – once so stirring and evocative – nowadays only served to underline the tedium.

Preema looked up from unenthusiastically picking at her food and we each offered the other that sullen stare that spoke of one thing: surely the ranger must turn up soon – for though the sea conditions remained brisk, there were days when it was even so possible to put a boat ashore upon the more sheltered western beaches. Failing that, couldn't he hire a bloody helicopter!

"I was reading that Bible of yours the other day," I dropped the admission into the stalled conversation – more so to puncture the awkward silence than to consciously invoke another of her juvenile sermons. However, having done so I guess I was unsurprised when she looked up again, this time her eyes glinting a little brighter in the glow from the brazier.

"You have? I mean, you did?"

"*'But Jonah rose up to flee unto Tarshish from the presence of the Lord and went down to Joppa; and he found a ship going to Tarshish. So he paid the fare thereof, and went down into it, to go with them unto Tarshish from the presence of the Lord,'* – Jonah Chapter One, Verse Three," I recited word perfect – much to Preema's surprise and delight. She commended me accordingly.

"I read the whole book too, you'll be pleased to know."

"Bravo, Mr Wez – though it is one of the smallest books in the Bible," she reminded me lest I boast too fulsomely about my foray into the Scriptures.

Maybe so. However, there was another reason why I thought she might be intrigued – one that had nothing to do with my restless eyes having read from cover to cover every one of the ranger's vapid paperback novels!

"I suppose you could say it caught my interest because its principal character sounds a bit like me. You see, this Jonah bloke appeared bored with life at home and so took himself off elsewhere…"

"No, Mr Wez, he disobeyed the command of the Lord to preach to the people of Nineveh," the evangelist's daughter corrected me with an eager smile.

"Yeah, well, whatever! Anyway, while he's off gallivanting – or 'fleeing from the presence of the Lord', as the Bible has it," I pre-empted the further correction that was twitching on her lips, "the ship he's aboard is caught up in a terrible storm that threatens to sink it. However, while the crew are praying for their lives, Jonah is snoring his head off below deck.

"A bit like Jesus when the boat he is in encounters a storm," Preema giggled.

"Yes, exactly. So anyway, the captain prods Jonah – knowing he's religious, like – and asks him to call upon God to calm the storm. Meanwhile though, the sailors have sussed out that Jonah himself might be the reason why God is angry and has sent the storm. So, in desperation, they throw the poor chap overboard in the hope that ditching him will appease – what does 'appease' mean?" I fired, pointing to her in expectation.

"It means to make an angry god less angry," she remembered.

"...Absolutely! They toss him into the sea in the hope that it will appease God: which it appeared it did; for calm returned. Meanwhile, Jonah finds himself being swallowed up by a whale. Or so the story goes."

"Bravo again, Mr Wez. You have remembered a story from the Bible – like I had to do lots of times to win first prize in Sunday school," she enthused, bobbing up and down on her stool in a sedentary rendition of one of her little happy dances.

"Yes, I thought you'd be impressed," I feigned modesty.

However, the well-pleased grin that greeted this news began to falter when my gaze lifted to stare her out. Meanwhile, it was the turn of my own lips to twitch as if I too was motioning to blurt something out. However, struggling to remember the passage in question, I stood and wandered over to her shelter. Reaching into the corner where she kept that well-thumbed Gideon Bible, I pulled it out and began flicking. However, in my inadequacy I was forced to use the contents list to find the Minor Prophets. Flicking with greater precision this time, I located the passage in question. I drifted over to the brazier, availing myself of its swirling luminescence to read from the Book of Jonah again.

> *"Then Jonah prayed unto the Lord his God out of the fish's belly. And said, 'I cried by reason of mine affliction unto the Lord, and He heard me; out of the belly of hell cried I, and Thou heardest my voice. For Thou hadst cast me into the deep, in the midst of the*

seas; and the floods compassed me about: all Thy billows and Thy waves passed over me'.

"Then I said, 'I am cast out of Thy sight; yet I will look again toward Thy holy temple. The waters compassed me about, even to the soul: the depth closed me round about, the weeds were wrapped about my head. I went down to the bottoms of the mountains; the earth with her bars was about me for ever: yet hast Thou brought up my life from corruption, O Lord my God'.

"When my soul fainted within me I remembered the Lord: and my prayer came in unto Thee, into Thine holy temple. They that observe lying vanities forsake their own mercy. But I will sacrifice unto Thee with the voice of thanksgiving; I will pay that that I have vowed. Salvation is of the Lord.

"And the Lord spake unto the fish, and it vomited out Jonah upon the dry land."

For several long seconds a silence ensued between us that was disturbed only by the crackling of the fire and the distant sibilance of the ocean from which we had both, by differing means and on different days, been 'vomited upon the dry land'. Meanwhile, in the reflection of that flickering fire she noticed that my eyes were watering.

"Why, Preema. Why me? Why did I deserve to live when all those other poor people aboard that plane died?" I begged, those eyes no longer able to dam the tears that were streaking from them. "Why did I survive when your parents perished – good people; Christian people; people who prayed to God; and who trusted in Him too," I implored her.

She stared up at me, for once lost for an answer.

"Does that not trouble you?" I put it to her again, placing the Bible down on the table and squatting on my haunches to grip one of her tiny hands. "Do you not ask yourself why they were not spared? Why instead God spared me – a lousy, godless, good-for-nothing womaniser; a man who abandoned his kid in England so that he could squander his life in Australia?"

"What's a womaniser?" she replied naively, ignoring the string of self-derogatory adjectives and quizzing the noun instead.

I screwed my eyes shut and shook my head, though still gripping her tiny hand. Come back, Anila Patel: all is forgiven. Oh, for someone who might understand the depths of my remorse for my misspent life! However, this russet-skinned moppet was the only earthly confessor I'd been granted. I snuffled and drew breath, hoping I could make her understand.

"Preema, a womaniser is a man who goes with women purely for what he can get out of them: sexually, I mean – like that man who you told me you saw doing those things to that woman in the forest. The only thing I would say in my defence is that, like her, the women I went with looked upon what they were doing in the same relaxed way: because they were probably going with me for not dissimilar reasons."

"You mean 'fornication'?" she proffered blandly, recalling that unseemly seventeenth century idiom, the meaning of which I'd enlightened her. Gosh, this conversation was surreal!

"Yes. And I did lots of it while I was in Australia."

"But that doesn't mean you're a bad man. In fact, I think you're a very good man. Besides, my father once told me that even good men and women sometimes do naughty things – like fornication. The Bible says we are all sinners, Mr Wez; it's why Jesus came to save us," she reminded me with a consoling smile. Perhaps her parents (or at least her father) had not been so unforthcoming about sex after all.

"So why is the story of Jonah on the ship causing you to cry?" she pressed me, brushing away from a grown man's hot, stubbled face those tears that must have seemed so incongruous.

What a can of worms I had carelessly opened up! Indeed, was my skirt-chasing really so bad in the great scheme of things that I needed to confess the salacious details to an (admittedly no longer quite so innocent) eight-year-old child? However, if screwing a gaggle of strumpets had been my only crime, then I might have desisted in the telling. After all (as her father had conceded), plenty of 'good men and women' had been tempted by the prospect of an extramarital thrill. And yet how could she ever hope to make sense of my tears unless I explained the relevance of the story of Jonah and the whale to my own predicament?

"It was me," I wept, snatching my hands back and sinking my face into them. The dreadful truth was out at long last.

"You, Mr Wez?"

"Yes, Preema. Like Jonah aboard the 'ship of Tarshish', I was the reason why that plane we were on crashed. I was the one whom God's anger was upon."

When I did eventually deign to open my eyes, I could see that my listener was none the wiser.

"But that is silly, Mr Wez. You didn't crash the plane. You told me that something went wrong with it. It was an accident."

Having ventured thus far there could be no turning back now. Dabbing at my eyes with my clammy palms, I drew breath again and pressed on.

"You remember this morning you said you could tell me your 'biggest, bestest secrets'? Well, Preema, can I tell you mine?" I begged, not knowing how the revelation was going to land, but sensing the 'prompt' of the Almighty in what I was about to do.

She smiled and nodded in willing affirmation.

"You see, there was one woman in particular who I went with; a woman who, as it would turn out, I fell very much in love with. In fact, had I had the chance I would have willingly taken her as my wife," I sighed wistfully.

"Was she beautiful, this woman? And did she make you very happy? Is that why you wanted to marry her?" my listener enquired upon offering me the serenest of enchanted expressions (and betraying the wondrous fairy-tale workings of a mind that had perhaps not entirely lost its innocence).

I smiled dreamily. "Yes, Preema. She was very beautiful. And I was always happy whenever I was with her. However," I knew I had to reveal the story's darker side, "she was already married."

"But it is wrong to be with another man's wife," she pointed out, her own smile ebbing warily. "It is adultery," she elaborated with unflinching grown-up frankness.

"I know it was wrong, Preema. I did a very bad thing," I confessed and looked away.

"But if you are sorry for doing this wrong thing – which I can see you are – then God will forgive you," she pointed out. "After all, He forgave King David when he went with another man's wife," she assured me, reaching for the Bible to alight upon the tale in question. However, I stayed her hand. Was there no seediness in that book that her old man hadn't regaled her with!

"I know that, Preema. However, like King David's adultery, what I did had far, far greater consequences – consequences that would lead to the death of your parents; and to you and I ending up together on this island."

Now she really was looking me up and down, mystified. I had absolutely no idea how what I was about to say would land but, again, having come this far there was no way I could avoid placing before her this final, momentous piece of the jigsaw.

"You see, the man whose wife I went with was an evil man; a man with a very bad temper whose mind was unbalanced – just like King Saul in the Old Testament," I explained by means of yet another story I'd discovered while secretly page-flicking her Bible. "What's more, this man was an airline pilot. He flew big passenger jets all over the world. As it happens, he was also piloting the plane you and your parents were aboard that night it took off from Singapore.

"That man was very, very angry with his wife over what she had done. So angry, in fact, that before he boarded that flight he murdered her and dumped her body into the sea."

The revelation visibly shocked my confessor. However, she listened in silence as I swallowed hard and pieced together the ominous strands of a truly incredible set of coincidences.

"He was also very angry with me, Preema. What's more – and I don't know how he did it – but he found out I was aboard the plane that night. And so angry was he with me that I'm convinced he deliberately crashed it into the ocean so that he could kill me. But, of course, by so doing he killed all those other poor people aboard it too – including your parents. Don't you see, Preema: it was my fault that they died. I'm the man who's responsible for everything that happened that night."

I'd finally verbalised the awful truth – upon which, for once, the loquacious little girl who had the answer for everything (and invariably too the question that occasioned it) was dumbstruck. Through those nerdy specs, her wide brown eyes examined me with an ambivalent lustre that suggested she was either crestfallen on my behalf or utterly appalled – or maybe even both – even as I was still shedding remorseful tears.

Finally, having had long enough to ponder something to say (or to prolong my torment), she placed a hand upon my shoulder.

"You must not blame yourself, Mr Wez," she protested. "It was not you who crashed that plane. It was all the fault of that wicked man who did a terrible thing because he was angry – just like it's the fault of the nasty people on the ground who fired the missile that has caused this other plane to crash. You are a good man, Mr Wez. After all, you helped me escape from the plane when you could have left me there to die. Remember?"

I did indeed – and I remembered my angst that she'd been shoved from my grasp in the crush for the exit. I wept again. However, this time it was my turn to come over all taciturn – lost for something to say amidst my pitiful wailing. In time however, I remembered something else: an even more out-of-character act on my part that I'd undertaken amidst those most desperate of circumstances.

"You know, the funny thing is…" I said, shaking my head at the confession, "… at that point when the plane was about to hit the waves – and when I was adrift in the ocean afterwards – I prayed to God. I really did. And though I feared He wouldn't hear me, it seems He did. He spared my life and I cannot think why. Why would He want to do that, Preema? Why would He spare my life and allow all those other people to die?"

She thought about my observation while I dabbed at my tears. In those moments when I elected to study her I thought she was wrestling to alight upon not just *an* answer, but the *correct* answer given the shocking revelation she'd just heard.

"Because He loves you, Mr Wez. He doesn't need another reason. You are very special to Him. Maybe He put me on this island so that I might tell you how special you are – and that you would understand all the things I have been telling you."

Funnily, her response sounded neither trite nor stilted. Even so (and to make the point), she took the Bible from the table and began flicking for another passage – this time in the Gospels.

> *"And Jesus spake this parable unto them, saying, 'What man of you, having a hundred sheep, if he lose one of them, doth not leave the ninety and nine in the wilderness, and go after that which is lost, until he find it? And when he hath found it, he layeth it on his shoulders, rejoicing. And when he cometh home, he calleth together his friends and neighbours, saying unto them, 'Rejoice with me; for I have found my sheep which was lost'.'*
>
> *"'I say unto you, that likewise joy shall be in Heaven over one sinner that repenteth, more than over ninety and nine just persons, which need no repentance'."*

"You are that 'lost sheep', Mr Wez – the one that Jesus set out to find. And He made all these frightening things happen so that you would be found by Him. Remember," she bade me again, "we were both together on the plane, seated almost next to each other – even though you spent the first part of the flight upstairs where you met that rich Indian lady you told me about, and which is where I think you wished you had spent the whole flight so that you could carry on talking to her," she offered me a knowing smirk. "However, if later on you had not been seated next to me then you would not have been able to help me out of my seat and I would not have been able to escape from the plane.

"So do not be ashamed to say you love God, Mr Wez. Understand that He loves you too and forgives you of *all* these wrong things you have done. Instead say thank you to Him: for finding you; but also for setting you free from your sins."

* * * * *

'The lost sheep' that God had searched for… and found. I liked that metaphor and felt humbled by it. With my heart now open to such things, as Preema and I continued to touch upon spiritual matters over the coming weeks (and I discovered other passages in the Bible that talked about God's measureless love for repentant sinners), I began to appreciate how wise this mere child was – far beyond her years. I suppose it helped, of course, that her father had been a famous international preacher and that she'd imbibed such wisdom listening to him practising his sermons.

And yet this time it was impossible not to detect a certain detachment in the dialogue – as if her estimation of me had been irreparably pricked by the secret I'd confessed to her. Was that seeming forgiveness for my part in her parents' death just a front; a charade she felt compelled to act out because to 'forgive' others (as Jesus had 'forgiven' others) was something her father had drummed into her from a very young age? Suddenly I had the sense that I was no longer Preema Patel's shining hero. Indeed, despite her lofty and reassuring words, over the coming weeks – and ridiculous as it seemed that a 'Christian' could think that way – I was tempted to believe the little girl whose life I'd saved (and had preserved ever since) actually despised me.

19

"I was surpriz'd, when turning my eyes to the sea, I presently saw a boat at about a league and a half's distance, standing in for the shore... the wind blowing pretty fair to bring them in... Upon this I call'd Friday, and bid him lie close, for these were not the people we look'd for, and that we might not know yet whether they were friends or enemies."

Robinson Crusoe

It was one of those stiflingly hot days relieved only by the stiff south-easterly breeze that never seemed to relent. Six long months we'd been marooned on the island and still we were no nearer to being discovered and rescued.

Seeking relief from the insufferable ennui – as well as from Preema's lingering, yet unspoken reproach – I'd therefore taken off by myself to the windward side of the island, there to enjoy some time alone. Indeed, with no telephones, no television, and no access to the internet, one of the more exquisite blessings of being a castaway (even if it didn't seem that way at first) was that, away from such distractions, it had afforded me all the time in the world for reflection. My erstwhile addiction to being 'busy' and 'going places' had meant that I'd permitted so many vain fancies to crowd my life, while the things that truly mattered had passed me by unnoticed. Indeed, I could now perceive just how perniciously the 'false god' of worldly success had served to shorten my attention span and to cocoon me from ever having to think seriously about eternal matters. As I strolled naked and barefoot along the shore – reminiscing and giving thanks for God's goodness towards me – it really did feel like a wiser and more chastened Wes Smith was emerging at last from the old impatient, irascible one who had died to his sinful past.

It was while rounding the headland, lost in such meditation, that I spotted a boat – some way off in the distance to be sure; yet appearing to be heading inshore. Rescue at last!

At first elated, soon enough a healthy suspicion born of experience intruded upon my rejoicing. Donning my shorts, I clambered up onto the dunes for a better view. While crouching in a hollow to make myself less visible, I studied it further and estimated it to be about twenty metres long with a high prow and its superstructure abaft. A fishing boat, perhaps. What's more, I could have sworn it was drifting (for there was no hint on the prevailing breeze of engines throbbing). Had I possessed a pair of binoculars I might have been able to pick out the assortment of souls who were crowding its decks. However, even from this distance I could make out the grubby, unkempt exterior of the vessel – as well as the melanoid complexions of those souls.

"Oh, no!" my heart sank. "Here we go again!"

* * * * *

Racing back to the camp, I was unsurprised to find Preema had taken herself off upon what I assumed to be a contemplative stroll of her own. After several minutes of cantering up the beach calling after her, soon enough her more familiar melanoid face emerged from the treeline to greet me. Sprinting across the expanse of sand that separated us, I grabbed her by the shoulders.

"What is it, Mr Wez?" she enquired with startled eyes.

"It's a boat, Preema."

"A boat? You mean we are finally going to be able to leave this island?" she said, tempering her trepidation with relief.

"I don't know," I puffed. "It might be…"

"You mean it's… another pirate ship?"

I knew what her thoughts were even before she'd swallowed hard and verbalised them: after weeks of putting our camp back together, we might have to witness it being trashed all over again – or even being compelled to trash it ourselves and go into hiding once more in fear of our lives.

"Hopefully not," I placated her. "For some reason though the vessel is attempting to put ashore on the eastern side of the island.

But that's madness!" I shook my head, genuinely perplexed.

* * * * *

"Surely they can see those nasty reefs," Preema exclaimed as she re-joined me to squat out of sight in the dunes, there to study this strange craft that was adrift beyond the foaming white waters.

I'd assured her often enough that any visitors who sought to come ashore would have to do so on 'our' side of the island, where the sea was calmer and there were breaks in the reefs. To do otherwise would be to risk their vessel being dashed apart by the violent surf – as that German cruiser had been a hundred years earlier after its captain had beached it to escape a fatal mauling by a more powerful, pursuing Australian warship.

Instead we could only look on as the afternoon progressed and this latest arrival continued bobbing aimlessly towards its peril. Either it had broken down; or to beach their craft was indeed the intention of whoever was in charge.

"There are lots of people aboard, Mr Wez," my fellow observer added by-and-by. "And look! There are children aboard too!" she pointed out, glancing back at me in excitement.

Though I strained to make them out, there were indeed. Suddenly, my hope that the vessel would be consumed by the swell long before its occupants could put ashore and molest us was supplanted by concern that its appearance might not herald ill-intent after all. Why would a band of ruthless, yet supremely calculating pirates take hostage skinny little dark-skinned waifs whose value on the international ransom market was surely outweighed by the hassle of tending to them at sea? And then drive both them and their vessel onto a deadly reef?

Furthermore, as the boat edged closer to the shore and I was able to better survey the human cargo milling about on deck, it was apparent that there was no sense of any of them being under duress; just gathering anxiety about how they would make it ashore in the face of the huge, thundering waves that were starting to batter the creaky boat with their backwash.

"Maybe we should help them," Preema turned to me again and ventured with a dolorous sigh.

She was right. Whoever these people were, surely their terrified children deserved help. Moreover, studying them further, I'd come to the conclusion that, rather than pirates, these particular voyagers were probably asylum seekers fleeing some conflict or other and hoping to make it to Australia.

"But how? We have no way of crossing that reef," I noted, for in my haste I'd omitted to put my boots on when I'd hurried through the camp. "Neither do we have any ropes that are long enough to throw them a line."

"But we can't just leave them to drown, Mr Wez. Even if they can swim the sharks will eat them."

Reluctantly, I rose to my feet and ambled over the brow of the dune, marching down to the water's edge. There, having caught their attention, I tried to make gestures to indicate to whoever was skippering their boat that they desist from coming in any closer.

"No...! Go back...! It is not safe to land here...!" I cried.

However, it was to no avail. Either through lack of choice, or willing recklessness, they were determined to come ashore. Some of the more able-bodied passengers on deck were even readying themselves to swim for it.

All at once, a huge wave lifted the boat and slammed it into the coral, impaling its hull and jolting those passengers overboard. Panic ensued. It was every man for himself. Even those woman and children who'd hung back and had managed to cling on for dear life were emptied into the surf when a second enormous wave capsized the vessel.

There was no time for me to return for those battered Timberlands now. Unless I acted fast there would be only corpses to retrieve from the churning waters. Even as I hesitated, some of the non-swimmers were giving up the struggle.

I waded into the sea as far as I dared before my toes flinched upon bumping jagged coral. However, another huge wave came thundering in, knocking me off my feet, but also rushing the first of those frantic swimmers into the shallows – a stocky young male who, upon righting himself and planting his limbs upon *terra firma*, immediately re-joined me wading back out into the swell to rescue his compatriots.

Soon we'd managed to grasp and haul in other struggling

survivors: a woman here, another man there; children too, who we scooped up into our arms to convey to the safety of the beach, where Preema was dancing about impotently, wishing she could help (but no doubt praying instead).

Soon enough, we'd hauled at least a dozen people onto the sands. Together with my fellow rescuer, I ventured in again to haul a few more from the water – some of them barely clinging to life; most of them badly blooded from being dashed against the coral. Finally, spotting a child flailing helplessly – and putting all concern for my own safety aside – I raced back into the waves and swam through the surf for all I was worth. I managed to grab the mite – a little girl. Remembering the life-saving skills I'd learned at school, I swam back through the breakers with her in my clutches.

No sooner had I struggled ashore with her in my arms than a man who I took to be her father came bounding up to fret over her lifeless form. Nudging him and other onlookers aside, I laid the child down on the sand and checked for vital signs. I placed my ear to her nose and mouth. She wasn't breathing. Neither could I detect a pulse. I pressed my hand on her chest and pumped. However, though it expelled water from her airways, still she didn't respond. Tilting her head back, I pinched her nose and locked my mouth onto hers, blowing hard to fill her lungs with my own breath. This too expelled more water from her lungs but failed to revive her. I continued both procedures again, watched over by her distraught father. Anxious onlookers were meanwhile chanting prayers to their gods. Preema too was looking on tearfully through the gaps in the crowd that had gathered, silently petitioning hers.

"Come on! Don't you give up on me! Don't you dare!" I wailed at the infant, administering CPR one final time.

However, it was useless. She was dead. Barely four-years-old – five at a push – her brief little life had ended here in the middle of nowhere. Meanwhile, God had stood by and watched it unfold; and yet He had chosen not to intervene.

I rose from my knees and permitted the child's father to clutch her in his arms, speaking tender words to her that I couldn't understand. Then he looked up to tearfully implore Heaven in that same tongue – anguished pleas that were pitiful to behold and which left me with a numbness in my soul.

"*'O Allah,*" someone who'd spotted my angst quietly translated, having sidled up alongside me, "*make her a preceding reward and a stored treasure for me... O Allah, unite her with the righteous believers; place her under the care of Ibrahim – peace be upon him; and protect her by your mercy from the torment of Hell'...*"

The torment of Hell? The residual sceptic in me wanted to scream 'what crime had this helpless little one ever committed that might warrant facing the 'torment of Hell?'! However, instead I lowered my gaze to inspect the cuts and grazes upon my own limbs and torso. Then – upon spotting Preema still glaring at me as if to scoff at both my lack of proficiency and my lack of faith – I paced over to direct her gaze away from the lifeless infant, ushering her away from this morbid gathering.

* * * * *

"You tried your best, Mr Smith. You should not reproach yourself. You could not have saved her."

I was waiting for my comforter to remind me that it was 'the Will of God' (which I'd gathered one or two of his fellow passengers were muttering to justify casting today's tragedies from their minds). Perhaps they were right. After all, the loss of twelve out of the thirty-two people who'd been tipped into the sea (not counting the two who died beforehand during the crossing) was everybody's fault and nobody's.

However, either Aavannan Loganathan wasn't a desperately religious man or he was aware that these senseless deaths were sore trying my newfound faith (and so graciously elected to forego trying it any further). Neither did he trumpet that it was his skills as a doctor that had enabled him to revive all four of the lifeless passengers that had been dragged up the beach for his attention. The other victims had yet to be recovered.

Otherwise, he was right. As he explained to me how this assorted boatload of wanderers had wound up here, I sensed it was no time to wallow in my feelings of failure. Suddenly, the island's population had increased tenfold; and if the challenge of feeding and sheltering two people who spoke the same language had been daunting, how much more so would be tending to all these extra mouths – men, women and children who hailed from places as diverse as Syria, Iran and Pakistan (but mostly, he told me, from Sri Lanka), of whom only a handful appeared to speak passable English.

Fortunately, Dr Loganathan was one of them. A balding, mild-mannered man of modest stature and with a pleasant, rounded face, I guessed him to be of my age (his own teenage daughters had been among those thankfully plucked from the waves, along with his wife). He now elaborated upon why he himself had forsaken a successful medical practice back in Sri Lanka to journey across the ocean in an unseaworthy old pinnace.

"We thought the end of the civil war five years ago would also end the bitterness and division that had torn my country apart. However, it has not. Though we have 'democratic government', it is a democracy by and for the Sinhalese majority, who have not been magnanimous in their victory. Instead, we Tamils have become second-class citizens in our own country. Many people have been arrested or interned; others have been hounded from their jobs. I myself was told I had no future in the country because the government has not forgotten that my brother fought with the Tamil Tigers. They would not listen when I told them that I'd pleaded with him that violence only breeds more violence and that making war on the Sinhalese was not the answer to our country's problems.

"Therefore, with great reluctance, I decided my family could no longer stay in Sri Lanka. My wife has relatives in Melbourne. Therefore, we resolved to go to Australia in the hope that we would be permitted to enter the country as refugees fleeing persecution. It is why we boarded that boat – that we should cross the Bay of Bengal to Sumatra and then sail down the coast of Indonesia to Kupang. From there we would cross the Timor Sea to Darwin.

"However, things went wrong no sooner we left Batticoloa. It turned out that the person in charge of the boat – which we had paid good money for places aboard – knew next to nothing about navigation; nor how to work such a boat on the open sea. Running low on food and water, we thought of turning back. However, the government of Sri Lanka has made it illegal for its citizens to leave the country without permission. To return would have meant facing jail for certain; or maybe even worse.

"Then, after three weeks of not sighting land, we saw your island. Maybe, we thought, we had reached Australia at last."

I huffed with an air of irony and amusement.

"You've reached Oz alright, mate. However, I'm afraid there's not much of it to see on this lonely outpost. Besides, you do know that Australia deals firmly with people who turn up on its shores unannounced," I thought it as well to point out. "At best they'll pack you off to a detention centre on some other godforsaken island. Failing that, you'll most likely be bungled back onto a plane to where you've just come from."

From the absence of a spoken response, I could read my raconteur's face and discern the trepidation he felt that the 'Lucky Country' he'd heard about held promise only for those similarly lucky (and invariably First World) denizens like me who arrived *with* an invitation, *possessed* a marketable skill of some sort that the Australian economy could make use of, and could command a salary that would keep that economy purring nicely. The outcasts and ne'er-do-wells of Third World countries turning up in leaky boats were categorically not welcome. In fact, the government had announced a policy of 'zero tolerance' towards them.

However, that was by-the-by. Right now, with dusk drawing in and hope of finding his missing comrades fading, the more immediate task was to bury the dead and then corral those who'd survived round to my camp on the far side of the island, there to tend to their wounds. The two-kilometre trek along the beach and around the headland would hopefully afford me time to think how I was going to cater for all the other needs of this unexpected and uninvited caravan.

20

*"My island was now peopled, and I thought my self
very rich in subjects; and it was a merry reflection
which I frequently made, how like a king I look'd...
They all owed their lives to me, and were ready to lay
down their lives, if there had been occasion of it, for
me. It was remarkable, too, (that) they were of three
different religions. However, I allowed liberty of
conscience throughout my dominions."*

Robinson Crusoe

"Hey, Mr Wez. There plenty good meat on this one," my
fellow hunter laughed, having wrung the bird's neck. He then
held it aloft for me to admire both his handiwork and its
contribution to filling our bellies. I could only fret on behalf of
the absent ranger for this sudden spike in the plundering of the
island's protected wildlife.

I ascribed the deftness with which Soroush Najafzadeh
collared and despatched seabirds from around the lagoon to the
fact this beefy twenty-eight-year-old had once been a petty officer
in the naval branch of the Iranian Revolutionary Guards, where
he'd presumably learned a thing or two about how to despatch
things with his bare hands. It was in this elite force that he'd
probably honed his seafaring skills too (and which was why he'd
proved so deft at first swimming ashore and then back out again
to rescue his fellow passengers). As he recounted his military
career to me in broken English I imagined the machete in my
hand was unlikely to provide much defence should this muscular
man decide to employ those martial skills upon me!

Not that I needed to fear: there was a gentleness and bonhomie
about my new hunting companion that seemed remarkably at
odds with his previous life as a trained and ruthless killer. So

what had occasioned this transformation? And why had he suddenly decided to turn his back on the Islamic Republic he'd sworn to defend?

"Iran no longer good place," he grunted as we wandered back to the camp with our trophies. "Government no good. Full of much corruption. And Government make many people in Iran much poor because no like Americans."

I took it he meant the tough economic sanctions that the Western world, led by the United States, had imposed on his country to thwart its ambitions to possess a nuclear bomb. However, Soroush himself had made his peace with the 'Great Satan' – as he elaborated further in the quaint third person manner with which he discoursed with me in broken English.

"Soroush he leave Iran and go Australia. Or even better: he go America. Soroush he like America. Soroush he hear it good country. But first Soroush he travel to India; then to Sri Lanka, where he pay money and board boat. However, boat no good. It go nowhere. So Soroush end up here – on no good island!"

I was tempted to reel off the more delightful pleasures this place held in store for those seeking to escape crass modernity – or even sanctions-induced penury. However, taking his point, I consoled him that washing up here was infinitely better than drowning at sea! However, as with Dr Loganathan, I thought it only right to warn my dewy-eyed raconteur that, with the announcement of *Operation Sovereign Borders*, Australia was now dealing brusquely with migrants who arrived by boat. Why, he could even find himself placed aboard a plane back to Tehran.

"Uh!" he grunted defiantly, shaking his head. "Soroush no go back Iran. Soroush go America. America 'Land of Free'."

One had to admire his determination. Were things really so bad back home? Apparently so.

"Soroush no go back Iran, Mr Wez" he continued to mutter elliptically as we strolled along the beach. "Iran now bad place. So Soroush he go America. America 'Land of Free'."

For all his touchiness about the prospect of being returned to where he'd escaped from, after six months of having only Preema for company it felt good to be able to converse with an adult again – man to man, as it were (even if I had to constantly explain the English idioms by which I recounted how I too came to be washed ashore on 'no good island').

* * * * *

For all its remoteness and insignificance, 'no good island' was managing to yield up enough of its bounty to provide for all the extra people who'd found themselves stranded here – for now, at least. What's more, Soroush and I had managed to swim out to what was left of the boat and retrieve items of supply and equipment that would assist in that task. Otherwise, hopefully its hulk grinding back and forth on the coral would alert any further overflights by the Australians that there were people ashore on the island – at least until the relentless surf carried it out to sea to a more permanent watery grave.

Meanwhile, from being a sleepy little hideaway overlooking the beach, my camp had suddenly been transformed into a bustling village. Back and forth hurried menfolk salvaging further spare timbers from the *ataps*, availing themselves of my tools to fashion them into shelters for their families. Darting among them were their womenfolk, bearing fish they'd caught in the shallows or crabs they'd cornered in the forest. Meanwhile, the brazier they cooked them over was being fed by driftwood that Preema and the children gathered from the beach (the youngsters' anxiety about their new home allayed upon discovering that it counted a brown face like theirs among its existing inhabitants). What's more, following Preema's lead, they too (like Soroush) had taken to addressing me as 'Mr Wez' (although, unlike Soroush, they would refer to the place more fawningly as 'Mr Wez's island'). In fact, with my knowledge about what to gather and where to find it (including the medicinal properties of the local plant life that had enabled Dr Loganathan to balm their wounds), everyone seemed to regard me as the island's 'king', to be deferred to and respected.

However, lest this sudden sensation of power go to my head, I remained conscious that mine was a 'kingdom' that existed on the margins of survival. Like me, Dr Loganathan (along with his educated family, the only person to address me by the more formal 'Mr Smith'!) had voiced his concern that sustaining this many people on such a small island would prove progressively more difficult. Already, the presence of all these voluble newcomers tramping about the place was spooking both its bird life and its shy forest-dwelling crustaceans. Meanwhile, binding up all those cuts and grazes had depleted altogether my meagre supply of bandages, ointments and sticking plasters.

There were undeniable tensions in the camp too, which I feared its multinational complement was carrying over from the weeks they'd spent cooped up at sea. While Dr Loganathan and his fellow Tamils were mostly Hindus, others among his countrymen were Muslims (as were those from elsewhere – like Bassam Al-Asali, the father of the little girl I'd fought to save, who, with his wife and older son, had fled the vicious civil war that was raging in Syria). Furthermore, there were even different sorts of Muslims too, Dr Loganathan explaining to me that one or two of the young men from Pakistan were Ahmadiyyas – a branch of Islam that the others regarded as heretical and whose adherents faced persecution at home (and, in some instances, death). Hence why they'd journeyed across south Asia to join him aboard that shambling seaborne mystery tour.

Though it was heartening to observe all these people rubbing together for now, I wondered how long this new 'kingdom' of mine would remain a harmonious one once its subjects succumbed to the ennui of being marooned on a tiny (and now rather crowded) island.

* * * * *

Undoubtedly, the most intriguing character among this polyglot human soup remained Soroush. Apart from the fact that, at six-foot-five, he stood head-and-shoulders above the rest of us, there was something about his manliness that I warmed to. Dr Loganathan might be the 'brain' on 'my island' (both his medical and his organisational skills having proved invaluable from the moment he'd swum ashore); however, it was Soroush who provided its 'brawn'. Hefty timbers from the *ataps* that otherwise required two men to lift and carry had proved no match for his weight-lifting talents. Meanwhile, shinning up even the tallest coconut tree was a breeze to this accomplished former commando.

As such, I often chose him to accompany me on my foraging of the island. In particular, I was intrigued to learn more about the circumstances in which he'd fled Iran; and, more pertinently, why he'd instead fallen in love with his country's arch-enemy. Somehow, I suspected he wasn't telling me the whole story when he regaled me with all this gushing bumph about the 'Land of the Free' being such a compelling foil to the dour, oppressive theocracy that was his benighted homeland. Perhaps he'd fallen foul of the mullahs who ran the place. However, although I angled to coax the secret from him, he remained tight-lipped.

Furthermore, watching him at play with the other children on the beach – showing off his acrobatic skills; or piggy-backing them on his big, broad shoulders – reminded me that there was something manly about Soroush that Preema had warmed to as well – albeit for different reasons. Symbolically, he'd earned his place in her undying affection when he'd miraculously stumbled upon her beloved Rubik's cube further up the beach where Cyclone Kiona had deposited it (and which had occasioned one of her more ecstatic happy dances!). Yet the growing bond between them pointed to something much more profound that I couldn't quite put my finger on. Not for nothing did I begin to suspect that the burly Iranian had supplanted me as the new hero in her life.

* * * * *

Though it galled to think that Preema was disillusioned with me, at least it was heartening to observe how well she'd slotted into her appointed role in my 'kingdom' as 'princess' in charge of keeping the children occupied (and through whom they were daily discovering that 'no good island' could actually be quite a fun place for youngsters). For example, Preema took it on herself to organise games for them: building sandcastles and then decorating them with different sorts of shells – though repeating my admonition not to touch the gaily-patterned, but deadly cone snail shells (as well as the manmade explosive variety to be found in the abandoned ammunition dump!). Likewise, copying one of my more inspired initiatives, she organised 'lessons' to further their education, teaching them new phrases in English to supplement the smattering they'd already acquired. Like a true pedagogue, she even drew everyday objects in the sand with a stick, instructing them how to pronounce and spell them. Inevitably, she soon had them pronouncing the words 'Jesus' and 'Bible' too. It would have been churlish not to have chuckled: maybe it was all part of a crafty scheme on the part of the evangelist's daughter to preach the Gospel to them!

And not just the youngsters either: looking to improve his own ropey command of the Queen's tongue, I would frequently spot Soroush sitting cross-legged at the back of these beachside classes, eagerly imbibing her instruction.

"Jee-zus...! Bi-bul...!" this sporting giant of a man would hold his hand aloft and call out, basking in the approbation of his prepubescent teacher.

"Soroush he like Jee-zus. He like Bi-bul too," he would add, as if to further ingratiate himself with her.

Furthermore, on evenings lounging in my hammock, I would overhear Preema reading the Good Book aloud to him by the glow from the brazier – offering Soroush extracurricular instruction, as it were. While a part of me was amused to earwig her explaining terms like 'justification', 'remission' and 'propitiation', another part of me was needled by jealousy that my little companion now had a new mature student upon whom she could practice her evangelism.

Meanwhile, Preema's didacticism among the children was laced with practical demonstrations of God's love too. In particular, she'd taken under her wing two shy little Sri Lankan girls – Sathiri, her own age; and her smaller sister, Niralya – whose parents had been washed out to sea during the landing attempt on the reef (trauma that no doubt explained their glumness and taciturnity). When she wasn't recounting Gospel stories to them too, Preema would show off how her Rubik's cube worked before handing it to each of them in turn, commending the youngsters when they too eventually managed to line up the colours. Touched by the bond that was deepening between these three orphaned playmates, my thoughts turned to words I'd read in John's First Epistle: *'if we love one another, God dwelleth in us, and His love is perfected in us'*.

Inevitably, it was not just Preema's religious beliefs that were on display. The Hindus too would offer obeisance and thanksgiving to their deities. Likewise – after I'd pointed out to them where Mecca was in relation to 'no good island' – five times a day the Muslims would congregate on the beach to kneel in prayer – most of the island's *umma* at one end of it while the Ahmadiyyas discreetly performed *salat* at the other.

Interestingly, they were collective acts of worship that Soroush elected not to partake of. Perhaps, I thought, being an Iranian Shia (while Bassam and his cohorts were Arab Sunnis) then never the twain shall meet. Then again, it was always possible that his estrangement with his country and with its zealous brand of Islam went deeper than he was letting on.

* * * * *

Even a king in his kingdom is frequently unhappy. While I rejoiced that, by our acts of kindness, Preema and I were making life comfortable for desperate people who'd fled persecution in their respective countries (as well as for Soroush, who appeared to have fled for no better reason than straitened economic circumstances), the instinctive loner in me yearned for the tranquillity I'd once known. Nowadays the camp was invariably bedlam, with someone or something always requiring my attention – even if it was just the children excitedly looking to practise their English upon me and to enquire thereby whether I supported Chelsea or Manchester United!

More worryingly though, more than once Dr Loganathan and I had to diffuse spirited arguments among the camp's young male occupants that came close to fisticuffs. How much longer could we keep the lid on these simmering tensions? How much longer before that accursed ranger returned to discover, to his horror, that his 'uninhabited' wildlife refuge had been overrun by a boatload of migrants?

Today, therefore, I felt I simply had to escape the mayhem and head off alone around the southern headland, where I might unclutter my head and reflect upon all the crazy events of the last few months. Solitude regained, I lingered at the graves of those German sailors who'd perished offshore in 1914. Like them, who among my friends and family back home would credit that the impetuous and adventurous young man from Solihull who they once knew would wind up in this remote place?

Sure enough too, I was once again drawn to that old Jap fighter that lay half-buried in the sand – another rusting reminder of the island's past. True to form, I was unable to resist cocking a leg inside to squat down on what was left of the pilot's seat. Who among *his* friends and family back home in Japan would have credited that the young airman they'd once waved off to war would wind up in this remote place too? Now, as then, I gripped the rusty stump that was the joystick he'd once clutched and daydreamed a while longer.

"Banzai!" I eventually hollered, thrusting it forward to place the Zero into an imaginary steep dive. For a few brief moments, Wesley John Smith – crack fighter ace – was an impetuous and adventurous young man all over again.

"Nya-a-a-a-a-a-r-r-r-r-r-r!" I screamed at the top of my voice in an impersonation of it swooping out of the sun upon some unsuspecting enemy patrol. Having selected my victim, I thumbed the imaginary trigger, juddering the stick in my hands.

"Dagga-dagga-dagga-dagga-dagga-dagga-dagga-dagga...!"

"Nya-a-a-a-a-a-r-r-r-r-r!" I screamed again, this time pulling back hard to climb steeply, glancing back over my shoulder at my imaginary foe spiralling to Earth in flames.

Except over my shoulder I spotted instead a familiar bespectacled face staring at me through trailing windswept hair.

"Oh... I didn't hear you approach," I twittered.

To which Preema's visage remained gloomy.

"Hey, why the long face?" I countered, releasing the joystick and hauling myself out of the plane.

"It's Babo," she announced. "They've killed him."

"Who has?"

"Some of the men. And now they're going to eat him."

I ought to have expressed outrage. However, with the wild birds around the lagoon increasingly playing hard to get, it was inevitable that sooner or later the more impatient young males would eye up Babo, whose tame and trusting disposition rendered him easy prey. How could they possibly know this particular booby bird held a special place in a little girl's heart.

"I'm sorry," was all I could think to say, ashamed that the king in his kingdom had proved powerless to save one of its feathered subjects – along with Clive the giant coconut crab, who they'd also gleefully polished off.

It was the cue for Preema to launch her arms around my waist and bury her sobbing face into my chest. In response, I drew her in tight and rushed a hand through her sable mop. Furthermore, in that moment of tenderness and accord we were both conveying without recourse to words things that had been on our hearts since the night I'd confessed my shameful secret to her.

"I'm sorry too, Mr Wez: for ever thinking badly of you," she eventually snivelled, seeking forgiveness.

What she didn't say – but which was implicit from the depth of her remorse – was that I was her hero once more. For my part, the tears I was shedding unnoticed were an admission of how much I'd missed being in her confidence. For all that I'd enjoyed male company these last few weeks (of both the learned and the rugged variety), I realised that it was Preema's girlish chattiness that had come to mean more to me. As she broke from my embrace to skip across those unspoilt sands alongside me, I yearned for those times when I would playfully chase her across them to the sound of laughter flowing over her shoulders. Truly this sassy little lass had become the second daughter I'd never had.

"When will all these people leave, Mr Wez?" she pined. "I miss those times when it was just you and me on this island."

"I miss them too, Preema. So right now – while no one else is about – let's enjoy them again, shall we," I insisted, looping my fingers around my eyes like flying goggles and making some more aeroplane noises in the hope it might cheer her up.

Whereupon, I chased my little friend around the beach in a large figure of eight, eventually coaxing that laughter from her.

"Look… maybe we'll *all* be gone… from this island… soon," I continued, stooping to press my knees and catch my breath, "you; me… and these other people too."

"I do hope so, Mr Wez. Every night I pray it will happen. After all, we have been on this island a very long time."

"We certainly have, Preema," I hummed. "We certainly have."

21

*"I forgot not to lift up my heart in thankfulness to
Heaven; and what heart could forebear to bless
Him, who had not only in a miraculous manner
provided for one in such a wilderness, and in such a
desolate condition, but from whom every deliverance
must always be acknowledged to proceed."*

Robinson Crusoe

My ears pricked up. So did everyone else's. It was the gathering
roar of a warplane – a jet fighter, if I wasn't mistaken. Like the
others in the camp, Preema and I stopped what we were doing and
raced onto the beach to spy it as it soared along the shoreline at
treetop height.

It was a Boeing F/A18 Super Hornet of the Royal Australian
Air Force. Surely its pilot couldn't fail to spot all these people on
the beach waving at it as it sped past. Then again, maybe he had:
for a few anxious moments, Preema and I stared at each other
with that familiar mien of dejection, fearing that we'd been
overlooked once again. However, upon observing the mighty
warbird climb and bank with a thunderous roar, it quickly became
apparent that it was manoeuvring to make a second pass.

This time I hauled off my shirt when I caught sight of it again,
waving the garment about my head spiritedly. As the jet streaked
in low a second time, its pilot acknowledged me with a wave of
his gloved hand. As if to confirm this, the jet tilted its wings in
salute as it made off into the distance – the deafening blast of its
afterburners lingering on the morning breeze. It was Friday,
September 26th 2014 – our twenty-eighth week on the island –
and at last somebody was aware that we were here!

To say I was ecstatic was an understatement! Snatching
Preema and whirling her around in my arms, I then repeated my

joyful dance with each of the other children in turn before racing across the beach to offer the grown-ups my rapturous embrace. I seized Dr Loganathan's hand and shook it heartily.

"We're going home, Mr Wez! We're really going home!" squealed Preema, who'd been endeavouring to keep up with me. I turned and seized her a second time, scooping her up and spinning her around again, savouring the child's voluble elation.

However, even as we continued to rejoice I sensed our ostensibly jubilant onlookers were receiving this news with, at best, equanimity; at worst, foreboding. For unlike the euphoric Mr Smith and Miss Patel, *their* imminent deliverance from this lonely place promised to be a less than unalloyed blessing.

"Hey, Soroush, mate: it looks like you'll finally be leaving 'no good island'," I bounded up to the strapping Iranian, who'd been stood at a distance, offering him a matey hug.

"Soroush go America then," he burbled as if in a daze. "America – 'Land of Free'."

For once, I could tell he didn't really believe the hopeful, mantra he was always repeating in my hearing.

"Maybe, Soroush. I certainly hope so," I gripped his shoulder, hoping to dispel his gloom.

"Soroush must go America, Mr Wez. Or if he no can go America, he go Australia, eh?" he repeated, looking me in the eye before adding that "Soroush no can go back Iran."

"I know that, mate. Iran is no longer a very nice place. But look, well… it might not be that easy," I felt compelled to temper a dream that the prospect of rescue appeared to have popped.

"You no understand, Mr Wez. Soroush he no can go back Iran," he insisted again, hesitating. "… Because Soroush, you see, he Christian. Love Jesus; read Bible. You understand? If he go back Iran then Pâsdârân they kill Soroush," he said, gesturing across his throat with the edge of one of his huge hands, "because he no longer Muslim. Soroush he Christian."

The sudden revelation stopped me dead in my tracks. In my surprise at hearing this confession for the first time, perhaps he sensed I didn't believe him; or that I was annoyed that he hadn't told me this pertinent fact sooner. My subconscious facial contortions couldn't have dispelled that impression, for I just knew there had to be some ulterior reason why this bullish and boisterous tough-guy had proved so open to a small girl regaling him with Bible stories. Had he been cynically availing himself of Preema's instruction to rehearse his lines in readiness to convince sceptical immigration officials that he'd fled his country out of a 'well-founded fear of persecution' – well-founded because of this dramatic renouncing of its fanatical brand of Islam?

"Please, Mr Wez. Soroush no can go back Iran. Soroush Christian. Soroush love Jesus," he repeated, almost tearfully.

In the meantime, Preema had sidled up to me again, this time to insert herself beneath a possessive arm I opened to curl around her. The jolly little lass then stared up at me and fired off a barrage of questions about when and how I thought the Australian authorities would likely turn up to extract us. Soroush brushed away his tears with a knuckle that he then used to playfully pinch one of her smooth, dusky chops.

"You go home soon, Preema, eh? To India," he forced a smile for her. "And Soroush? Maybe he no go America after all; or Australia. But maybe he go England instead... with Mr Wez," he half-pleaded, training those dark, rheumy eyes upon me again. "Soroush he hear England good country too."

It was my turn to force a weak smile. Upon which, the downcast former commando turned and drifted away, resigned that – when that rescue vessel did finally appear over the horizon – his fate would not be mine to determine.

* * * * *

"Why is Mr Soroush so sad?"

The child's innocent question begged a response. Yet what could I say? That once the immigration authorities had given his testimony short shrift there was no guarantee he wouldn't be packed off to face the gallows in Iran?

"He tells me he's a Christian," I replied, subtly angling to get to the bottom of whatever cock-and-bull story he might have been feeding Preema during all those chummy conversations they'd had while huddled together over her Bible.

As we strolled up the beach alone together on what I reasoned might be the very last time we would get to enjoy the solitude of this place I tried to suppress an irrational frisson of jealousy upon recalling their closeness. Presumably informed of our presence, already that afternoon the Australians had despatched another plane (this time an Orion reconnaissance aircraft) to undertake a more leisurely study of how many people were ashore on the island and what they were up to. It would not be long before the park ranger turned up to enquire in person – along with an accompanying border protection team.

"But he *is* a Christian, Mr Wez," Preema protested. "He told me all about how he discovered Jesus through a friend in Iran; and how he joined a secret church but was forced to flee his country when the other believers were arrested. Please, Mr Wez, he is telling the truth."

I must have offered the credulous child a suitably wary glare.

"So why did he not tell *me* any of this?" I put it to her, indignation mixed with disappointment in my manner. "After all, he led me to believe his escape was predicated solely upon a hankering to seek a better life somewhere else."

"He shared his story with me because I showed him my Bible and told him I was a Christian too. That's why he kept asking me to read it to him. There are very few Christians in Iran; and even fewer Bibles. I'm sure he would have told you, Mr Wez; but perhaps he thought you weren't a believer because he doesn't see you praying or reading the Bible every day like I do."

Was that perchance a subtle rebuke for my reluctance to trumpet my newfound faith with the same fervour that Preema did? Even so, I was tempted to enquire what dramatic 'Damascus Road' experience had caused this erstwhile Iranian Revolutionary Guard to suddenly turn his back on his country (as well as on the uncompromising faith he'd once sworn to uphold) and instead embrace the creed of a despised and persecuted band of 'infidels'. How was such a thing possible? But then was it any less credible than the 'Damascus Road' conversion of the Apostle Paul himself that I'd read about in the Book of Acts – a man who'd made it his mission to similarly persecute the despised Christian church in its birthplace (and by no less brutal means)? Was it any less credible too than the twenty-first century 'Damascus Road' conversion of a cynical, career-obsessed Englishman who – having miraculously survived a plane crash and wound up with just a small Indian girl for company – had similarly experienced a life-changing encounter with the Living God? And just as that encounter was now softening my heart, might it likewise explain why the brawny Iranian had defied the stereotype to reveal himself to be such a jovial and considerate human being?

"They call what Soroush has done apostasy: rejecting Islam to become a Christian," I lamented, feeling chastened. "And in Iran the punishment for apostasy is death."

"I know that," Preema gulped despondently. "But is there nothing we can do to help him? Can't we at least pray that the men who come to rescue us from the island will believe his story; and that they will allow Soroush to live in Australia; a country where people don't have to be afraid to read the Bible and talk about Jesus."

Preema's touching innocence never ceased to amaze me; as did the simple faith that it spurred.

"You and I can certainly put a good word in for him. However, I'm afraid it will be down to the government whether he's allowed to stay in the country or whether he's sent back to Iran. So yes: let us pray that they will give him the benefit of the doubt, shall we," I suggested, halting her and turning her to face me.

And right there – alone together on the beach – that's exactly what we bowed our heads and did: Preema taking the lead and then me following. It was the first time in my life that I'd ever prayed aloud – and in earnest – in the presence of another human being. Against all my expectations, it felt strangely liberating.

* * * * *

If concern for the fate of Soroush was playing on our minds that day, it couldn't wholly supplant the joy of knowing we would finally be going home. Inevitably though, neither could rejoicing about our imminent rescue supplant a tinge of sadness that we might never get to wander these deserted sands again. Paradoxically, the tiny island that had been our prison had also been exceedingly good to us. Not only had its bounty provided for our material needs, but its tranquillity and its natural beauty had aided us during more than a few passing moments of thanksgiving for both our temporal and our eternal salvations. As we walked, we continued to reminisce upon the remarkable trials and tribulations that had spangled our sojourn in this lonely place, as well as the unlikely, yet endearing friendship between us that facing and overcoming them had forged.

"So what will you do when you get back to England, Mr Wez?" Preema enquired as we waded barefoot in and out of the surf that was lapping at the water's edge,

"Oh, I don't know," I chuckled, risking her dismay by impiously joking that "I suppose after I've given Emily a nice big hug I'm going to sit myself down in a quiet little pub somewhere and savour a long, refreshing ice-cold beer."

"No, silly!" she scowled playfully. "I mean will you leave England again to take up that new job in Canada that you were on your way to when all these things happened?"

It was a question I'd genuinely given little thought to. After all, with almost seven months having passed during which the world had written me off as dead, someone else had almost certainly been headhunted to that well-remunerated management post in British Columbia that I'd been looking forward to taking up. However, for all her childlike naivety, I suspected Preema knew that too; and that instead her question hinted at a more profound concern about the future direction of my life.

"I'm guessing the airline company must owe us both a fair bit of compensation. However, that money will only go so far. I'll still have to work for a living," I explained. "Besides, I'm a mining engineer; it's one thing in this world that I'm good at."

"But surely you are good at other things too," she insisted, gripping and swinging my hand merrily in her own as we walked.

"Look, Mrs Where-Why-What. If what you're driving at is: do I intend to be a better father to Emily, then the answer is yes. If being with you has taught me anything then it's that the relationship a man has with his child is more important than anything money can ever buy."

"And the relationship he has with God too," she insisted, the playful scowl putting in a second appearance.

"Of course."

"If you like, you can join the church that my sister, Ramila, goes to. It's near the university in Birmingham. My parents used to go there too. It's a very friendly church, Mr Wez – with lots of music and singing and dancing. I'm sure you'd enjoy it. You can bring Emily with you too – to the Sunday school. It's where I won first prize for remembering verses from the Bible!"

An equally playful smirk flitted across my face. Aside from the fact that I reckoned I'd have to be broken in gently to her family's brand of happy-clappy Pentecostalism, I feigned chariness at the prospect of making the acquaintance of yet another beautiful and self-confident Indian lady who went by the name of Patel!

"Gah!" I suddenly sucked in breath, halting and glancing down at my foot. Whatever it had struck it hurt. Without thought of asking, I availed myself of Preema's shoulder to balance upon as I bent my knee back and lifted my heel to examine it.

"What is it, Mr Wez?" she arraigned me anxiously.

To my horror, I spotted exactly what it was I'd trodden on.

"Oh – my – God!" I exclaimed as my heart sank.

Preema was about to arraign me again – perhaps for taking the Lord's name in vain; but more likely because she too was equally horrified upon spotting it.

"Mr Wez! Look! It's a cone snail shell! Like the ones you told me not to touch!" she fretted, pointing out the rounded diamond shape half-buried in the sand, as well as the tell-tale mottled tawny brown pattern upon its ivory-coloured shell.

"Too right it is! And whatever's inside it has just stung me!"

The harpoon-like dart that the creature had, with lightning swiftness, fired into my heel (and which it employed to paralyse the small fish that were its prey) indeed felt like the sting of a bee or a wasp. And although the initial sharp pain eased, I'd read enough about these animals in that wildlife book to know that, in extreme cases, their venom could prove fatal. Each year dozens of people on tropical islands died from cone snail stings, often when gathering up their gaily-coloured (and highly-prized) shells. It was why I'd always cautioned Preema to be careful when paddling in the shallows in her bare feet.

"Are you going to be okay, Mr Wez?" she worried aloud.

"I hope so. But look, to be on the safe side we'd better get back. Maybe Dr Loganathan can take a look at it for me."

My bland assurance only went so far to allay the youngster's patent concern. As such, she was eager that I quicken the pace. However, after a few hundred metres she could see that I was limping. As we progressed closer to the camp the limp worsened. Far from being in pain though, my heel had gone numb. What's more, I was perspiring heavily; and I was increasingly breathless. After attempting a few more weary steps I halted and slumped down on the sand.

"Mr Wez! What's wrong?" Preema fretted again.

"Look... I'm alright. Just let me... rest... a while," I panted.

"No, Mr Wez. I'll go and get help," the child protested, fearful of what these symptoms portended.

Then – in a spontaneous act that both heartened me, yet left me with a strange, sobering premonition that what had just happened might prove terminal – she threw her arms around me and gripped me tight in her sobbing embrace.

"I will always love you, Mr Wez – for everything you have done for me!" she insisted.

Eventually, I broke free. Upon which the tearful lass sprinted up the beach for all she was worth. As I sat there palpitating, it was as much as I could do to prop myself up and observe her desperate flight.

* * * * *

Of all the people Preema could have bumped into, mercifully the first person she spotted was the one who was most able to convey a stricken six-foot, one-hundred-kilo Caucasian male. Having discovered the former Iranian trooper sat on his haunches on the beach, disconsolately tossing pebbles into the shallows, I can only imagine the urgency with which she must have seized this gentle giant by the hand and hurried him back to where she'd left me. By the time they arrived, I was spread out on my back – my breathing laboured, my speech increasingly incoherent.

"Hey, is okay, Mr Wez. Soroush here. He help you," he dropped to his knees and poured those tender words into my ear. Then he scooped my limp frame into his muscular arms and began to leg a passage back to the camp. Though my head was hanging limp and my vision increasingly blurred, I could make out Preema bounding alongside him, gawping through watery eyes at what a curious little creature no bigger than her hand had so quickly reduced her grown-up best friend to.

"I will keep praying for you, Mr Wez," she cried insistently as she jogged along to keep up.

"Yes. And Soroush… he pray for you too, Mr Wez," my human ambulance chuntered as he bore me in his arms. "He pray to Jesus... Because Jesus make people better... Jesus He die for us, Mr Wez… to make us free... And now He live again… to make us go Heaven... Hey, Heaven even better than America, Mr Wez... Heaven real 'Land of Free'!" he declared exuberantly.

As I struggled to slur a response I feared Soroush had spoken truer than he knew: I was indeed going to be knocking on the door of that celestial kingdom rather sooner than I'd imagined. The numbness had spread from my foot and had now engulfed my entire lower body. However, I was still sufficiently lucid to remember my arrival back at the camp, where the gentle Iranian laid me on the ground while anxious fellow islanders crowded around me. Preema hurriedly sought out Dr Loganathan and dragged him over to examine me, pointing out to him how blue my poorly foot had turned.

"Cyanosis," the learned Sri Lankan medic replied as he peered into my glassy eyes, checking my vital signs. "It is the result of loss of blood flow to the affected limb."

"Oh, no. Will he be okay?" Preema squealed.

I would have loved to have cheered the tearful lass with a quip from my repository of wise cracks. However, with not just numbness but paralysis now wracking my body whatever I struggled to mouth must have made no sense. With what vision I had left I could make out the good doctor firing off a battery of orders to those around him to assemble the things he would need to prevent my weakened form passing the point of no return – which it surely would if the paralysis spread, causing my heart and lungs to cease pumping.

"Listen, Mr Smith," I heard him holler as if to make me understand, "I will try as best I can to help you using what things I have to hand – until the Australians arrive and they can get you to a hospital. However, while no one has developed an anti-venom to the sting of a cone snail, I have treated many patients before in Sri Lanka, where we also have these snails. They survived. I am confident you will also."

I tried to acknowledge him as best I could. Over his shoulder I vaguely recalled Bassam and his family praying over me in Arabic. Around him, the other asylum seekers were also petitioning their deities on my behalf.

In his concern to bolster his patient's morale, I guess what Dr Loganathan purposely didn't tell me was that my recovery would depend upon which of the over six hundred species of Indo-Pacific cone snails I'd had the misfortune to step on. For example, the geography cone snail was one of the most venomous creatures known to man, an encounter with one of these critters all too frequently proving fatal. If such had been my nemesis, then death would swiftly ensue.

"Come on, Mr Wez. We will get you to a hospital soon," Preema chivvied, feeling obliged to echo the doctor's assurance.

I ventured to summon a supportive smile. However, if – as he'd been frank enough to explain – there really was no anti-venom then it was unlikely that Australian health care would be able to do much for me either.

"Hey, Mr Wez. Soroush he still praying for you," I made out my Iranian friend demonstratively press his hands together and close his eyes for my encouragement.

Maybe I was approaching the point where I'd ceased caring – resigned to my fate. In the fuzziness of my thinking I made my final peace with God – thankful that I now knew that, upon my confession of faith, He had forgiven my many sins and, by His grace and goodness, had made a way for me to stand redeemed in His presence. If I had any regrets at all in those final few moments of consciousness it was that I was not going to be granted the opportunity of similarly making my peace with those I'd wronged during the life that was now deserting me: with my ex-wife, Leanne, who I now realised I'd never ceased loving; with my parents – and especially with my father, who had always feared that chasing those false dreams of career success overseas would be my undoing; and most of all with Emily – my beautiful, loving daughter, who had surely deserved a better father than the one she'd been handed.

"Please, Mr Wez, don't leave me. Not now. Not after all we've survived together," Preema implored, sobbing. I tilted my head to make out Soroush placing his arm around her, employing his free hand to dab away his own tears.

What a ridiculous end to my story: to have survived against the odds every peril that nature (as well as errant human nature) had thrown against me, only to fall victim – on what, in all probability, would have been my last day on the island – to the lethal barb of a small, startled snail.

"… Dear Father God, Mr Wez is my bestest, bestest friend. Please help him… please…" Preema was weeping.

By now my head was awash with a strange, loud, whirring noise and a tempest like a sandstorm had suddenly clouded my vision. Perhaps this was it: a few more short shallow gasps of breath and my spirit would depart this world for good.

"…Try to keep calm and keep still, Mr Smith. Help is arriving…" I heard Dr Loganathan admonish me above the roaring clamour. One had to admire his optimism.

"… Please, Jesus. You help Mr Wez, eh… He good man... He no must die…" Soroush had meanwhile joined Preema to beseech Heaven.

"… *The Lord is my shepherd; I shall not want……*" I overheard my little companion mouthing the Twenty-third Psalm – and from memory too. In my head I tried to repeat it as best I remembered – which I'm afraid was not very well.

"*…He maketh me lie down in green pastures…*"

In those final moments of utter helplessness, how I wished it were possible for me to live my life on Earth all over again. There would be so many things I would do differently this time.

"*… He leadeth me beside still waters…*"

But it was too late. Rather than still waters, the whooping noise in my head was growing louder.

"*...He restoreth my soul; He leadeth me in the paths of righteousness, for His Name's sake...*"

By now I guess I was hallucinating – for amidst the jumble of faces I could make out what appeared to be Europeans; and caught the rasp of their once-familiar accents.

"*...Yea, though I walk through the valley of the shadow of death, I will fear no evil...*"

"...What's happened to him, guys...?"

"*...For Thou art with me. Thy rod and Thy staff they comfort me...*"

"... He has trodden on a deadly cone snail. I'm afraid the venom is advancing through his bloodstream..."

"*... Thou preparest a table before me in the presence of mine enemies...*"

"...You help him, eh. He good man..."

"*... Thou anointest my head with oil; my cup overflows...*"

"...No worries. We'll deal with this...?"

"*... Surely goodness and mercy shall follow me all the days of my life...*"

"...Hang on in there, mate. We're gettin' yer' outta' here...!"

"*... And I will dwell in the house of the Lord forever...*"

22

> *"And thus I have given the first part of a life of*
> *fortune and adventure, a life of Providence's*
> *chequer-work, and of a variety which the world will*
> *seldom be able to show the like of: beginning*
> *foolishly, but closing more happily than any part of*
> *it ever gave me leave so much as to hope for."*

> *Robinson Crusoe*

Five years later...

It had taken almost three hours for the lumbering Royal Australian Navy auxiliary vessel to arrive at this precise spot. Meanwhile, the ship's meteorologist had assured us that the skies would remain clear for the rest of the day and that a moderate sea state would prevail. Now, at last, the vessel's propellers ceased churning and all that could be discerned of its engines was a gentle hum that carried on the breeze. Overhead, only a few high-drifting clouds ventured to intrude upon the tranquil blue canvas from which the midday sun was shining. As if by divine appointment, the perfect moment had presented itself for the passengers to gather on deck to reflect and remember.

To be sure, only a handful of the relatives of those who'd been aboard that doomed flight had been able to undertake the arduous journey to the Cocos Islands – and thence by ship to this point in the Indian Ocean where what remained of the giant airliner lay scattered on the ocean floor four thousand metres beneath them. Neither was it any surprise that most of those who had were Australians – whose loved ones had also comprised the lion's share of those who'd perished.

Having travelled all the way from England with my daughter, Emily, yesterday we'd joined Preema (who journeyed from India with her grown-up sister, Ramila) to attend the ceremony on the main island to unveil a memorial to the victims. Upon it had been inscribed the names of all four hundred of its passengers and crew – including their parents. Today's voyage had brought us to their final resting place on this, the anniversary of that terrible disaster. Though we'd kept in touch by social media, this week of special events would be the first occasion I'd had chance to meet up with Preema in person since I'd reeled from the cone snail's venom coursing through my body. Like Emily, she was now thirteen-years-old and blossoming into a beautiful young lady.

With a microphone set up on deck in readiness, today's proceedings commenced with ministers from the different religions represented stepping forward in turn to offer up prayers for those victims. All the time, while our heads were bowed, the solitary television crew that had been permitted to accompany us angled discreetly to record this solemn occasion for posterity.

Then, in what was undoubtedly the most poignant and moving act in this service of remembrance, four volunteers from among those relatives – including Ramila – were ushered forward to take turns reading out the names of those deceased passengers' (along with the many countries from which they'd hailed). Meanwhile, like the relatives, the sailors who'd also gathered on deck to observe proceedings could be seen nursing stray tears.

"… Adam Lim – Singapore… Anila Patel – United Kingdom…"

Into my thoughts there flitted the memory of the elegant and self-confident fashion entrepreneur. Suddenly, it was my turn to shed a tear, recalling that we never did get to meet up again in London (and which might have been the prelude to a beautiful and exhilarating affair). However, to such wistful contemplation was added a more sobering one: had not a previous adulterous liaison I'd ventured upon turned out to have had consequences more devastating than anyone could ever have imagined?

Truth to tell, even before they'd been able to unexpectedly avail themselves of my testimony, detectives in Perth had established beyond reasonable doubt that, having dared to announce that she was leaving him, Willow Mackenzie had indeed been murdered by her husband. His resentment fuelled by psychopathic fury, this 'crime of passion' had then morphed into the nihilistic deed that had claimed all these innocent lives. Furthermore, upon me appraising them of the aircraft's likely resting place, the eventual recovery from the seabed of its cockpit voice recorder had enabled air accident investigators to listen in on the desperate struggle that had taken place when her husband – whose name was purposely *not* read out today – had murdered the flight crew and seized control of the plane. After cunningly flying it along the boundaries of the different air traffic control authorities (the better to lull them into assuming the other was directing it), once out into the Andaman Sea he'd then set that southward course towards oblivion – jettisoning its fuel as it went. What investigators had not been able to determine was why, instead of plunging the airliner into the ocean at speed, its deranged first officer had then attempted to land it on the ocean in such a way that suggested he might have been intending to spare his passengers from instant death. Belated remorse for what he'd done? Or one more instalment in the sadistic mental torture he'd already put them through? That we would never know.

What investigators *were* able to confirm was that Willow had been very much alive when that curious valedictory text message had been sent to me the day before. However, network issues had delayed its transmission so that I would only receive it minutes before the plane departed Singapore – by which time her body had been dumped in Fremantle harbour. The implication was that, in all likelihood, when Rick Mackenzie had embarked upon his wicked suicide bid he'd been oblivious that, ironically, aboard his plane would be the very man who'd cuckolded him!

"… Paul Patel and Charita Patel – India…"

Ramila suppressing a frisson of emotion to read out the names of her deceased parents briefly jolted me from such musing.

Yet bizarrely, far from feeling empowered to absolve myself of any part in their deaths, this awareness of the utterly senseless nature of what had been done would serve to reignite the survivor's guilt that would again assail me upon my return to England. On this day too, I was tempted to run my mind over all the many 'what-could-have-beens' if only I'd never forsaken my country's shores in the first place.

Perhaps sensing this, Preema selflessly brushed aside tears of her own to slip an arm around me. It was the kind of fortifying gesture she would often volunteer when we'd been castaways together and which I'd not experienced in a long time. Through watering eyes, I returned the hug she bestowed upon me. Without a word being spoken, her heartening smile then assured me that such unhelpful introspection no longer had any place in my life.

You see, to all the many blessings that had enabled me to survive that horrific air crash there would be added a final one. On that fateful afternoon, a border protection squad had been despatched by helicopter to investigate reports of an incursion upon the island by suspected asylum seekers. To their surprise, upon discovering a missing Englishmen ashore – and one on death's doorstep at that – they promptly evacuated him aboard that same helicopter to the hospital on the main island, where his condition was stabilised and he would eventually make a full recovery. And while I can't say those hours I'd spent perilously hovering between this life and the next were the most pleasant I'd ever experienced, it is apt that their lasting legacy has been an even greater awareness of the God to whom I owe not only my eternal salvation, but my physical one too. Oh, and a residual wariness of walking barefoot on foreign beaches!

It was from my bedside that the world would first get to hear my remarkable story – recounted firstly to incredulous Australian officials, and then to a succession of equally astonished reporters. Another visitor I would entertain was the park ranger himself – who – as well as being apologetic about his tardiness in calling on the island – explained how, as a Christian himself, he'd felt led to place that Gideon Bible in the survival pod on the off-chance a visitor should ever find himself stranded on the island.

Meanwhile, the loquacious little girl who'd first planted the seeds of my own faith would also be flown to the main island to be checked over by medics (who were impressed by how well I'd managed to reset a broken bone on my first amateurish attempt at doing so!). Thereafter, she too would be interviewed by Australian officials, as well as by a child psychologist – who was also pleasantly surprised to observe how well she'd withstood both the traumatic loss of her parents and eight months of subsisting on a diet of crabs, coconuts, and Pisonia leaves! Perhaps it was a testament to the fortitude and resilience of the human spirit (though I'm sure Preema lost no time explaining to them that she owed her own miraculous survival to the grace and goodness of a far more awesome 'spirit' – as well as to the 'angel with a man's body' in whom He'd entrusted her care.

In Daniel Defoe's eponymous novel, Robinson Crusoe observed that when he'd finally returned to England after an absence of almost three decades he'd been 'as perfect a stranger to all the world as if I'd never been known there'. Alas, once discharged, issued with a new passport, and then repatriated back to the United Kingdom, I would discover that my face was rather more familiar. For as well as those disbelieving members of my family who'd been present at Heathrow Airport to greet me, it really did seem as if the entire world media had turned out to report this latest chapter in one of the most 'incredible' and 'heroic' survival stories of modern times.

At first, I was flattered by all this fawning attention. Why, I would even be approached by a well-known movie mogul offering to turn my story into a Hollywood blockbuster to rival the one Tom Hanks had produced and starred in! Soon enough though, I would tire of it; and of the repeated assertion that I was in any sense a 'hero'. Indeed, when the revelation broke that I'd been conducting an illicit affair with the wife of the man who'd crashed that airliner and murdered its passengers my 'heroic' status would be viewed in a more ambiguous light – and which fed a darker side to the newspapers' prurient obsession with dissecting every aspect of my life.

Consequently, I've since shunned requests to be interviewed (or, God forbid, agree film rights). Upon her own return home, Preema's family too would zealously shield her from uninvited media intrusion, permitting her to participate in just one documentary account of her spectacular tale that would be broadcast on Indian television.

Alas – despite entreaties Preema and I would make on their behalves – for those who'd latterly joined us on the island there would be neither welcoming fanfares nor reporters and movie directors jostling for their stories. Soon enough, they would be quietly despatched to the network of migrant detention centres that Australia had established away from its shores – including to the notorious Manus Island in Papua New Guinea.

Sadly, it would be there that my good friend Dr Loganathan would succumb to an attack of pancreatitis that would have been easily treatable had the camp's doltish, rule-bound overseers permitted him to be flown to Darwin for surgery. In response to the resulting scandal, as well as a much-publicised hunger strike among his fellow detainees, his wife and daughters would finally be permitted to enter Australia – reunited at last with their relatives in Melbourne. Meanwhile, the public outcry over their treatment would be instrumental in forcing the closure of the Manus Island camp in October 2017, whereupon many of its remaining detainees would be accepted for resettlement by the United States. Thankfully, among those who would make the journey to the 'Land of the Free' was a thirty-one-year-old Iranian Christian who went by the name of Soroush Najafzadeh.

With the final names read out, it remained only for a representative from the Australian government to draw forward and offer a brief eulogy of his own on behalf of his country. Thereafter, the sailors who been looking on began handing out wreaths and flowers to those relatives who wished to undertake their own personal acts of remembrance for their loved ones. Touchingly, it was Preema's turn to receive a hug – this time from Emily – as she stared sorrowfully at the posy in her hand. Steeling herself to honour the memory of a devoted father and mother, she stepped up to the deck rail and cast it upon the waves.

* * * * *

With the ship's engines stirring and the propellers churning once more, what had once taken me over twelve lonely, terrifying hours to drift towards would appear over the horizon barely fifteen minutes later – for there was one more special place that the ship was scheduled to visit today. Though we would not be permitted to land (predictably, the surf crashing over the reef was too rough for a boat to put us ashore anyway), the captain had very kindly announced that on our return we would be detouring around the island upon which the only two passengers to survive that disaster had once been marooned.

As that lonely, windswept speck drew closer – and Preema and I could take turns through a pair of binoculars to view again its lazily swaying palms – we found ourselves buffeted by all manner of conflicting emotions: fondness and joy at being reacquainted with the sheer, idyllic beauty of the place; and yet sorrow and humility at recalling the daunting array of challenges we'd faced during our seven-month exile there – of which, with hindsight, the absence of most of the civilised comforts we'd previously taken for granted was perhaps the least. Throughout it all we'd had to bear separation too from families and friends back home who we knew were in mourning for us.

"How did we ever do it, Preema?" I sighed rhetorically as we leant together side-by-side upon that deck rail. "How did we ever overcome those odds to survive in such a place?"

"I often ask myself the same thing, Wes. But we did. And for that, we should always be grateful."

As the ship continued its circumnavigation of the tiny island, I levered those binoculars to my eyes again and strained to make out familiar landmarks that I plaintively surmised had long since forgotten us – even as *we* would never forget them. I spied the pebbled escarpment into which I'd dug my first primitive shelter upon wading ashore; that haunting lagoon just visible through a gap in the forest at the point where it had once been open to the sea; the wild, rugged headland at the island's most northerly point, where I'd oft times strolled naked and alone; the bleached white sands of its more sheltered western beaches, beyond which I'd established my camp; the southern shore upon which I could just about make out the weathered graves of those German sailors whose warship lay broken and submerged beneath its roaring breakers. Meanwhile, above us, the island's colony of seabirds circled in curiosity – as if they too had never known us. Had this remote and unvisited place really once been our home?

"I know it is only by the grace of God that we triumphed over all those many ordeals. Thankfully, even you can see that now,

Wes," said Preema, the smile having returned to a face that had this day been tempered again by sadness. "May that same grace make you and I better people; people who respond to the trials of this life with joy, peace, patience, kindness, goodness, faithfulness, gentleness and self-control."

"The 'fruits of the Spirit', eh!" I guessed correctly, nowadays *au fait* with the place in the Scriptures where those commendable qualities are lauded.

As I rested an arm upon Preema's shoulder and planted a gentle kiss upon her forehead, Emily too nestled up to permit me to drape the other around her paternally. I acknowledged her too with a gentle kiss, trusting that she, of all people, could testify that nowadays joy, peace, patience, kindness, goodness, faithfulness, gentleness – and, yes, greater self-control – did indeed infuse my dealings with those who knew me.

"Daddy, do you think you will ever go back to that island again?" she looked up at me and probed, perhaps aware of the clawing sentimentality that had overcome me as I watched it retreat from view.

I squeezed her a little tighter and reined in the temptation to reply. After all, what need had I of the place now? The time I'd passed there had worked its bane and enlightenment upon me. Otherwise, it was a chapter in my life that was closed.

Our mission today accomplished, the two teenagers eventually slipped my embrace and drifted away to enjoy what remained of this most memorable voyage, giggling together while trading snapshots of people and places they taken on their phones – as girls of their age nowadays do. In their place, a beautiful South Asian lady – who'd meantime been sharing her thoughts with the television reporter – strolled up to lean against the deck rail beside me, having spotted an apposite opportunity to articulate something else that was this day on her heart.

"Once again, Wes: a huge thank you. May the Lord always bless you for everything you did for my sister," said Ramila, her gorgeous brown eyes searching out mine before alighting upon her beloved sibling, who was busy revelling in this touching new friendship she'd struck up with my daughter.

I glanced over my shoulder before hauling in a humble smile.

"No worries," I shrugged.

She smiled gratefully, fleetingly resting a delicate hand upon my sun-bronzed arm. She too then drifted away, leaving me alone once more to glance out to sea at that distant dot on the horizon. Whatever my part in the tragic events that had brought us here today, I knew I stood forgiven – by Preema and her family, by my own family, and indeed by Heaven itself.

Confident of this, henceforth Mr Smith could view his time on North Keeling Island in a positive light – as he would always the inestimable privilege of having passed it in the company of the Miss Patel who'd been his soulmate there.

Just after midnight local time on Saturday, March 8ᵗʰ 2014, a Boeing 777 belonging to Malaysian Airlines took off from Kuala Lumpur bound for Beijing. At 0119 hours, over the South China Sea, its captain radioed cryptically: "Goodnight, Malaysian Three-Seven-Zero." It was the last message ever broadcast from the airliner. Minutes later it disappeared from the radar screens of watching air traffic controllers.

However, military radar continued to track Flight MH370 as it executed a series of bizarre manoeuvres that took it back across the Malay Peninsula, whence they too lost contact with it. Hours later, it was announced that the flight and its two-hundred-and-thirty-nine passengers and crew were presumed lost.

When Inmarsat communications subsequently hinted that Flight MH370 had thereafter veered south, Australia offered to co-ordinate a huge search of the southern Indian Ocean, where it was feared the jet had crashed upon running out of fuel. Involving ships and aircraft from several nations, sophisticated sonar was deployed to scour the seabed in a desperate race to locate its crucial 'black box' flight data recorder. However, despite promising leads, they failed to locate either the plane or its 'black box'. After three months, the recovery operation was scaled back – by which time the hunt for the missing airliner had become the costliest air accident investigation ever mounted.

Finally, in July 2015 – seventeen months after it had disappeared – wreckage from an airliner was discovered washed up on a beach on the Indian Ocean island of Réunion. Subsequent analysis confirmed it belonged to missing Flight MH370.

To this day, no evidence has come to light confirming why it diverted so tragically from its course – including whether foul play on the part of a crew member was responsible.

The disappearance of Malaysian Airlines Flight MH370 remains the greatest unsolved mystery in aviation history.

* * * * *

At 0150 hours on June 30ᵗʰ 2009, a Yemenia Airlines Airbus A310 flight out of Sana'a crashed in the Indian Ocean as it approached the Comoros Islands. All one-hundred-and-fifty-three of its passengers and crew perished – except one.

Twelve-year-old Bahia Bakari could barely swim and had been thrown from the aircraft before she'd had chance to don a life jacket. However, despite suffering a fractured pelvis and collarbone, by clinging to a piece of wreckage she managed to survive thirteen hours in rough, shark-infested sea – much of it in darkness – until she was rescued by fishermen.

When news of her ordeal broke in her native France, the press promptly christened her the 'Miracle Girl', while the government minister despatched to bring her home declared that "her absolutely extraordinary battle for survival (sends) a message to the world that almost nothing is impossible."

The following year, she released a ghost-written account of her story entitled 'Moi Bahia, La Miraculée' ('I'm Bahia, the Miracle Girl'). It was reported that Steven Spielberg subsequently sought permission to turn the book into a movie.

However, Bahia declined, citing concern that not even the most accomplished child actress would be able to convey the terror and despair she felt upon finding herself adrift and alone in the middle of the ocean.

* * * * *

At 1041 hours on March 24ᵗʰ 2015, all one-hundred-and-fifty passengers and crew aboard a Germanwings Airbus A320 were killed instantly when it crashed into a mountainside in the French Alps while en route from Barcelona to Dusseldorf.

Upon investigation, the cause of the crash was determined to be suicide on the part of the co-pilot, twenty-eight-year-old Andreas Lubitz, who had locked the captain out of the cockpit before launching the plane into a steep descent. During the ten minutes it took to impact, the cockpit voice recorder picked up the sound of crew members attempting to break down the cockpit door; and in the final minute the sound of passengers screaming.

Lubitz had a history of mental health issues – including suicidal thoughts – which he'd concealed from his employer.

Pilot suicides involving civil airliners remain extremely rare.

I do hope you have enjoyed reading *'Mr Smith & Miss Patel'*. If so, then can I beg one final indulgence: that you very kindly leave a review of this book on the Amazon site you purchased it from:-

United Kingdom/Ireland – amazon.co.uk
United States – amazon.com
Canada – amazon.ca
Australia/New Zealand – amazon.com.au

Reviews greatly assist authors to promote their books as widely as possible. A review needn't be a long essay. Even a simple 'I enjoyed this book' will suffice.

Thank you, and God bless.

Ray Burston

If you have enjoyed reading this, why not search out another gritty thriller about a psychopath's ruthless and calculating determination to wreak revenge upon those who he perceives have done him wrong…

The Black Country Gigolo

Ray Burston

Tom Simmons has everything: he is tall; he is charming; he is self-assured; and he is strikingly handsome – the kind of guy who will always command the attention of the opposite sex.

Ben Hingley is none of these things. Gullible, obsessive, and emotionally illiterate, this unprepossessing little man seems destined to live out his days a despised and misunderstood loner.

Yet these two contrasting characters *do* share something in common – the gathering indulgence of three very different women: a raffish, thrill-seeking author; a crestfallen politician; and a kindly church-goer who bears the scars of a truly shocking crime.

Three women who find themselves caught up in a bizarre love tangle – as well as an even deadlier tangle with a past that is catching up with each one of them.

ABOUT THE AUTHOR...

Ray Burston was born and lives in the English Midlands and has so far published eleven novels.

In 'ANGELS UNAWARES', a well-meaning recluse wins a huge lottery prize and, through misplaced altruism, ends up becoming roped into a violent terrorist plot.

'OPERATION SPREAD EAGLE' follows the eventful story of an aid convoy put together by British volunteers to repair and re-equip a maternity hospital in impoverished southern Albania, and is based on his own experiences as a member of just such a mission in 1993.

Shadowing his own experiences as a politician, 'THE MAKING OF THE MEMBER' follows the turbulent careers of two ambitious parliamentary candidates set against the backdrop of British political life during the 1980s. The sequel – 'THE MAKING OF THE MINISTER' – follows them into parliament and takes the story up to 2010. A final book in the trilogy is planned for after the next General Election!

'ACT OF ATONEMENT' is an intimate study of friendship, love and betrayal set against the backdrop of the bitter war that France fought in Algeria between 1954 and 1962.

Waged across three oceans, two continents and one desert, 'THE SOUGHING OF THE WIND' chronicles the final fateful voyage of Admiral Graf von Spee's German cruiser squadron at the outset of the First World War (and has been knitted together from true accounts of this incredible story).

'TO REACH FOR THE STARS' tells the enchanting and often harrowing tale of a young woman who breaks out of a claustrophobic home environment to enlist in Britain's Women's Auxiliary Air Force (and is based around the story of his own late mother's wartime service with RAF Bomber Command).

Confronting every woman's worst nightmare, 'THE BLACK COUNTRY GIGOLO' is a gripping psychological thriller in which a strikingly handsome young man captivates three very different women, only to confront them again with a truly shocking event from their pasts.

Set on the Isle of Wight during Britain's most memorable long, hot summer, 'THE SUMMER OF '76' is a tale of two young people from different sides of a big, wide ocean uncovering dark secrets about their families' pasts.

Set in Ray's native Black Country during the 1960s, in 'THE SNAKEMAN OF SNEYD END' an eccentric local campaigner unearths the truth about the mysterious disappearance of young people in the town, and which takes place against the backdrop of the controversial closure of its railway.

Ray's latest novel – 'MR SMITH & MISS PATEL' recounts how a an ambitious and successful divorcee winds up a castaway on a remote uninhabited island, his perilous exile given an unexpected twist when he discovers he's sharing it with a most unusual and illuminating companion.

Ray's reasons for becoming a writer are many, but one is that he has always been fascinated by history - and in particular by how ordinary people can find themselves caught up in the sweep of its happenstance. The story of mankind has often hinged on the deeds of such people – "whose names are found inscribed on war memorials, but not in history books" (as the French novelist Jean Lartéguy once observed). Most of Ray's novels echo this theme of ordinary people shaping larger events.

YOU CAN FOLLOW RAY ON FACEBOOK BY SEARCHING FOR 'RAY BURSTON - AUTHOR'.